William E. Schenck

Nearing Home

comforts and counsels for the aged

William E. Schenck

Nearing Home
comforts and counsels for the aged

ISBN/EAN: 9783337268046

Printed in Europe, USA, Canada, Australia, Japan

Cover: Foto ©Andreas Hilbeck / pixelio.de

More available books at **www.hansebooks.com**

NEARING HOME.

COMFORTS AND COUNSELS FOR THE AGED.

BY

WILLIAM E. SCHENCK, D.D.

PHILADELPHIA:
PRESBYTERIAN BOARD OF PUBLICATION,
1334 CHESTNUT STREET.

CONTENTS.

3

CONTENTS.

4

CONTENTS.

CONTENTS.

CONTENTS.

PREFACE.

In this day, when so much labour is expended in producing almost innumerable books for the young, there is danger of our neglecting the aged ones who are about to pass off the stage of life. Yet there is a host of men and women in the decline of life who will be glad to receive a few words of instruction, of sympathy and of kindly cheer. For such this book has been prepared. May God bless it and make it a blessing to all such readers!

It will be seen that the materials for the volume have been gathered from a great variety of sources. Special acknowledgment is due to a volume entitled "Life's Evening Hour," published by the Religious Tract Society of London, from which several of the excellent anonymous pieces have been taken.

W. E. S.

Nearing Home.

Would you be Young Again?*

CAROLINE, BARONESS OF NAIRN.

WOULD you be young again?
   So would not I ;—
One tear to memory given,
   Onward I'll hie ;—
Life's dark wave forded o'er,
   All but at rest on shore,
Say, would you plunge once more,
   With home so nigh?

If you might, would you now
   Retrace your way?
Wander through stormy wilds,
   Faint and astray?
Night's gloomy watches fled,
   Morning all beaming red,
Hope's smiles around us shed,
   Heavenward, away!

* Written in the author's seventy-sixth year.

Where are those dear ones,
    Our joy and delight,
Dear and more dear, though now
    Hidden from sight?
Where they rejoice to be,
    There is the home for me;
Fly, time, fly speedily;
    Come, light and life!

The Review of Life.

ANONYMOUS.

THE busy day of life is over. Its pleasures, its duties, and its anxieties have passed away. The sunshine and the shade, which alternately marked its path, have alike disappeared; and the soft tints of evening are gathered over the sky.

The evening of life! Yes: life has its sunset hour, its twilight season. The dim eye, the silvered lock, and the feeble step indicate that the closing period of earthly existence has arrived. How rapid has been the flight of time! How near must be the approach of eternity!

The gradual decline of health and strength is a kind and merciful preparative for the solemn change which awaits us. It seems to lessen the reluctance which our nature feels to give up life; to wean us from the varied attractions of earth; to soften the abrupt transition from the present to a future state of being. It accustoms us to the consideration of death: it assists us in the realization of immortality.

The evening of life! Evening is the time for rest.

13

The little bird seeks its leafy roost; the rosy child throws aside its playthings and falls asleep; the weary labourer comes home from his work. The cares of the day are forgotten; and all is hushed and quiet. And life's closing hours, Christian reader, should be distinguished by serenity and repose. You must not harass and perplex yourself now with occupations which were once both appropriate and necessary, nor repine because you are unable to exert yourself as in former days. Your strength is to sit still. Old age is the resting-place in the journey of life; and the feverish heat of noontide is exchanged for the refreshing coolness of twilight.

An impatient, restless, grasping, or dissatisfied spirit is not consistent with the character of an aged pilgrim. Habitual quietude and self-possession should mark his demeanour. Neither the excitements of the world, nor the agitations of the professing church, should ruffle your equanimity; for you are too experienced a traveller in this vale of tears to be discomposed by the distractions around you, or to doubt the wisdom and faithfulness of Him who makes all things work together for good.

Your rest in Christ, your trust in him as your Saviour, should be more perfect, more unwavering than in earlier years. "I know whom I have believed, and am persuaded that he is able to keep that which I have committed unto him against that day,"* should be the assured expression of your confidence in him. Firmly placed on the Rock of ages, and fully conscious of the security of your position, your closing life should be a realization of that promise in which God has engaged to keep in "perfect peace" those whose minds are stayed on him.† The cheerful, all-sustaining faith of an aged Christian is one of the best testimonies to the worth and reality of religion, and furnishes a bright and encouraging example to the lambs of the flock. Weary and distressed by the arduous conflict in which he is engaged, the youthful Christian is frequently too ready to conclude with the desponding patriarch, "All these things are against me;"‡ or to exclaim with the sorrowful Psalmist, "I shall perish one day."§ At such seasons in his experience his faith is strengthened and his hope is revived as he beholds the tranquillity and peace of some advanced believer, who has safely passed through similar trials and successfully surmounted similar temptations to his own, and who is now enjoying a foretaste of that rest which remaineth to the people of God.

* 2 Tim. i. 12.   † Isa. xxvi. 3.
‡ Gen. xlii. 36.   § 1 Sam. xxvii. 1.

Such repose is to him a pledge of his own partial deliverance from toil and conflict; and the contemplation of it enables him to gird up the loins of his mind, and to run with patience the race set before him.

Then let those around you, Christian reader, see that your hope is like an anchor sure and steadfast; that you are now confidently resting upon those principles which have hitherto sustained and guided you.. Let no doubt shadow your peace; no anxiety ruffle your composure. You have struggled long with trial and temptation; you have tested in your own experience the truth of God's promises; you have done his work among your fellow-men; and now you must calmly wait until your Father's loving voice bids you welcome home.

The evening of life! Evening is the time for reflection. Amidst the busy and exciting occupations of the day there is seldom much opportunity for serious consideration. Well-disciplined minds, it is true, can control their thoughts, and gather them around high and holy subjects, even in those moments which are necessarily devoted to worldly business; but most persons are so harassed and engrossed by the constant claims upon their time and attention as scarcely to be able to cast a hurried glance on things which are unseen and remote; and they feel how welcome and how desirable is the evening hour for quiet meditation, for self-examination, and for the formation of wise and good purposes.

Now, reader, your eventide of life should be consecrated to calm and elevated thought. Through the long period which is passed you have not perhaps redeemed much time for hallowed consideration. Martha-like, you may have been cumbered with much serving; or, Israel-like, you may have forgotten the Lord your God. But whatever has been your previous history, you are now, by the infirmities of age, withdrawn from active duties, that you may muse upon coming realities. How thankful should you feel that there is yet a brief space allotted you for pious thought and preparation, before you go hence and be no more seen!

In the peaceful twilight hour, when we sit alone and commune with our own hearts, our thoughts naturally turn to the occurrences of the past day. Little incidents, too trifling perhaps to speak about, are reviewed and dwelt upon; virtuous actions which have been performed win the approval of conscience, and wanderings from duty call forth feelings of regret; pleasing events and painful trials have each a share in our pensive musings; varied indeed are

3

the scenes which one day's panorama brings before our view. And then we generally glance at the future. We arrange our plans for the coming day; we look forward with glad expectance to the joys which are in store for us; or we shrink in fear and despondency from the troubles which seem associated with the morrow; and will not your thoughts, aged reader, thus chiefly divide themselves into retrospection and anticipation?

Retrospection! "Thou shalt remember all the way which the Lord thy God led thee these forty years in the wilderness."* Old age is the most appropriate season for this consideration of the past. The judgment is not so likely to be warped by the heat of excitement, nor the feelings to be swayed by the influence of passion, as in youthful days. The veteran, as he recalls the battle-field, can mark events and form opinions far more advantageously than the soldier who is engaged in the midst of an action. Contemplate, then, your whole life from the dawn of infancy to its present decline; trace out the many windings of your pathway through the world; survey each minute feature of your changeful history.

But is it pleasant to look back? Are there not

* Deut. viii. 2.

many places in our pilgrimage where memory dis-
likes to linger? are there not many facts in life's
early records which we feel happier in forgetting?
True, the remembrance of our imperfections and our
sins is painful and self-condemning; yet it is always
best to open one's eyes to the truth. Enter, then,
into a full and faithful examination of your past
history. Scrutinize your motives by the tests with
which God's word furnishes you; and try your conduct by his holy law. Let neither pride nor prejudice hide the real state of things from your view.
How important is it that, on the confines of eternity,
you should be kept from self-deception! Ask God
himself to be your teacher. Make this your prayer:
"Search me, O God, and know my heart: try me,
and know my thoughts: and see if there be any
wicked way in me, and lead me in the way everlasting."*

What, then, is the result of your investigation?
What verdict does conscience, enlightened from
above, give concerning the past? It may be, nay, it
must be, that you find enough in your recollections
to overwhelm you with sorrow and confusion. So
much selfishness and worldliness have mingled with
your brightest deeds; so much unfaithfulness has

* Psa. cxxxix. 23.

been connected with your professed allegiance to Christ; so much impurity of heart and defilement of life are discovered by your rigid self-inspection, that you are ready to exclaim with the Psalmist, "Enter not into judgment with thy servant, O Lord: for in thy sight shall no man living be justified."* Or perhaps your reflections on the past have convinced you that you have hitherto been living without God and without Christ in the world; that you have been so absorbed with the trifles of earth as to have forgotten the attractions of heaven; that, although a responsible being, and liable to be summoned at any moment to your final account, you have gone carelessly on in the ways of sin, and have disobeyed the commands of the Most High.

The retrospect in either case is *humbling.* Yet it leads to hope, and peace, and salvation. Both to the troubled Christian and the penitent sinner the cheering annunciation of the gospel is, "The blood of Jesus Christ cleanseth us from all sin."† "Believe on the Lord Jesus Christ, and thou shalt be saved."‡ Then, "though your sins be as scarlet, they shall be as white as snow; though they be red like crimson, they shall be as wool."§ "Come unto me, all ye that labour and are heavy laden, and I

---

* Psa. cxliii. 2.   † 1 John i. 7.   ‡ Acts xvi. 31.   § Isa. i. 18.

will give you rest."* Full and free forgiveness is
offered to all who seek it at his cross. Cast yourself
with all your sins, however great their number or
aggravated their guilt, at the Saviour's feet, saying,
"Lord, save me: I perish!" and his gracious response will be, "Thy sins are forgiven;—go in
peace."†

Let the sorrowful and self-abasing remembrance
of your iniquity make Christ in your estimation
increasingly precious. Your sin is the dark back-
ground which throws his love and his atonement into
strong relief. Without his sacrifice and intercession,
how dark would be life's evening! Not one star of
hope would illumine the sky; not one ray of gladness would beam on your spirit. But now the light
of the knowledge of the glory of God in the face of
Jesus Christ casts a lovely and softened radiance
on all around you and before you. Oh, as you behold by faith the Lamb of God which taketh away
the sin of the world, as you thankfully recognize
in him your gracious Mediator and ever-prevalent
Intercessor, can you not exclaim with the aged and
rejoicing Simeon, "Lord, now lettest thou thy servant depart in peace: for mine eyes have seen thy
salvation?"‡

* Matt. xi. 28. † Matt. viii. 25; Luke vii. 48–50. ‡ Luke ii. 29.

But the consideration of the past should not only awaken penitence, it should excite gratitude. You have been wonderfully preserved from many dangers; you have been safely guided through many difficulties; you have been continually enriched with numberless blessings. Surely goodness and mercy have followed you all the days of your life. Recall some of the multiplied proofs which you have had of God's tender, parental care over you. It would be impossible to recount every instance of his goodness towards you, for memory, always imperfect, is now sadly impaired; but "forget not *all* his benefits." Each comfort which you have enjoyed through life came from his beneficent hand; each impulse to good and each resistance to evil which you have felt was through the impartation of his grace. Can you not heartily acknowledge the truthfulness of that charge which the dying servant of the Lord pressed home upon the Israelites around him?—"Ye know that not one thing hath failed of all the good things which the Lord your God spake concerning you; all are come to pass unto you, and not one thing hath failed thereof."* Oh yes! every aged believer will testify to the faithfulness of God in the fulfilment of his promises. You can look back to several points in

* Joshua xxiii. 14.

your history, where, but for the interposition of God's providence, or the aid of his Spirit, you must have been overwhelmed by temptation and sorrow. Many have been the occasions when you have had to set up your stone of remembrance, and to confess that hitherto the Lord hath helped you. Even as to your trials, you can see now, with regard to some of them at least, that they were "blessings in disguise;" and you are sure that they were all sent for some wise and loving purpose. With what grateful emotions, then, should your recollections of by-gone days be accompanied!

And should not gratitude for past mercies be combined with hope for future favours and deliverances? "He thanked God, and took courage."* When you think of the increased weakness and perhaps suffering which you have yet to bear; of the inevitable separation between yourself and those whom you love which will soon take place; of the valley of the shadow of death through which you must pass, and of the solemn moment when your spirit shall depart from this world,—natural feeling shrinks from the scene before you. "Cast me not off in the time of old age," is the language of your heart; "forsake me not when my strength faileth."† Hearken to

---

* Acts xxviii. 15.   † Psa. lxxi. 9.

the immediate reply of the God of your salvation:
"I will never leave thee nor forsake thee."* "Fear
thou not; for I am with thee: be not dismayed; for
I am thy God: I will strengthen thee; yea, I will
help thee; yea, I will uphold thee with the right
hand of my righteousness."† Ah! you can read'
these assurances in the page, not of inspiration only,
but of experience. You can infer with certainty,
from God's conduct in past days, what its complexion
will be in future moments. He is the same yesterday, to-day, and for ever; and therefore in the
loving-kindness which he has hitherto manifested
towards you, you have the surest pledge of the continual exercise of his power and goodness. He *hath*
delivered; he *doth* deliver; in whom you trust that
he *will yet* deliver. "The God who hath fed you all
your life long" is your God for ever and ever; and
he will be your guide even unto death.

Anticipation! Looking back should be combined
with looking forward. The weary pilgrim, who recalls with mingled sorrow and gladness the events
which have occurred during his journey, will also
think of the rest and the welcome which wait for
him in his happy home. The Christian traveller, as
evening is closing in around him, and the objects

* Heb. xiii. 5. † Isa. xli. 10.

of earth are fading from his gaze, loves to let his
imagination dwell upon the many mansions in his
Father's house, where a place is being prepared for
him.

> "A little while, and every fear,
>   That o'er the perfect day
> Flings shadows dark and drear,
>   Shall fade like mist away;
> The secret tear, the anxious sigh,
>   Shall pass into a smile;
> Time changes to eternity—
>   We only wait a little while."

The morning of joy is close at hand; the things
which are not seen and eternal are every moment
drawing nearer to you; the promised inheritance,
incorruptible, undefiled, and never-fading, will soon
be actually yours. Meditate on the glory which
shall presently be revealed. Consider how perfect
in its nature, and how perpetual in its duration, is
the happiness which God has provided for you in his
everlasting kingdom. An eminent minister, who
was spending an afternoon with some Christian
friends, was observed to be unusually silent. On
being aroused from his reverie by a question which
was addressed to him, he said that he had been
absorbed in the contemplation of eternal happiness.
"Oh, my friends!" he exclaimed, with an energy

4

which arrested the attention of all present, "think what it is to be for ever with the Lord; for ever, for ever, for ever!"

But is the prospect of heaven thus attractive to you? Have you any true sympathy with its joys, any congeniality of spirit with its bright inhabitants? You of course hope, when you die, to go to heaven; the most thoughtless and worldly-minded characters hope that, not because they aspire after more intimate communion with God and closer conformity to his image, but because they associate the idea of happiness with heaven; and it is the instinctive desire of their nature to wish to be happy. But unless we are made meet for the inheritance of the saints in light, the enjoyments of heaven, were we allowed to be there, would be positively distasteful to us. The unjust and the unholy would be unjust and unholy still, and in a world of perfect truth and purity would find no source of satisfaction. A clergyman was conversing with an intelligent woman in his parish, who was ill and dying. After he had ceased talking to her, she said with an expression of much distaste, "If heaven be such a place as you describe, I have no wish to go there." Such an avowal may seem unnatural, but it would be the confession of every unsanctified heart, if men seriously considered the character of celestial happiness. The songs of the redeemed cannot change the heart, nor the glory of the heavenly city transform the spirit. What fellowship can light have with darkness?

Aged reader, rest not satisfied with anything short of a true preparation for everlasting bliss. It is easy to bear the name of Christian. But without "holiness" no man shall see the Lord.* "Except a man be born again, he cannot see the kingdom of God."†

How shall you attain this preparation? By simple faith in Christ, by the grace of the Holy Spirit. External acts of devotion, alms-giving, self-denial, or large charitable bequests, cannot purchase your passport for heaven. The righteousness of God, which is unto all and upon all them that believe, and the sanctification of the heart which is effected by the power of the Holy Spirit, must be yours before you can enter into everlasting glory. And they may be yours—yours now. Put your trust in that Saviour who has declared he will in no wise cast out those who come to him; and seek for the gift of that Holy Spirit which is promised to all who earnestly and perseveringly ask for it; and you shall have everlasting life.

* Heb. xii. 14.   † John iii. 3.

But it is possible that some humble-minded and timid Christian hesitates, from a fear of being presumptuous and self-deceived, to appropriate those joys which are at God's right hand. Gladly would you anticipate the moment of your departure hence, could you be sure that an abundant entrance would be ministered unto you into Christ's kingdom. But although you cling to the Saviour as your only hope of salvation, and are anxiously striving to bring forth the fruits of the Spirit, you cannot rise to that happy confidence which many Christians feel in the prospect of eternity. You cannot echo their peaceful and unwavering declaration, "We know that if our earthly house of this tabernacle were dissolved, we have a building of God, an house not made with hands, eternal in the heavens."* You are like the pilgrims on the Delectable Mountains, whose hands shook so that they could not look steadily through the perspective-glass at the gate of the celestial city.

Yet, fear not! it is your Father's good pleasure to give you the kingdom; the promised possession is secured to you, although you are unable to realize your interest in it. It is both your privilege and your duty to seek earnestly the "assurance of hope;"

* 2 Cor. v. 1.

but remember, for your consolation and encouragement, that the weakest believer in Christ is as safe as the most rejoicing Christian. Keep your eye fixed upon your Saviour; strive to follow in his steps; use with constancy and diligence the means of grace which he has provided; and you shall eventually attain to that perfect peace which casteth out fear. "At evening time it shall be light."*

Happy are those whose hope is clear, whose faith is strong, and who, in the consciousness that the time of their departure is at hand, can look to the past and to the future, and meekly but confidently affirm with " Paul the aged," " I have fought a good fight, I have finished my course, I have kept the faith; henceforth there is laid up for me a crown of righteousness."† Joyful assurance! Bright anticipation! Well may such aged believers have an ardent desire to depart, and to be with Christ; well may they long for that rapidly approaching hour when he shall present them faultless before the presence of their God with exceeding joy.

The evening of life! Evening is the time for prayer. Then the lisping babe folds its little hands and utters its simple words of supplication and thanksgiving; then the pious family assemble round

* Zech. xiv. 7.   † 2 Tim. iv. 6.

the domestic altar; then the thoughtful Christian retires into his closet, shuts his door, and prays to his Father who seeth in secret. The comparative quietude which exists in the world around him, and the repose which spreads itself over the face of nature, seem to soothe the spirit of the wearied believer, and to invite him to calm and hallowed intercourse with his Maker.

And should not life's evening thus tranquillize and elevate his feelings? Private prayer, the delight and duty of all who have been taught of God, is an employment peculiarly appropriate to the aged Christian. Compelled to relinquish the active occupations of former days, unable to read much even of the best of books, and frequently deprived, perhaps, of the long-valued ministrations of the sanctuary, how thankfully does he retain the inestimable privilege of pouring out his heart in secret before God, and in holding sweet converse with his heavenly Father! "I can very seldom talk or read now," said a venerable servant of God, whose days were almost numbered; "but," he added, as a happy smile lighted up his withered features, "I can pray. In my weakest moments, without opening my lips, I can make known my requests unto God, and praise him for his never-changing goodness towards me."

Let the evening of your life be much devoted to prayer; for at the close, no less than at the commencement of your Christian experience, you are entirely dependent upon Almighty succour. Go therefore with boldness to the throne of grace, that you may still obtain mercy, and find grace to help you in every time of need.* Old age has its especial wants and trials; but, "Ask, and it shall be given you,"† is the inscription which is ever written over the mercy-seat. Implore that strength which you require in order that you may cheerfully bear God's will now; that support which you will need in the hour of death, when heart and flesh shall fail; that consolation and guidance which you desire to have imparted to those whom you must leave behind in a world of grief and danger. He who is able to do exceeding abundantly above all that you can ask or think, will hear and answer your feeble but heart-felt petitions.

The evening of life! Have these words a melancholy sound? They tell, it is true, that the bright sunshine of youth and manhood is past; that the health and the energy which impelled our steps in the path of usefulness and renown have departed; that the night of death will soon gather round us,

* Heb. iv. 16.   † Matt. vii. 7.

when we must close our eyes upon all that is loved
and lovely here.

But are these facts unwelcome to the Christian?
Nay, are they not rather the incentives of his hope
and his joy?   Long a stranger and a pilgrim upon
earth, do they not assure him that he is now on the
borders of that country which he has so earnestly
been seeking?   The worldling may mourn over the
flowers which have withered in his grasp, but the
Christian has a treasure laid up in heaven, and his
heart is there also.   The orphan spirit may shrink
from the prospect of an unknown eternity; but the
child of God cannot but rejoice in the thought of
soon going home.

The evening of life!   Aged Christian, an everlasting morning will soon dawn upon your redeemed
and perfected spirit.   "Now is your salvation nearer
than when you believed."*   Mark with thankfulness
the shadows of evening as they deepen around you,
for they are the necessary precursors of the coming
day.   Calmly and trustingly as an infant that slum-
bers on its mother's bosom, you will soon "sleep in
Jesus," to awake in that purer and happier world,
which has "no need of the sun, neither of the moon,
to shine in it; for the glory of God doth lighten it,

* Rom. xiii. 11.

and the Lamb is the light thereof."* "Absent from the body," you will at once be "present with the Lord;"† you will "behold his face in righteousness;" you will "be satisfied, when you awake, with his likeness."‡

* Rev. xxi. 23.   † 2 Cor. v. 8.   ‡ Psa. xvii. 15.

The Old Folks.

ANONYMOUS.

Ah! don't be sorrowful, darling,
  And don't be sorrowful, pray;
Taking the year together, my dear,
  There isn't more night than day.

'Tis rainy weather, my darling,
  Time's waves, they heavily run;
But taking the year together, my dear,
  There isn't more cloud than sun.

We are old folks, now, my darling,
  Our heads are growing gray;
But taking the year all round, my dear,
  You will always find a May.

We have had our May, my darling,
  And our roses long ago;
And the time of the year is coming
  For the silent night of snow.

34

And God is God, my darling,
　Of night as well as day;
And we feel and know that we can go
　Wherever he leads the way.

A God of the night, my darling,
　Of the night of death so grim;
The gate that leads out of life, good wife,
　Is the gate that leads to Him.

Nightfall.

MARGARET JUNKIN.

The calm, full day, so flushed with light,
    So draped in placid majesty,
    Has sunk beneath the mystic sea
That shrouds the immortal from our sight.

We revelled in its affluent rays,
    We sunned us in its atmosphere;
    We drank its beauty—breathed its cheer,
And felt its bliss a thousand ways.

What princely flowers filled its morn!
    What rich results its noontide hours!
    How nobly its unresting powers
Have all the heat and burden borne!

'Tis well that kindly night should come
    With precious silence and release:
    So in our souls we whisper " peace"
At such a tranquil sinking home.

36

But while we miss the golden bars
    That bounded in this day so bright,
    We look aloft—and lo! the night
That closes round us throbs with stars!

Father, I Know.

MISS A. L. WARING.

FATHER, I know that all my life
   Is portioned out by thee,
And the changes that will surely come
   I do not fear to see;
But I ask thee for a quiet mind,
   Intent on pleasing thee.

I ask thee for a thankful love,
   Through constant watchings wise,
To meet the glad with cheerful smile,
   And to wipe the weeping eyes;
And a heart at leisure from itself
   To soothe and sympathize.

I would not have the restless will
   That wanders to and fro,
Seeking for some great thing to do
   Or secret thing to know:
I would be dealt with as a child,
   Led, guided where to go.

Wherever in the world I am,
  In whatsoe'er estate,
I have a fellowship with other hearts
  To keep and cultivate;
And a work of holy love to do
  For the Lord on whom I wait.

I ask thee for the daily strength
  To none that ask denied,
And a mind to blend with outward life
  While keeping at thy side—
Content to fill a little space,
  So thou be glorified!

And if some things I do not ask
  In my cup of blessing be,
I would have my spirit filled the more
  With gratitude to thee.
More careful than to serve thee much,
  To serve thee perfectly.

There are thorns besetting every path,
  That call for patient care;
There is a crook in every lot,
  And a need for earnest prayer;
But a lowly heart that leans on thee
  Is happy everywhere.

In a service that thy love appoints
    There are no bonds for me;
For my secret heart is taught the truth
    That makes thy children free;
And a life of self-renouncing love
    Is a life of liberty.

Our One Life.

HORATIUS BONAR, D. D.

'Tis not for man to trifle! life is brief;
    And sin is here.
Our age is but the falling of a leaf,
    A dropping tear.
We have no time to sport away the hours;
All must be earnest in a world like ours.

Not *many* lives, but only *one* have we—
    One, only one:
How sacred should that one life ever be—
    That narrow span!
Day after day filled up with blessed toil—
Hour after hour still bringing in new spoil.

Our being is no shadow of thin air—
    No vacant dream—
No fable of the things that never were,
    But only seem;
'Tis full of meaning as of mystery,
Though strange and solemn may that meaning be.

Our sorrows are no phantom of the night—
　　　No idle tale;
No cloud that floats along a sky of light,
　　　On summer gale;
They are the true realities of earth;
Friends and companions even from our birth

O life below—how brief, and poor, and sad!
　　　One heavy sigh.
O life above—how long, how fair, and glad!
　　　An endless joy.
Oh, to be done with daily dying here!
Oh, to begin the living in yon sphere!

O day of time, how dark! O sky and earth,
　　　How dull your hue!
O day of Christ, how bright!　O sky and earth,
　　　Made fair and new!
Come, better Eden, with thy fresher green;
Come, brighter Salem, gladden all the scene!

Retrospect.

MARTIN F. TUPPER.

How many years are fled!
How many friends are dead!
    Alas! how fast
    The past hath passed!
How speedily life hath sped!

Places that knew me of yore
Know me for theirs no more;
    And sore at the change,
    Quite strange I range
Where I was at home before.

Thoughts and things, each day,
Seem to be fading away;
    Yet this is, I wot,
    Their lot to be not
Continuing in one stay.

A mingled mesh it seems
Of facts and fancy's gleams;

43

I scarce have power,
From hour to hour,
To separate things from dreams.

Darkly, as in a glass,
Like a vain shadow they pass;
    Their ways they wend
    And tend to an end—
The goal of life, alas!

Alas! and wherefore so?
Be glad for this passing show;
    The world and its lust
    Back must to their dust,
Before the soul can grow.

Expand, my willing mind,
Thy nobler life to find;
    Thy childhood leave;
    Nor grieve to bereave
Thine age of toys behind.

Reflections on Old Age.

ARCHIBALD ALEXANDER, D. D.

The autumn of our life has actually arrived. The scenes of our youth have fled for ever; and the feelings and hopes of that period have passed away also, or are greatly changed. When we take a retrospect of the past, several weighty reflections cannot but press upon our minds and sadden our hearts. How true do we now find that trite remark, that the longest life in the retrospect appears exceedingly short, though in prospect the same period appeared almost interminable! Old age has come upon us (though its approaches were very gradual) by surprise; and even now, except when feeling something of the infirmities of age, or when viewing our altered image in the mirror, we are prone to forget that we are old; and often are impelled to undertake labours to which our strength is no longer competent. Truly our life of three-score, or more, appears like a dream when we awake from sleep. And as the past years have passed

45

so quickly, the few that remain will not be less rapid in their flight. Indeed, to the aged, except when they are suffering protracted pain, time appears shorter than it did when they were young. Thus at least it seems to the writer; the year, when its days and weeks and months are numbered, is as long as ever, but to our sense it seems to grow shorter. We are less absorbed and interested in passing scenes than the young. Life has with us become a sober reality. The enchanting visions of a youthful imagination have now entirely vanished. But it brings a solemn and tenderly melancholy feeling over the minds of the aged to inquire for the friends and companions of their youth. How few of these can we now find upon earth! The ministers whose labours were made useful to us, and the very sound of whose voice was sweeter than the richest music, are now lying beneath the clods of the valley. The beloved friends with whom we were wont to take sweet counsel, and to whom we could confidingly open our whole hearts, have been torn from our side. Many dear relatives, loved it may be as our own life, have slept the sleep of death. Time may have healed the painful wounds made by such bereavements, but their loss often leaves a chasm which can never be supplied, and, at any rate, a scar which we shall carry to the grave. There is one reflection connected with this subject still more sad; it is, that some in whom we once delighted, and in whom we reposed strong confidence, have turned aside from the ways of truth and righteousness in which they appeared to be walking, and, though they may be still walking up and down upon the earth, are dead to us and to all those interests which once seemed to be common to them and us. And as to those who remain steadfast, and have continued their pilgrimage without turning aside into crooked ways, what a sad change has time made upon their persons! Where is the bloom of youth, the robust strength of manhood, the eye sparkling with intelligence, and the countenance beaming with animation? Alas! they are fled; and in their place we see the decrepid body, the sunken eye, the withered countenance, and the tottering gait. All are not equally changed by the ravages of time. Indeed, to some the access of gray hairs and old age brings an addition of comeliness. There is something peculiarly lovely, as well as venerable, in the silvery locks and placid countenance of a good old man. There is in his countenance a chastened expression of benignity and sobriety which long experience alone can produce.

But the bitterest of all reflections to the aged is that of sins committed, duties omitted, time wasted, and opportunities of doing good neglected. Reflections of this kind, at certain times, become insufferably painful. And although we could not wish to go a second time through such a pilgrimage, yet we cannot but wish often that with our present views, and with the aids of experience, we could enjoy again the opportunities of usefulness which were suffered to pass without improvement. But even in these painful regrets and this bitter repentance our deceitful hearts often impose upon us, and we give ourselves more credit for present good feelings than we deserve. For let us only ask ourselves, whether we now avail ourselves of all the advantages of our situation to do good. Are we not now guilty of as gross neglects as when younger? The probability is, therefore—yea, the certainty—that if left to ourselves as much as we were, we should do no better if we were permitted to live over our unprofitable lives a second time.

But while we should lay aside all fruitless wishes, we ought certainly to reflect upon our sins and short-comings, until our godly sorrow is so enkindled within us as to work a repentance not to be repented of. We cannot atone for our sins by tears of penitence; for this we must have recourse to another fountain, even the blood of Christ, which cleanseth from all unrighteousness; but the flow of ingenuous, godly sorrow has a tendency to soften and purify the heart, and our iniquities are rendered by this means odious; so that while we are penetrated with unfeigned gratitude to God for pardoning mercy, we are rendered more watchful against our besetting sins, and made to walk more tenderly and circumspectly, and more humbly too; for I have thought, that the reason why a covenant-keeping God sometimes permits his children to fall into shameful acts of transgression is because nothing else but such a sight of themselves as these falls exhibit would sufficiently humble their proud hearts. The recollection of such sins serves all their life long to convince them that they ought to place themselves among the "chief of sinners" and "the least of saints." And this view of our exceeding depravity of heart serves to show us the faithfulness and loving-kindness of God in the strongest light. According to that which he speaks in Ezek. xvi. 62, 63, "And I will establish my covenant with thee; and thou shalt know that I am the Lord; that thou mayest remember, and be confounded, and never open thy mouth any more because of thy shame, when I am pacified toward thee for all that thou hast done, saith the Lord God."

My aged friends, permit me to counsel you not to

7

give way to despondency and unprofitable repining at the course of past events. Trust in the Lord, and encourage your hearts to hope in his mercy and faithfulness. Your afflictions may have been many and sore, and your present circumstances may be embarrassing, and your prospects for the future gloomy. Providence may seem to have set you up as a mark for the arrows of adversity. Stroke upon stroke has been experienced. Billow after billow has gone over you, and almost overwhelmed you. Truly the time has come when you can say, "My joys are gone." But though friends have been snatched from you or have proved unfaithful; though children, once your hope and joy, are numbered with the dead, or what is far worse, profligate or ungrateful; though your property has wasted away, or your riches suddenly taken wings and flown like the eagle to heaven; though bodily diseases and pain distress you,—still trust in the divine promise, " I will never leave thee, nor forsake thee." Though friends die, God for ever liveth. Though your earthly comforts and supports are gone, you are heir to an inheritance "incorruptible, and undefiled, and that fadeth not away." Take for your example the prophet Habakkuk, who triumphantly declares, "Although the fig tree shall not blossom, neither shall fruit be in the vines; the labour of the olive shall fail, and the fields shall yield no meat; the flock shall be cut off from the fold, and there shall be no herd in the stalls; yet I will rejoice in the Lord, I will joy in the God of my salvation." Learn to live by faith: no class of people need the supports of faith and hope more than the aged. And not only believe, but act. "Work while it is called to-day." "To do good, and communicate, forget not, for with such sacrifices God is well pleased." Your work is never ended while you are in the body. It is a sad mistake for aged persons to relinquish their usual pursuits and resign everything into the hands of their children. Many have dated their distressing melancholy from such a false step. The mind long accustomed to activity is miserable in a state of stagnation; or rather, having lost its usual nutriment, it turns and preys upon itself. Lighten your burdens, but do not give up business, or study, or whatever you have been accustomed to pursue. Imbecility and dotage are also prevented, or postponed, or mitigated, by constant exercise of the mind.

Keep also as much of your property, if you have any, in your own hand as is necessary for your own support, and make not yourselves dependent on the most affectionate and obedient children. They will be more affectionate and more respectful when you are not dependent.

Dismiss corroding cares and anxieties about what you shall do to get a living. How strange it is that the nearer men come to the end of their journey, the greater concern they feel as to the means of future subsistence! God's hand will provide. His command to us is, " Be careful for nothing; but in every thing by prayer and supplication with thanksgiving let your requests be made known unto God."

"And the peace of God, which passeth all understanding, shall keep your hearts and minds through Christ Jesus."

Christian Graces for the Aged.

ANONYMOUS.

BE *patient*—life is very brief,
    It passes quickly by;
And if it proves a troubled scene
    Beneath a stormy sky,
It is but like the shaded night
That brings a morn of radiance bright.

Be hopeful—cheerful faith will bring
    A living joy to thee,
And make thy life a hymn of praise,
    From doubt and murmur free;
Whilst like a sunbeam thou wilt bless,
And bring to others happiness!

Be earnest—an immortal soul
    Should be a worker true;
Employ thy talents for thy God,
    And ever keep in view
The judgment scene, the last great day,
When heaven and earth will pass away.

53

Be holy—let not sin's dark stain
  Thy spirit's whiteness dim—
Keep close to Jesus 'mid the world,
  And trust alone in him;
So, midst thy business and thy rest,
Thou shalt be comforted and blest.

Be prayerful—ask, and thou shalt have
  Strength equal to thy day;
Prayer clasps the Hand that guides the world:
  Oh, make it then thy stay!
Ask largely, and thy God will be
A kindly Giver unto thee!

Be ready—many fall around,
  Our loved ones disappear;
We know not when our call may come,
  Nor should we wait in fear;
If ready, we can calmly rest;
Living or dying, we are blest.

Bridges.

A. D. F. RANDOLPH.

I.

A BRIDGE within my heart,
   Known as the " Bridge of Sighs,"
That stretches from life's sunny part
   To where its darkness lies.

And when upon this bridge I stand,
   To watch the tides below,
How spread the shadows on the land !
   How dark the waters grow !

Then as they wind their way along
   To sorrow's bitter sea,
How mournful is the spirit-song
   That upward floats to me,—

A song that breathes of blessings dead,
   Of joys no longer known,
And pleasures gone ;—their distant tread
   Now to an echo grown.

And hearing thus, beleaguering fears
　　Soon shut the present out;
The good but in the past appears,
　　The future full of doubt.

Oh, often then doth deeper grow
　　The night that round me lies;
I would that life had run its flow,
　　Or never found its rise.

II.

A Bridge within my heart,
　　Known as the Bridge of Faith;
It spans by a mysterious art
　　The streams of life and death.

And when upon this bridge I stand,
　　To watch the tides below,
How glorious looks the sunny land!
　　How clear the waters flow!

Then as they wind their way along,
　　And to a distant sea,
I listen to the angel-song
　　That sweetly floats to me,—

A song of blessings never sere,
  Of love beyond compare;
And life so vexed and troublous here,
  So calm and perfect there.

And hearing thus, a peace divine
  Soon shuts each sorrow out,
And all is hopeful and benign
  Where all was fear and doubt.

Oh, ever then will brighter grow
  The light that round me lies;
I see from life's beclouded flow
  A crystal stream arise!

A Little While.

GREVILLE.

A LITTLE while, and every fear
　　That o'er the perfect day
Flings shadows dark and drear,
　　Shall pass like mist away;
The secret tear, the anxious sigh,
　　Shall pass into a smile;
Time changes to eternity,—
　　We only wait a little while.

A little while, and every charm
　　That steals away the heart,
And earthly joys that warm
　　And lure us from our part,
Shall cease our heavenly views to dim;
　　The world shall not beguile
Our ever-faithful thoughts from Him
　　Who bade us wait a little while.

A little while, and all around,
　　The earth, and sea, and sky,

The sunny light and sound
   Of nature's minstrelsy,
Shall be as they had never been,
   And we, so weak and vile,
Be creatures of a brighter scene,—
   We only wait a little while.

The Fruitless Tree.

JOHN M. LOWRIE, D. D.

"Nothing but leaves;" so the Saviour said,
    And then he blasted the fruitless tree;
And I ponder his curse with trembling dread,
    Lest just such a word he might speak of me:
I have known his name from my early youth,
    And my outward homage his cause receives;
Yet his judgment upon my life in truth
    Might render the verdict, "Nothing but leaves."

"Nothing but leaves," though the ground was choice;
    In the Lord's own garden the tree was set;
And loving parents by life and voice
    Gave cheerful care to nurture it; yet,
Though of rapid growth and comely form,
    No answering fruit their toil retrieves;
The blossoms fell off in the first spring storm,
    And autumn found on it "nothing but leaves."

"Nothing but leaves;" yet the church of God
    Wide open her doors every Sabbath threw;

6)

And faithful preachers proclaimed aloud
  His fearful wrath and his mercy too;
And the showers of grace, as dew, came down,
  And the Spirit called who never deceives;
How many the blessings my life has known!
  And still my returns are "nothing but leaves."

"Nothing but leaves;" yet I might have won
  More hearts than my own to taste his grace;
But the world's gay rounds my feet have run,
  Ever prone to the broad and downward ways;
Had I entered with zeal his harvest field,
  And now filled my arms with gathered sheaves,
What happy reflections my life would yield!
  How fearful the contrast, "Nothing but leaves!"

"Nothing but leaves;" though it has been so,
  Yet a remnant still of life remains;
Great God, thy renewing mercy show—
  I plead by the dying Saviour's pains!
May my zeal be warm, may my life be new,
  While every power of heart believes,
And holy influences ever show,
  That I give no longer "nothing but leaves."

Afternoon.

MARGARET JUNKIN.

You say the years have sadder grown
   Beneath their weight of care and duty,
That all the festive grace has flown,
   That wreathed and crowned their earlier beauty.

You tell me Hope no more can daze
   Your vision with her bland delusions,
Nor Fancy, versed in subtle ways,
   Seduce you to her gay conclusions.

The rapturous throb, the bound, the flush,
   That made all life one strong sensation,
Grow quiet now, beneath the hush
   Of time's profounder revelation.

You have it still—the inviolate past,
   So pure, so free from gloss and glitter:
The wine runs limpid to the last—
   No dregs to dash its beads with bitter.

Vixi:—thus looking back you write;
    The best that life can give, you've tasted;
And drop by drop, translucent, bright,
    You've sipped and drained—not one is wasted.

'Tis not in retrospect your eye
    Alone sees pathways pranked with flowers;
You knew the while the hours flew by,
    They were supremely blissful hours.

The sun slopes slowly westering still,
    Behind you now your shadow lengthens;
And in the vale beneath the hill
    The evening's growing purple strengthens.

The morning mists that swam your eye
    Made large and luminous life's ideal:
Now, cut against your clearer sky,
    You comprehend the true—the real.

Time still has joys that do not pall,
    Love still has hours serene and tender:
'Tis afternoon, dear,—that is all!
    And this is afternoon's calm splendour.

God grant your cloudless orb may run
    Long, golden cycles ere we sever;
Or, like the Northern midnight sun,
    Circle with light my heart for ever!

Old Age Anticipated.

REV. REUBEN SMITH.

You are now descending into the valley of declining years. That valley, we are persuaded, need not be dark if you but carry into it the lamp of true wisdom. To meet it aright requires reflection and experience. There is what may properly be called, perhaps, *the art of growing old.* But where shall it be found? or what are those precepts and appropriate considerations and practices by which we may sustain and comfort ourselves when found falling "into the sear and yellow leaf" of our earthly existence? To answer these questions is the design of the present undertaking.

Cicero, the heathen philosopher, has written something on this subject; nor do we think that his beautiful thoughts, so far as they go, are to be despised or wholly neglected. According to him, the different sources of molestation in old age are these four: 1. Our necessary withdrawing from the more active

64

pursuits of life. But he tells us there are other employments more appropriate to this condition; and these are specified and recommended. Then comes, 2. The loss of our voluptuary enjoyments; but these were never worthy of man, and their loss cannot be an annoyance when they are no more desired. 3. The failure of our *mental faculties* comes next, but this is not necessarily or universally true. Even memory need not essentially fail in old age, when it is cultivated; and he adduces many examples to show that it may still be strong. 4. But the most formidable of all the evils of old age is, *in that it compels us to contemplate a near approaching death;* and it is instructive to observe here by what an unsatisfying train of thoughts heathen philosophy attempts to meet this want. The argument of the aged Cato is essentially this: that death is not an evil to be dreaded, because it either ends our being, and then it is nothing; or there is an immortality, and then it leads to eternal felicity. There is, he thinks, no third estate. For himself, he is inclined to believe in immortality, and then he solaces himself with the thought that he shall meet there the spirits of the illustrious and beloved dead, who, like him, will have escaped from *t*his perturbed and transitory life! " O illustrious day!" he exclaims, "when this shall once be!"

9

Now, we are free to admit that all this, or most of it, is true and very interesting, with one exception. There are thoughts and precepts here not unworthy of a reflecting old age. But we are sure you feel their defectiveness. The last argument, in particular, is not only defective, but in part false. There *is* a third estate. Yes, we may live beyond time and *not* be happy. And then the *kind of solace* he seeks there is inferior, and ought not to be confined to the few things here specified. We need on every account a larger and securer instruction. In nothing, perhaps, does the superiority of the blessed gospel above the teachings of heathenism more strikingly appear than in what it teaches of future happiness and the true secret of a tranquil old age. The gospel brings life and immortality to light; the gospel does not vainly deny that old age is an evil in itself, but it admits its trials, and then provides appropriate alleviations.

I. Would we learn to bear the ills of old age so as to be happy under them? therefore, *let us learn, first of all, to expect it, and submit to it when it comes as a providential event.* We should learn, says the proverb, *to be seasonably old*, that we may be *long old*. By this it is not meant that we should antedate old age, or be too often dwelling upon it in our minds.

But since we know it must come, and has its annoyances, and that all this is the order of Providence, it is best to admit the truth freely, and make the best provision for it that we can. The man who denies his age, or attempts to conceal its approach from himself, acts unworthily both of his nature and condition. The consistent man rather faces his trials, anticipates them, and submits to them as they arise, because they are from God. And when he can say with John the Baptist, " He must increase, but *I must decrease*," and yet rejoice in the providence, the half of his difficulties are thereby removed.

II. Here also we may properly *look at and estimate the amount of these trials as they are usually seen to occur.* Some trials of age are inevitable, and others *may* come whence they ought not. We shall undoubtedly find some of our faculties and some of our enjoyments decreasing in that state. We may find ourselves pushed out of our places by those who are coming after us, and not always without a rough or thoughtless touch. The young do not in all cases honour gray hairs as they should. Some instances of vain and fanciful self-conceit will undoubtedly annoy us. The changes and wastings of things must constantly meet us—the thoughtlessness of the age aggravated to us by the too ready forgetting of what has gone before·—

jealousy of improvements because they are new, and grief for the loss of other things because they are old ;—all these are to be met perhaps in our own case, together with poverty, darkness and neglect; and then the inevitable necessity of being swept away at last by a " rude stream that must for ever hide us,"—this is more or less to be expected, and it is no wonder if the anticipations of such things do at times shake our faith and gather clouds over our future experience.

III. And yet it is comfortable to be able to believe *that the anticipations of abandonment and extreme trials in old age are not often realized.* On the contrary, except where vicious habits or peculiar circumstances have rendered escape impossible, the wants of age are remarkably provided for, and most persons are comparatively happy in that condition. They have many sources of enjoyment (as we shall soon see), and they have learned better to appreciate them. They have surmounted their annoyances, and their estate is generally tranquil, sometimes truly enviable. Their old age is peaceful, resigned, cheerful and deeply respected. " The apex of old age," says Cicero, " is *authority;*" by which we suppose to be meant that respect and influence to which a virtuous old man usually attains. For the attainment of this state, however, means are undoubtedly to be used. *The art* is to be learned and practised. We proceed to say, therefore,

IV. That an important means of rendering old age happy *is to have a sufficiency of appropriate employment.* Agriculture and gardening are particularly to be recommended. Let the old men plant trees, though they may never expect to eat the fruit of them; let them cultivate a cheerful intercourse with children— let them bring forward and encourage all virtuous and enlightened progress—let them sympathize with, and, as far as possible, relieve the afflicted—let them sedulously cherish the confidence of the young and seek to do them good—let them furnish the world with the results of experience and observation—transmit facts and recollections—set a goodly example of patience, prayer and steadfastness, in attachment to all good institutions; and if they have the proper furniture for it let them become authors. Old age, other things being suitable, seems the very time for authorship. We are told that Plato wrote at eighty-one years of age, and Isocrates at ninety-four. We might even recommend the study of languages, since every new language or science is an enlargement of mind, and a most absorbing employment. Cato is said to have learned Greek in his old age, and Socrates to play on musical instruments.

V. Again : *we should cultivate most carefully those faculties which are most usually impaired in old age.* *Memory* is one of these. The memory soonest fails undoubtedly; but it need not be altogether so; nor do we see why we should not remember all we desire to remember, as well in old age as at any other period. The reason why we do not probably is, that to many things we attach less importance than we did in earlier life. Seldom does any man forget his legal titles to property; the Christian never forgets the name of his Saviour. We should occupy our memories, therefore, with things most worthy to be remembered; and then much may be done by practising them. Sloth and neglect will ruin any faculty. "If the instrument be blunt, then must he put to the more strength."

VI. On the same principle, it is important *to keep alive our hope and ambition in old age.* The affections of the mind can in many things control bodily infirmities, and among these affections there are none stronger than those of hope and ambition. "An old man can do something," says one; "I will show it," cries another; and "I shall succeed," says a third. And now by believing, feeling, and *trying*, success and great usefulness are finally attained; while on the other hand many no doubt have sunk prematurely, through mere discouragement or retiring too early from the activities of life. Cases are occurring to show that health and physical strength may be greatly extended by determined and appropriate efforts, and why should it not be so with mental activities? Let us never give up hope.

VII. Let us learn *to avoid and resist as far as possible those things which may be called the besetting infirmities of this condition.* These are jealousy of neglect, an undue valuation of old things, peevishness, neglect of personal appearance, moroseness, or discontent with our whole condition. These are natural tendencies undoubtedly, and great annoyances where they exist; but much may be done by foreseeing and avoiding them. It was Dean Swift who wrote his resolutions as to *what he would not do* in old age. But the better recommendation is prayer, watchfulness, and a constant exercise of patience.

VIII. Another rule is, *to think as little as possible of our losses in old age, and more of the blessings which still remain.* No doubt natural differences of disposition will have influence here, and some cases are so providentially afflictive that human efforts can do little to modify them. But in general we believe that cheerfulness and entire contentment may be secured in the way now suggested; and we have wit-

nessed some cases of this that were truly edifying.
"See," said an old lady of eighty-six to her pastor,
"how well I can read without spectacles!"   "Yes," said
he, "and you have all these other comforts.   Here
are your convenient accommodations, your dutiful
children, and, above all, your Bible with all its precious promises."   "I know it, I know it," said she,
with rising animation; "I am only afraid that I am
not thankful enough."   Now that individual would
have been cheerful in almost any condition.   The
happiness we recommend is not of indifference, however—not of a mere animal, but of a rational being,
and therefore it is reflective.

IX. We must not omit now *those more direct exercises of prayer, and faith, and Christian meditation* so
necessary and so becoming the condition we are contemplating.   The aged should have opportunities for
these.   They should have retirement and freedom
from noise; and it is one of the greatest cruelties
practised upon them that these opportunities are
sometimes denied.   But what more pleasant, what
more appropriate and profitable, when they are enjoyed, than to

> "Walk thoughtful on the silent, solemn shore
> Of that vast ocean we must sail so soon;"

to spend much of our time in reading, meditation

and prayer; to withdraw our affections more and more from the world, like old Barzillai; to reflect much on God's dealings with us, like David in the 71st Psalm, and to seek the welfare of Zion, and all around us, as we find ourselves descending to the tomb!

"The land of silence and of death awaits my next remove:
  Oh may these poor remains of breath teach the wide world thy love."

X. But we come to the closing scene. We must all come there at last; and now the great question is—the only question worthy of much solicitude—*how shall we best be prepared to meet anticipated death?* Not, we answer, by the cold despisings of philosophy—not by mere natural resolution or vain speculation, as if death must either be nothing, or necessarily lead to eternal felicity. For, alas, we may live after death in a very different state! And no mere natural resources seem sufficient to face with calmness a responsibility like this. Nor yet is it a sufficient solace, in view of death, that we may say, We shall meet beyond death those with whom we held intercourse here on earth. No, we *feel*, we *know* that we want all this, *and more.* Now, the true Christian, and he alone, has this resource. To him the blessed gospel "has brought life and immortality to light." He believes this.

10

He has long obeyed the gospel, and tasted some of its blessed consolations; and now, in his old age, he lies down to die with infinitely more and better enjoyments than the wisest of heathens ever knew. He has all that Cicero wrote so pleasingly of; and then he goes much further. He knows he must die; he sees death near; and yet he does not shudder. He has heard his divine Redeemer say, "I am the resurrection and the life," and he responds, "I know that my Redeemer liveth." He is conscious, never more so than now, of his great sins and great deficiencies of obedience; but he knows also that he has a great and mighty Saviour, and "that the blood of Jesus Christ cleanseth from all sin." He expects a glorious resurrection also; and then as to the felicities that await him beyond the grave, he does not confine them to mere social intercourse, such as he possessed on earth, but expects these infinitely improved; and then the superadded and almost inconceivable fruition of a present God, an openly-beheld Saviour, and the society of all holy and elevated beings—angels and men—in one unwearying activity around the throne of God for ever. Illustrious day indeed, when all this is to be entered upon and enjoyed! As to leaving the world, he does not regret it, for he has enjoyed what of good it could ever afford, and finished his usefulness in it. Dear objects of his affection are there still, but he leaves his blessing with them, and hopes besides to meet them all again "at the great rising day." And thus he dies, easily, tranquilly, and with glorious hopes.

> "Sure the last end of the good man is peace.
> Night-dews fall not more gently to the ground;
> Nor weary, worn-out winds expire so soft."

Loving-Kindness.

REV. SAMUEL MEDLEY.

Awake, my soul, in joyful lays,
And sing thy great Redeemer's praise
He justly claims a song from thee;
His loving-kindness, oh, how free!

He saw me ruined in the fall,
Yet loved me notwithstanding all;
He saved me from my lost estate,
His loving-kindness, oh, how great!

Though num'rous hosts of mighty foes,
Though earth and hell my way oppose,
He safely leads my soul along,
His loving-kindness, oh, how strong!

When trouble, like a gloomy cloud,
Has gathered thick, and thundered loud,
He near my soul has always stood,
His loving-kindness, oh, how good!

Often I feel my sinful heart
Prone from my Saviour to depart;
But, though I oft have him forgot,
His loving-kindness changes not.

Soon shall I pass the gloomy vale,
Soon all my mortal powers must fail;
Oh, may my last expiring breath
His loving-kindness sing in death.

A Few More Days.

HORATIUS BONAR, D. D.

A FEW more years shall roll,
  A few more seasons come,
And we shall be with those that rest
  Asleep within the tomb.
Then, O my Lord, prepare
  My soul for that great day;
Oh wash me in thy precious blood,
  And take my sins away!

A few more suns shall set
  O'er these dark hills of time,
And we shall be where suns are not—
  A far serener clime.
Then, O my Lord, prepare
  My soul for that blest day;
Oh wash me in thy precious blood,
  And take my sins away!

A few more storms shall beat
  On this wild, rocky shore,

And we shall be where tempests cease,
  And surges swell no more.
Then, O my Lord, prepare
  My soul for that calm day;
Oh wash me in thy precious blood,
  And take my sins away.

A few more struggles here,
  A few more partings o'er,
A few more toils, a few more tears,
  And we shall weep no more.
Then, O my Lord, prepare
  My soul for that blest day;
Oh wash me in thy precious blood,
  And take my sins away.

Abide with Me.

REV. HENRY FRANCIS LYTE.

ABIDE with me!   Fast falls the eventide,
The darkness thickens; Lord, with me abide:
When other helpers fail, and comforts flee,
Help of the helpless, oh abide with me.

Swift to its close ebbs out life's little day;
Earth's joys grow dim, its glories pass away:
Change and decay in all around I see;
O thou, who changest not, abide with me.

Not a brief glance I beg, a passing word,
But as thou dwell'st with thy disciples, Lord—
Familiar, condescending, patient, free;
Come, not to sojourn, but abide, with me.

Thou on my head in early youth did'st smile,
And though rebellious and perverse meanwhile,
Thou hast not left me, oft as I left thee;
On to the close, O Lord, abide with me.

I need thy presence every passing hour;
What but thy grace can foil the tempter's power?
Who, like thyself, my guide and stay can be?
Through cloud and sunshine, oh abide with me.

I fear no foe with thee at hand to bless;
Ills have no weight, and tears no bitterness:
Where is death's sting? where, grave, thy victory?
I triumph still if thou abide with me.
11

God is my Light. *

HENGSTENBERG.

God is my Light!—Never, my soul, despair
    In hours of thy distress!
The sun withdraws, and earth is dark and drear;
    My light will never cease,
O days of joy with splendour beaming!
Through nights of grief, its rays are gleaming;
    God is my Light!

God is my Trust!—My soul, be not afraid!
    Thy Helper will abide:
" I'll not forsake thee!"—he has kindly said,—
    He's ever at thy side;
In feeble age will yet stand by thee,
No real good will he deny thee;—
    God is my Trust!

His is the power!—He speaks, and it is done;
    Commands, it standeth fast;

* Translated by Dr. Mills.

Ere hope of rescue is in me begun,
    Behold, the work is past!
When we our weakness most are feeling,
God loves to prove, his strength revealing,
    His is the power.

God is my shield!—Of me he takes the care
    As none beside could do;
He guards my head,—he watches every hair,
    All dangers brings me through;
While thousands, to vain helpers calling,
On right and left are near me falling,—
    He is my Shield!

God's my reward!—Well pleased I onward go
    The path that he has shown:
It has no trials but my God will know,
    When he awards my crown.
I'll gladly strive, the fight sustaining,
Until in death the victory gaining,—
    God's my Reward!

The Pilgrim's Retrospect.

REV. ROBERT F. SAMPLE.

"Call to remembrance the former days."—Heb. x. 32.

I'VE travelled a long and weary way,
   Through many a valley dim;
I have wept in the morning gray,
   And sobbed my evening hymn;
But 'tis the way that leads me home,
No more to weep, no more to roam;
     And like a Sabbath chime
     Along the by-gone time,
     The voice of Him who said,
     "'Tis I; be not afraid."

Sore conflicts oft with sin I've known,
   And tempest-tossed have been;
My heart was rent with many a groan;
   Alas, the power of sin!
But strength was given and armour bright;
I walked by faith, and not by sight;

84

And like a Sabbath chime
Along the by-gone time,
The voice of Him who said,
" 'Tis I ; be not afraid."

The light of cherished hopes went out,
   And dark'ning storms came on ;
In forests cold I roamed about,
   And refuge there was none ;
But Jesus came to my relief,
He hushed the wailings of my grief ;
      And like a Sabbath chime
      Along the by-gone time,
      The voice of Him who said,
      " 'Tis I ; be not afraid."

Soon on my home dark shadows fell,
   My dearly-loved was dead !
Then sadly tolled the funeral bell,
   And blinding tears were shed ;
But in the gloom arose a light,
As Jesus passed within my sight ;
      And like a Sabbath chime
      Along the by-gone time,
      The voice of Him who said,
      " 'Tis I ; be not afraid."

But mercies too have crowned my years,
  And many days were bright;
The lamps of heaven dispelled my fears,
  And bathed my path with light;
'Twas sweet to lean on Jesus' arm,
To feel secure from real harm;
    And like a Sabbath chime
    Along the by-gone time,
    The voice of Him who said,
    " 'Tis I; be not afraid."

Sympathy and Selfishness.

ANONYMOUS.

EACH season of life has its own peculiar tendencies and temptations. But selfishness is at all times and under all circumstances the common sin which doth so easily beset us. In early youth we are prone to imagine that everybody and everything about us ought in some way to minister to our gratification, and we therefore strive to employ them in the furtherance of the plans which we have arranged for our own happiness. In old age, when the infirmities of life compel us to withdraw from its activities and its pleasures, we are in danger of supposing that since we can derive but little enjoyment now from those sources which once yielded to us a rich supply, it is a matter of little importance to us whether others find any satisfaction in them or not. It often happens that old age narrows the channel of our benevolence and our sympathy; we have less to receive, and we think we cannot have so much to give. Our thoughts, allowed to take their natural course, become concentrated on "self;" all that personally con-

87

cerns us is so magnified as very much to hide from our view the interests of our neighbours; we look so steadily and so exclusively on our own good that we almost lose sight of the good of others.

Now, will you guard against the influence of these selfish feelings? Will you bear in mind how opposed, how thoroughly opposed, are selfishness and Christianity? Will you reflect upon the injury which you may do to religion by allowing an undue regard for self to be manifested in the little occurrences of your everyday life? A young man, who was urged by a pious friend to devote himself to the service of God, made this reply: "It is of no use to talk to me in this way; I have seen too much of religious people to desire to be like them. They pretend to be a great deal better than everybody else, but they are just the same underneath. Why, there's my uncle S———, an old man with one foot already in the grave; he calls himself a Christian, and yet he is as covetous and as selfish as possible. See him at home; *his* comfort, *his* ease, *his* wishes, must be first consulted; everybody must give way to him; and he is constantly taking offence because he thinks he has not sufficient attention and respect paid to him. What's the use of religion? it is all show—mere show."

It was not difficult to answer such an objection as this, but it was difficult to remove the prejudice and the misconception which had gathered around that young man's mind. The selfish behaviour of his aged relative, in conjunction with that of others, had so set him against religion that he would not listen to its claims; and, although moral and amiable in his conduct, he still remains estranged from God and from his people. It is true that the faults and inconsistencies of professed Christians will furnish no valid excuse for his refusal to love and serve his God and Saviour; but ought they not to excite the deepest grief and shame in those who have thus thrown additional stumbling-blocks in the way of a sinner's return? Ought we not earnestly to watch and pray that we do not bring reproach upon that holy name by which we are called, through our self-love and self-indulgence? It is not so much by flagrant departures from the ways of godliness that we exert a baneful influence over the undecided and the unconverted, as by our apparently careless disregard of whatsoever things are lovely and of good report. The warm and generous-hearted spirit of youth will shrink with distaste, if not with disgust, from a religion which our actions have led him to ally with meanness and selfishness. Our prayers, our zeal,

12

our alms-giving, our profession, will have but little
weight with him if they are associated day after day
with the unhallowed and unamiable endeavour to
secure our personal ease, in preference to the comfort
of others;—he will regard them but as sounding
brass or a tinkling cymbal. And will he not rightly
regard them? "Though I have all faith and knowledge; though I bestow all my goods to feed the poor;
and though I give my body to be burned, and have
not love—that love which seeketh not her own;
which vaunteth not itself, but which suffereth long
and is kind—it profiteth me nothing."*

Let not, then, the infirmities of age be a plea for
your lessened sympathy with others. Should the
graces of the Christian decline with his fading
strength? should the shadow of the tomb dim the
light of his heaven-born love? Surely the nearer
that he approaches to the pure and peaceful fellowship of the saints above, the more should his spirit
be conformed to theirs. And is theirs a spirit of
selfishness? Are they absorbed in their own interests, their own occupations, their own joys? are they
indifferent to the feelings and the pleasures of their
bright companions? No; they joyfully and fully
sympathize with each other; self is forgotten there;

* 1 Cor. xiii.

and if we hope, through a Saviour's merits, to reach the home where they dwell, let us endeavour to cherish corresponding emotions to theirs. Let us strive to follow them as they, when on earth, followed Christ. Ah, let us rather look at once at Jesus, our perfect model, our brightest example; let us ask to have the mind that was in him, and to be imbued with his Spirit. For then we cannot live day after day—as some who profess and call themselves Christians do live—cold and careless about the welfare of others, and at the same time intensely solicitous to promote our own. "Ye have not so learned Christ; if so be that ye have heard him, and have been taught by him, as the truth is in Jesus."* His doctrine which we have received into our hearts, and his example which we have chosen as the guide of our conduct, lead us to deny ourselves that we may benefit others, and to take the liveliest interest in all that relates to their happiness.

And we are not to retrace our steps as years increase. We are not to be peevish, discontented, or unreasonable because we are old or getting old. This is certainly not our creed, and, God helping us, it shall never be our practice. As we advance in life we should be more considerate, more kind, more

* Eph. iv. 20, 21.

like Christ, not less so; and if we abide in him, and his words abide in us, there can be no doubt that we shall thus grow in grace. The stream of Christian affection will become deeper, not shallower; the flame of unselfish love will burn more brightly, instead of almost going out.

Oh how delightful is the sight of an aged believer richly imbued with the loving and unselfish spirit of his Master! How refreshing is it in this dreary world to rest a while beneath some venerable palm tree, which spreads out its cooling branches as if the only object of its existence were to bless the passer-by! How cheering is it, amidst the selfish and dissatisfied throng around us, to meet with those who can smile through their own tears upon the happy and the gifted!

An aged servant of the Lord had survived all her near relatives; the last beloved object of her tender affections, of her constant recollection, was laid in the grave. Her life had been the scene of many sorrows, and there was but little sunshine to cheer the evening of her life. One day, as, lonely and blind, she sat by the fireside in her little parlour, a friend who called to see her found her—doing what? Murmuring over her desolate condition, and complaining that she was uncared-for and forgotten?

No, but rejoicing in the happiness of others. A family whom she had known and loved in early life was to be gladdened on that day by the return of a long-absent member; and, through its dull and silent hours, her lips were often unclosed to express her delight at the thoughts of their meeting, her prayers that they might be blessed. " Were this my case," thought the listener, " I should have been repining that others had the comfort of tender relatives and loving friends, while I was left alone in the world, looking for none whose approach could console and gladden my solitary existence." The latter feeling is the emotion of the natural heart—the former of the Christian spirit. Reader, which would have been *yours?*

Thy Saviour's Prayer.

ANONYMOUS.

"I pray not that thou shouldest take them out of the world, but that thou
shouldest keep them from the evil."—John xvii. 15.

PILGRIM in the path of life,
Fainting in the daily strife,
Wishing, longing to be free
From thy load of misery,
Panting for the heavenly home,
Where no blighting sorrows come:
List thy Saviour's prayer for thee,
Wait his time to set thee free.

Mourner, bending o'er the dead,
From whose cheek the bloom has fled,
Gazing in the glassy eye,
Vainly asking for reply,
Wishing that thy days were done,
And thou with thy beloved one:
List thy Saviour's prayer for thee,
Wait his time to set thee free.

94

Aged wanderer, sad and lone,
All thy youth's companions gone,
Like blasted trunk, round which the vine
Shall never more its tendrils twine,
Like stranger on a foreign coast
Weeping o'er his treasures lost:
List thy Saviour's prayer for thee,
Wait his time to set thee free.

" Not that thou should'st take away
These thy creatures of a day,
Pray I, Father, but that in
Thy mercy thou would'st save from **sin :**
Keep them from the evil one,
Till their course of life is run."
This thy Saviour prayed for thee;
Patient wait till thou art free.

The Aged Christian.

ANONYMOUS.

THE spring and summer time of life have long since
     pass'd away,
And golden autumn, with its leaves of sadness and
     decay,
Has come and gone; and winter shrouds each lovely
     scene in gloom,
And bids me mark across my path the shadows of
     the tomb.

Mine eye is growing dim with age, my step is feeble
     now,
And deeper lines of thought and care are graven on
     my brow;
But shall I murmur as I trace the rapid flight of
     hours,
Or grasp with trembling eagerness earth's fair yet
     fading flowers?

Oh no! a bright and happy home awaiteth me above,
And my ardent spirit longs to dwell where all is joy
     and love.

Does the wave-tossed mariner regret when he sees
    the haven near
Where his shattered bark shall safely rest, nor storm
    nor danger fear?

Will the toil-worn labourer sigh because his weary
    task must close,
And evening's peaceful shades afford him calm and
    sweet repose?
Or does the child with sorrow mark each swift re-
    volving mile
Which bears him to his cherished home and loving .
    father's smile?

And shall the Christian grieve because some gentle
    signs are given
That he is nearer to the bliss, the perfect bliss of
    heaven?
That every moment closer brings that mansion fair
    and bright,
Prepared for him with tender love in realms of pure
    delight?

Oh! with such brilliant hopes as these how can my
    heart repine,
Although I feel my vigour fade, my wonted strength
    decline?

13

Rather with gladness would I hail these messages of
     love,
Which tell me I shall quickly join the white-robed
     throng above.

My pilgrimage will soon be o'er, my arduous race be
     run,
And the bright crown of victory triumphant faith
     have won ;
No sorrow clouds the land of rest, hush'd is the thought
     of pain :
Oh ! if for me to live is Christ, to die indeed is gain !

The Voice from Galilee.

HORATIUS BONAR, D. D.

"Of his fulness have all we received, and grace for grace."—John i. 16.

I HEARD the voice of Jesus say,
 Come unto me and rest;
Lay down, thou weary one, lay down
 Thy head upon my breast.
I came to Jesus as I was,
 Weary, and worn, and sad;
I found in him a resting-place,
 And he has made me glad.

I heard the voice of Jesus say, .
 Behold, I freely give
The living water,—thirsty one,
 Stoop down, and drink, and live.
I came to Jesus and I drank
 Of that life-giving stream;
My thirst was quenched, my soul revived,
 And now I live in him.

99

I heard the voice of Jesus say,
    I am this dark world's light,
Look unto me, thy morn shall rise,
    And all thy day be bright.
I looked to Jesus and I found
    In him my star, my sun;
And in that light of life I'll walk
    Till travelling days are done.

The Father-Land.*

FROM THE GERMAN OF CLAUS HARMS.

Know ye the land—on earth 'twere vainly sought—
To which the heart in sorrows turns its thought?
Where no complaint is heard,—tears never flow,—
The good are blest,—the weak with vigour glow?
Know ye it well?
                    For this, for this,
All earthly wish or care, my friends, dismiss!

Know ye the way—the rugged path of thorns?
His lagging progress there the traveller mourns;
He faints, he sinks,—from dust he cries to God—
" Relieve me, Father, from the weary road!"
Know ye it well?
                    It guides, it guides
To that dear land where all we hope abides.

Know ye that Friend?—In him a man you see;—
Yet more than man, more than all men, is he:

*Translated by Dr. Mills.

Himself before us trod the path of thorns;
To pilgrims now his heart with pity turns.
Know ye him well?

　　　　　　　His hand, his hand
Will safely bring us to that Father-land.

The Palm.

JAMES HAMILTON, D. D.

"The righteous shall flourish like the palm tree."—Psa. xcii. 12.

THE Palm brings forth its best fruit in old age. The best dates are said to be gathered when it has reached a hundred years. So it is with eminent Christians: the older the better; the older the more beautiful; nay, the older the more useful; and, different from worldlings, the older the happier. The best Christians are those who improve to the end, who grow in grace and in the knowledge of Jesus Christ to the very close of life.

They loved him at first, but now they love him more. At first they were selfish, and only sought to escape from wrath; now they are jealous of the Saviour's honour, and long to be saved from sin. At first they only thought of the Priest; now they perceive the Priest upon a throne, and love not only the Saviour's cross, but the Saviour's yoke and the Saviour's laws. One Jesus is their King. And they grow in knowledge of themselves. The truth to

103

which they once assented becomes a deep-wrought experience. "In me, that is, in my flesh, dwelleth no good thing." And the discovery of this depravity, the knowledge how debased and worthless their nature has become, instead of making them morose and bitter towards their fellow-sharers in the fall, makes them lenient and considerate. They know themselves too well to expect perfection in their friends, and find brethren to whom they can stick close in the face of obvious failings; and even when they hear of awful wickedness, indignation is chastened by shame and self-consciousness. It is something of the old Reformer's feeling when he saw the malefactor led to prison:—"There, but for the grace of God, goes John Bradford." And they grow in wisdom. Long experience, and still more the secret of the Lord, dispassionate observation and heavenly-mindedness, have given them sagacity; and sometimes in homely adages, sometimes in direct and sober counsel, they deal forth that mellow wisdom. And they grow in spirituality. We have seen those aged pilgrims to whom earthly things at last grew insipid; they had no curiosity for the news of the day, and little taste for fresh and entertaining books. They stuck to God's testimonies, and you never went in to see them but the ample Bible lay

open on the table or the counterpane; and they could
tell the portion which had been that morning's food
or the meditation of the previous night. The word
of God dwelt in them so richly that you could see
they were becoming fit to dwell with God; for when
a mind has become thoroughly scriptural it wants
but another step to make it celestial. And the last
harvest came, and the last gleanings of their precious
words, and when next we went that way their place
knew them no longer. They were flourishing in the
courts of God's house on high, and we should sit
under their shadow and be regaled by their goodness
no more. But when we recollected how fair their
Christian profession was, how beneficent and service-
able they had ever been, and remembered that their
last days were their brightest, and their last fruits
their fairest, we said over to ourselves, "The righteous shall flourish like the palm tree. Those that
be planted in the house of the Lord shall flourish in
the courts of our God. They shall bring forth fruit
in old age; they shall be fat and flourishing; to show
that the Lord is upright; he is my Rock, and there
is no unrighteousness in him."

Dear Christian reader, when your own ear cannot
hear it, may this be your eulogy: when your own eye
cannot read it, may this be your epitaph. In the

14

meanwhile, for the sake of that Saviour who is dishonoured by proud and selfish and unlovely disciples, do you strive and pray for consistency. And for your own soul's sake, which is dulled by defective views, and depressed by each besetting sin, do you seek a serene and lofty faith—do you covet earnestly a blameless conversation. Let your triumphs over self, and your high-hearted zeal for the Saviour, let the largeness of your spirit and your heavenly elevation, let the exuberance of your goodness and the multitude of its special acts, let the fulness of your affections and the freshness of your feelings, and the abundance of your beneficence, make the Christian manifest and unmistakable. Let your happy piety be the far-eyed signal announcing an oasis in the desert, and pray that your church or congregation may become to weary pilgrims another Elim, where when they came they found "twelve wells of water, and threescore and ten palm trees."

God, my Exceeding Joy.

JAMES W. ALEXANDER, D. D.

Psalm xliii. 4.

EARLY my spirit turned
  From earthly things away,
And agonized and yearned
  For the eternal day;
Dimly I saw when but a boy,
God, my exceeding joy.

In days of fiercer flame,
  When passion urged me on,
'Twas only bliss in name—
  The pleasure soon was gone.
Compared with thee how all things cloy,
God, my exceeding joy!

At length the moment came—
  Jesus made known his love;
High shot the kindling flame
  To glories all above,

Now all the powers one theme employ—
God, my exceeding joy.

Shadows came on apace;
    Tears were a pensive shower;
I cried for timely grace
    To save me from the hour;
Thou gavest peace, without alloy;
God, my exceeding joy.

One trial yet awaits,
    Gigantic at the close;
All that my spirit hates
    May then my peace oppose;
But God shall this last foe destroy,—
God, my exceeding joy

A Name in the Sand.

HANNAH F. GOULD.

ALONE I walked the ocean strand,
A pearly shell was in my hand;
I stooped, and wrote upon the sand
    My name—the year—the day;
As onward from the spot I passed,
One lingering look behind I cast—
A wave came rolling high and fast,
    And washed my lines away.

And so, methought, 'twill shortly be
With every mark on earth from me;
A wave of dark oblivion's sea
    Will sweep across the place
Where I have trod the sandy shore
Of time, and been, to be no more;
Of me, my frame, the name I bore,
    To leave no track nor trace.

And yet, with him who counts the sands,
And holds the waters in his hands,

I know a lasting record stands
    Inscribed against my name,
Of all this mortal part has wrought,
Of all this thinking soul has thought,
And from these fleeting moments caught
    For glory or for shame!

Still will we Trust.

WILLIAM H. BURLEIGH.

STILL will we trust, though earth seem dark and
    dreary,
  And the heart faint beneath his chastening rod;
Though rough and steep our pathway, worn and
    weary,
      Still will we trust in God!

Our eyes see dimly till by faith anointed,
  And our blind choosing brings us grief and pain;
Through Him alone who hath our way appointed
      We find our peace again.

Choose for us, God!—nor let our weak preferring
  Cheat our poor souls of good thou hast designed;
Choose for us, God!—thy wisdom is unerring,
      And we are fools and blind.

So from our sky the night shall furl her shadows,
  And day pour gladness through his golden gates;
Our rough path leads to flower-enamelled meadows,
      Where joy our coming waits.

Let us press on in patient self-denial,
    Accept the hardship, shrinking not from loss—
Our guerdon lies beyond the hour of trial;
      Our crown beyond the cross.

A Prospect of Heaven.

ISAAC WATTS, D. D.

THERE is a land of pure delight,
　Where saints immortal reign;
Infinite day excludes the night,
　And pleasures banish pain.

There everlasting spring abides,
　And never-withering flow'rs;
Death, like a narrow sea, divides
　This heavenly land from ours.

Sweet fields beyond the swelling flood
　Stand dressed in living green;
So to the Jews old Caanan stood,
　While Jordan rolled between.

But timorous mortals start and shrink
　To cross this narrow sea;
And linger, shivering on the brink,
　And fear to launch away.

Oh could we make our doubts remove—
    Those gloomy doubts that rise—
And see the Caanan that we love
    With unbeclouded eyes;

Could we but climb where Moses stood,
    And view the landscape o'er,
Not Jordan's stream, nor death's cold flood,
    Should fright us from the shore.

Counsels to the Aged.

ARCHIBALD ALEXANDER, D. D.

As an aged man, I would say to my fellow-pilgrims who are also in this advanced stage of the journey of life, ENDEAVOUR TO BE USEFUL as long as you are continued upon earth. We are, it is true, subject to many peculiar infirmities, both of body and mind, to bear up under which requires much exertion, and no small share of divine assistance; but still we have some advantages not possessed by the young. We have received important lessons from experience, which, if they have been rightly improved, are of inestimable value. The book of divine providence, which is in a great measure sealed to them, has been unfolded to us. We can look back and contemplate all the way along which the Lord has led us. We can now see the wise design of our Father in many events which, at the time, were dark and mysterious. The knowledge to be derived from studying the book of God's providence cannot be communicated to

115

another; the lessons are like the name upon the white stone, which none can read but he that has it. The successive events of our lives we can make known, but the connection which these events have with our character, our sins, and our prayers can be fully understood only by ourselves. He who neglects to study the pages of this book deprives himself of one most important means of improvement; yet many professors of religion appear to pay little or no attention to the providence of God in relation to themselves. If they meet with some severe judgment or some great deliverance, their attention is arrested, and they acknowledge the hand of God in the dispensation; but as to the succession of ordinary events, they seem to have no practical belief that they are ordered by divine providence, or have any important relation to their duty or interest. I would affectionately entreat my aged brethren to make the dealings of God's providence towards themselves a subject of careful study. There is within our reach, except in the Bible, no source of instruction more important. And to aid you in this business permit me to recommend to your careful perusal two little volumes on Providence, which I have found useful and comfortable to myself. The first is Flavel's "Mystery of Providence Opened;" and the other is Boston's

"Crook in the Lot." These excellent treatises may be read over and over again with profit. Perhaps the best method of studying such books is, not to read the whole at once, or in a short time, but to peruse a few paragraphs at a time, and then reflect upon the subject, and make application of what we read to our own case. And while I am recommending works on this subject I ought not to omit mentioning Charnock's treatise on "Providence." I confess I am not so familiar with this as the treatises before mentioned, but I have found his other writings, especially those on the Divine Attributes, so surpassing in excellence that I feel willing to recommend any thing which ever proceeded from his pen.

I began this letter with an exhortation to endeavour to be useful while you live. To comply with this you should, in the first place, guard vigilantly against those faults and foibles into which old people are apt to fall. We must be careful not to mistake moroseness for seriousness, austerity for gravity, or discontent with our condition for deadness to the world.

Why should the aged be more peevish and morose than others? If they are pious, there can be no good reason for it; but it is not difficult to account for the *fact.* In the decline of life a gradual change takes

place in our physical system by which the mind is
considerably affected; and often positive disease is
added to this natural change. The nervous system
is debilitated and shattered; and in consequence the
spirits are apt to sink or to become irregular. To
these may be added the afflictions and disappointments which most experience in the course of a long
life, by which the temper is apt to be soured. And
when men, by reason of the decay of mind and body,
become disqualified for the same active services which
they were long accustomed to perform, and these fall
into the hands of juniors, whom they knew when
children, it is very natural to feel as if the world was
turning round—as if every thing was going wrong.
Old men have always been wont to laud the times,
long past, when they were young, and to censure all
the innovations which have come in since. Sometimes, also, the aged experience a neglect from the
young, and even a want of respect from their own
children, which is exceedingly mortifying, and tends
much to foster that acerbity of temper so frequently
found in the aged.

But although these and other similar things may
be truly pleaded in extenuation of the fault under
consideration, yet they do by no means amount to
an apology which exculpates us from blame. And

that old age is not necessarily accompanied by these unamiable traits of character is proved by many happy examples. Some aged persons exhibit an uniform cheerfulness and serenity of mind; and the remarkable fact has been recorded in regard to a few that a naturally irritable temper has been softened and mellowed, instead of being exacerbated by old age. If I recollect rightly, this is mentioned as true in relation to the Rev. Dr. Rodgers of New York by his biographer, my respected colleague, the Rev. Dr. Miller. The late venerable Dr. Livingston, of the Dutch Reformed Church, President of their College and Seminary, was distinguished by uniform cheerfulness to a very advanced age; and his cordial and affectionate manners were remarked and felt by all who approached him. The Rev. John Newton, of London, seems to have possessed, with large measures of divine grace, a very happy physical temperament. It is delightful to contemplate the old age of such a man. And while I am mentioning recorded examples of a temper in old age deserving of imitation, I would recall to the remembrance of my readers the case of the Rev. Dr. Thomas Scott, who, at a period of life when most men relinquish all severe labour, actually undertook to learn the Arabic language, that he might be able to give

instruction to the missionaries going to the East
It has often been noticed that piety is apt to decline
with the decline of manly vigour. If this be really
a common event, it is exceedingly to be deplored.
But perhaps it is more in appearance than reality.
It requires much stronger faith and feelings of
warmer piety to enable an old man to go forward in
his course with zeal and alacrity than for a young
man, who is buoyed up and borne along by the vigour
of youthful passions, to do the same. But I rejoice
to know that piety does not always even appear to
grow cold by the descent into the vale of years. In
some Christians it evidently goes on advancing; and
their growth in grace is much more rapid in this
period of life than any other. As they approach
nearer to heaven, their hearts and their conversation
are more in heaven. Oh that it might be thus with us
all! As these letters are intended also for my aged
friends of the female sex, I would recommend to
their notice and imitation the old age of Mrs. Hannah More. From her first appearance as a Christian
she seems to have gone on advancing in evangelical
knowledge and ardent piety until she was completely superannuated. And even then she lost nothing of the respect and affection which by her pious
and benevolent labours she had gained; for still,

when her memory was so impaired that she did not remember the books she had written; the elevation of her piety and the enlargement of her benevolence remained unimpaired. And it is truly a delightful thought that when in the wreck of mind the whole cargo of knowledge seems to be lost, and parents no longer recognize their own children, religion, where it was possessed, still remains. JESUS CHRIST IS NEVER FORGOTTEN. Pious sentiments are never obliterated. Cicero in his beautiful little treatise on Old Age, in which many judicious and pleasing sentiments are expressed, when speaking of the decay of the memory, says that he never heard of a miser forgetting the place where he had buried his treasure. What the mind prizes most is longest retained in memory. It is often remarked, and justly, "How beautiful does unaffected piety appear in youth!" But it may as truly be said, "How amiable and venerable is exalted piety in old age!"

It has been said that avarice is peculiarly the sin of age; we often hear of an old, but scarcely ever of a young, miser. This may be true in regard to those who have cherished the love of the world all their lives. They will hug their treasures with a closer grasp, and their affections will be more concentrated on them when other objects are removed; but this

16

vice does not originate in old age; it is only the ma
ture fruit of the seed planted in early life; and though
it becomes deeply radicated in old age, it is not now
so much the desire of acquiring wealth as of holding
fast what they have got. The folly of the miser who
hoards his money without a thought of using it is
easily shown, and has often been ridiculed. But the
truth is, that all ardent pursuit of worldly objects
beyond what is necessary for the real wants of nature
might be demonstrated to be equally absurd. But
whatever men of the world may do, let not Christians
dishonour their holy profession by an inordinate love
of the world. Especially, let not the aged professor
bring into doubt the sincerity of his religion by
manifesting a covetous disposition. "Take heed,"
said the Great Teacher, "and beware of covetousness;
for a man's life consisteth not in the abundance of the
things which he possesseth." Many begin the world
with little, and the claims of an increasing family
render it necessary to exercise much diligence and
economy to make a living; but thus it often happens
that an avaricious disposition under the semblance
of necessity, and even of duty, strikes its roots deep
into the soul ere the man is aware of any danger.
Indeed, it is almost impossible to convince a man of
the sin of covetousness while he avoids open acts of

injustice or fraud. Dear friends, it is time for many of you to give up the further pursuit of wealth, unless your object is to acquire the means of doing good. But beware of the deceitfulness of the heart. Covetousness will allow you to *promise* such an appropriation of your gains. But put yourselves to the test by a simple experiment. Ask yourselves whether you are now willing to make that use of the property which God has given you that his honour and the advancement of Christ's kingdom require. If you indeed find in yourself that disposition to consecrate all that you have to the glory of God, then it may be lawful to go on to acquire further means of usefulness. But whatever you now possess, or may hereafter acquire, of this world's goods, for your soul's sake set not your affections on these perishable things. Be not proud of your wealth. Neglect not while you live to do good and communicate. Remember that you are but the steward of the wealth which you possess, and therefore it is required of you to be faithful in the distribution of what is put into your hands. If you have tried the plan of parsimony lest you should lessen your estate, now try the plan of wise liberality, and see whether that saying of Christ is not verified by experience, that " It is more blessed to give than to receive."

Whether in the former periods of our lives we have had prosperity or have passed through the deep waters of affliction, it is nearly certain that in our old age we shall feel the strokes of adversity. If our friends have been preserved in life thus far, yet we know they must all die. If hitherto we have enjoyed uninterrupted health, yet now we must expect to encounter pain and disease. Old age itself may be called the common disease of our nature, which can only be escaped by death. Mr. Newton, in one of his last letters, says that he had but one disease, but that was incurable, which was old age. Then, my dear friends, let us set an example of patience and cheerful resignation under the afflictions which may be laid upon us. The passive virtues are more difficult to be exercised than the active, and God is perhaps more honoured by quiet submission to his will under sufferings than by the greatest achievements of zeal and exertion. But let us never forget that we have not the least strength in ourselves. We are dependent on the grace of God for every good thought and desire. But if we trust in him we shall never be ashamed.

Nearer to Thee.

MISS SARAH F. ADAMS.

"As the hart panteth after the water-brooks, so panteth my soul after thee, O God.

"My soul thirsteth for God, for the living God: when shall I come and appear before God?"—Psa. xlii. 1, 2.

"NEARER, my God, to thee—
Nearer to thee!"
E'en though it be a cross
That raiseth me;
Still all my song shall be,
" Nearer, my God, to thee—
Nearer to thee!"

Though like a wanderer,*
The sun go down—
Darkness comes over me,
My rest a stone;
Yet, in my dreams I'd be
Nearer, my God, to thee—
Nearer to thee!

* See Gen. xxviii. 10–22.

There let my way appear
　　Steps unto heaven;
All that thou sendest me
　　In mercy given;
Angels to beckon me
Nearer, my God, to thee—
　　Nearer to thee!

Then, with my waking thoughts
　　Bright with thy praise,
Out of my stony griefs
　　Bethel I'll raise;
So by my woes to be
Nearer, my God, to thee—
　　Nearer to thee!

And when on joyful wing,
　　Cleaving the sky,
Sun, moon, and stars forgot,
　　Upward I fly,
Still all my song shall be,
" Nearer, my God, to thee—
　　Nearer to thee!"

My Rest is in Heaven.

ANONYMOUS.

"Here we have no continuing city, but we seek one to come."—Heb.
xiii. 14.

My rest is in heaven, my rest is not here;
Then why should I tremble when trials are near?
Be hushed, my sad spirit; the worst that can come
But shortens thy journey, and hastens thee home.

It is not for me to be seeking my bliss
And building my hopes in a region like this;
I look for a city which hands have not piled—
I pant for a country by sin undefiled.

The thorn and the thistle around me may grow—
I would not lie down e'en on roses below;
I ask not my portion, I seek not a rest,
Till I find them for ever on Jesus' loved breast.

Let trial and danger my progress oppose,
They only make heaven more sweet at the close:
Come joy, or come sorrow, whate'er may befall;
A home with my God will make up for it all.

127

With a scrip on my back, and a staff in my hand,
I march on in haste through an enemy's land;
The road may be rough, but it cannot be long,
So I'll smooth it with hope and cheer it with song.

The Crown of my Hope.

WILLIAM COWPER.

My Saviour, whom absent I love,
  Whom, not having seen, I adore,
Whose name is exalted above
  All glory, dominion, and pow'r,—
Dissolve thou those bands that detain
  My soul from her portion in thee;
Ah! strike off this adamant chain,
  And make me eternally free.

When that happy era begins,
  When clothed in thy glories I shine,
Nor grieve any more by my sins
  The bosom on which I recline,
Oh then shall the veil be removed,
  And round me thy brightness be poured;
I'll meet him, whom absent I loved—
  I'll see, whom unseen I adored.

And then nevermore shall the fears,
  The trials, temptations and woes,

Which darken this valley of tears,
　Intrude on my blissful repose;
To Jesus, the crown of my hope,
　My soul is in haste to be gone;
Oh bear me, ye cherubim, up,
　And waft me away to his throne.

Home in View.

REV. JOHN NEWTON.

As when some weary trav'ller gains
   The height of some o'erlooking hill,
His heart revives, if cross the plains
   He eyes his home, though distant still.

While he surveys the much-lov'd spot,
   He slights the space that lies between;
His past fatigues are now forgot,
   Because his journey's end is seen.

Thus when the Christian pilgrim views,
   By faith, his mansion in the skies,
The sight his fainting strength renews
   And wings his speed to reach the prize.

The thought of home his spirit cheers,
   No more he grieves for troubles past;
Nor any future trial fears,
   So he may safe arrive at last.

131

'Tis there, he says, I am to dwell
   With Jesus, in the realms of day;
Then I shall bid my cares farewell,
   And he will wipe my tears away.

Jesus, on thee our hope depends,
   To lead us on to thine abode:
Assur'd our home will make amends
   For all our toil while on the road.

Evening Time.

JAMES MONTGOMERY.

Zechariah xiv. 7.

At evening time let there be light:—
   Life's little day draws near its close ;
Around me fall the shades of night,
   The night of death, the grave's repose;
   To crown my joys, to end my woes,
At evening time let there be light.

At evening time let there be light:—
   Stormy and dark hath been my day ;
Yet rose the morn benignly bright,
   Dews, birds and flowers cheer'd all the way;
   Oh for one sweet, one parting ray!
At evening time let there be light.

At evening time there *shall* be light:—
   For God hath said, "So let it be!"
Fear, doubt, and anguish take their flight ;
   His glory now is risen on me;
   Mine eyes shall his salvation see:
'Tis evening time, and there is light.

133

Husband to Wife,

ON ATTAINING A HALF CENTURY.

JOHN M. LOWRIE, D. D,

I REMEMBER, you remember, the days when first we
   met :

Those cheerful, pleasant hours of youth we never can
   forget;

And this our happiness was then, our happiness is
   now,—

No purer source of joy and peace is given man to
   know,—

That far above all earthly thoughts we had a common
   Friend,

A glorious Friend, around whose throne the hosts of
   heaven bend,

Yet dwells on earth the meek to bless, the humble to
   renew ;

We knew each other better then, because we knew
   him too.

134

I remember, you remember, how then we loved to
    trace,
With thankful hearts, yet now as then, the leadings
    of his grace;
For what were we that wrath should stay our guilty
    souls to spare?
Or why should we in grace so rich obtain the mean-
    est share?
And now, we trust with firmer faith, we bow around
    his seat,
As then to seek his guardian hand to guide our
    erring feet;
For still, as then, we walk by faith, observing his
    command,
And fall or falter save as he still holds us by the hand.

I remember, you remember, in days of gloom and grief,
We've shared their pains when we could find in him
    alone relief;
We knew they came at his command, we learned to
    bless him still,
To bow before his sovereign hand, submissive to his
    will:
And this upheld us many times when flesh and heart
    grew faint—
The cross and Calvary are still the strength of every
    saint—

That he was called this path to tread, this bitter cup
    to drink;
Should we not taste the griefs from which our Saviour
    did not shrink?

I remember, you remember, how little then we thought
Of anxious cares, dejecting fears, these later years
    have brought;
Though we had heard the world was cold—and
    thought we knew it too—
Yet sad experience impressed the lessons all anew;
But when our busy memory would the varied past
    recall,
With few regrets our thankful hearts would now re-
    view them all;
For ours has been a happy life, for every toil repaid,
"An hundred fold e'en in this life"—the Master's
    lips have said.

And we have learned, have fully learned, that all the
    toil and strife
Of these our changing years were but the discipline
    of life;
When friends that promised fair have changed to
    coldness and neglect,
When flaming pious zeal has cooled and lost our
    warm respect,

When hopes of good in youthful hearts have van-
    ished as the dew—
Such disappointments, ever met, yet still seemed
    ever new—
When death removed our best-tried friends to dwell
    before his face,
While we, alas! were left to mourn with none to fill
    their place:

Then have we learned, full well have learned—not
    only on one leaf,
But written clear on every page in plain and bold
    relief—
That though our souls have often felt discouraged by
    the way,
When rolling seas have tossed, or naught but deserts
    round us lay,
That still was ours a chosen way—the pathway of
    our God—
That wisdom chose out every grief, and mercy every
    rod;
And not one day, to cheer us still, did manna fail to
    fall;
And every hour of day and night the cloud was over
    all!

18

And we have learned, have partly learned, too much
    like them of old!

Forgive, O Lord, our unbelief and murmurings un-
    told!

The lessons which thy holy law from Sinai's summit
    gave,

And later lessons of thy word of him who came to
    save;

And not in vain—our life-long joy—and when our
    life is o'er,

Our nobler song with nobler tongues through ages
    evermore;

The song of all the Church of God when gathered
    round his throne,

Redeemed from sin, redeemed by blood of the Incar-
    nate Son.

So have we learned, have humbly learned, whatever
    be our lot,

That though deep darkness shrouds his ways, we
    comprehend them not,

'Tis ours to walk as duty bids, to find each daily
    care,

A joy which we may win, or else a cross that we must
    bear;

In either case his love may make the small or great
  impart

A portion of his grace to bless and purify the
  heart;

And thus we grow in faith and love, in fitness too for
  heaven,

By daily cares, all from above, just like the manna,
  given.

And I believe, as you believe, that nothing has been
  lost

Of all these lessons, oft impressed, at so severe a
  cost;

We needed each chastising blow the Father's hand
  has laid,

His strokes "according to our sins" his wrath has
  never made:

And though it may be we have failed to gather all
  we might,

To see the reasons of his love, to learn the way of
  right,

Yet slowly, oft unconsciously, his providence has
  wrought

To change our plans, our sympathies, our very modes
  of thought.

For we believe, with joy believe, that every passing
　　year,
Has better fitted us for life and for life's duties
　　here;
For though we do not yet confess we pass down life's
　　decline—
Though failing health may seem to make the sun less
　　clearly shine—
Yet hearts as warm for Christ's dear cause within
　　our breasts beat still,
And minds as clear to read his word and study out
　　his will;
And so the past has left its wealth that we may richer
　　prove,
To speak more wisely of his truth, more kindly of
　　his love.

And I believe, as you believe, that in these days by-
　　past,
The seed so freely scattered wide has not in vain
　　been cast;
Some have we seen spring up and fade e'er summer's
　　sun grew old,
But some has also borne its fruit, full to the hundred
　　fold;

And faith assures us that good seed, which fell we
    knew not where,
Left to the smiles and rains of heaven, of Providence
    the care,
Has brought forth fruit; no man can tell how far,
    how long, may spread,
Though planted by an infant's hand, the increase of
    one seed.

And I believe, as you believe, this life must soon be
    gone;
Our battles soon be fought, our crown for ever lost or
    won.
We hope that in that trial-day our ears may hear his
    word:
"Well done, good servants, share the joy for ever of
    your Lord;"
Yet in that gladsome hour our lips shall thankfully
    confess,
"Not unto us, O Lord, but to thy mercy and thy
    grace:"
But anxious fears and pains and sins and death
    itself shall cease,
While with the ransomed by his blood we'll taste his
    perfect peace.

To an Aged Unbeliever.

WILLIAM S. PLUMER, D. D.

Your life thus far has passed rapidly away. You felt surprise when you heard others speak of you as old. Perhaps even now you easily forget that you are no longer young. "Gray hairs are here and there upon Ephraim, yet he knoweth it not." It seemed hard for Samson to forget the feats of former days. Even when shorn of his strength he attempted new exploits. There is a vanity in some old persons which leads them to ape the young. Let every one act as best becomes his age. Paul says: "When I was a child, I spake as a child, I understood as a child, I thought as a child; but when I became a man, I put away childish things." It is a pitiable sight to see old and young trying to take each other's places. If you have passed middle life, admit the fact into your serious thoughts.

The Bible requires reverence for the aged. "Thou shalt rise up before the hoary head." I approach

142

you with the greatest respect. " I have a message
from God unto thee." I wish to deliver it meekly,
honestly, and solemnly. I beg you to hear it. I
will use neither many nor vain words.

I hope you believe the great truths of the Bible.
If you doubt any of them, I beseech you to give
yourself to prayer and to the word of God itself, that
you may know the truth and be persuaded of it. An
honest desire to know the truth, shown by prayer
and searching the Scriptures, God will bless. He
can teach you as no other can. Cry mightily to him.
Wisdom comes " from above."

No doubt you have sometimes said, " Let me die
the death of the righteous, and let my last end be
like his." But do not your actions show that while
you would die the death of the righteous you are not
leading his life? Remember, you have a soul. To
save it is " the one thing needful." He who is poor,
sick, and despised may save his soul, and so be happy
for ever. He who is rich, strong, and full of all
earthly good may lose his soul, and so be eternally
undone. Because it is immortal the soul is of priceless value. Many have undervalued it. None ever
thought it worth more than it is. God alone can
know its full value. No man can pay a ransom for
it, for its redemption is precious.. To save it God

gave his dear Son. To save it, Jesus wept, and bled, and died. To save it, the Holy Spirit calls you to repentance.

If you are not a true Christian, *your soul is now in a lost condition.* So the Bible teaches: "The soul that sinneth, it shall die;" "Except ye repent, ye shall all likewise perish;" "He that believeth not shall be damned;" "If our gospel be hid, it is hid to them that are LOST." So righteous is God, and so holy is his law, that many an aged person has felt the power of a fiery condemnation in his conscience before he left this world. William the Conqueror, of England, was a great king, warrior, and statesman. In his last days he wept, he groaned, he confessed, but no comfort came. He said: "Laden with many and grievous sins, I tremble; and being ready to be taken soon into the terrible examination of God, I am ignorant what I should do. I can by no means number the evils I have done these sixty years, for which I am now constrained, without stay, to render an account to the just Judge." Many a monarch has died in anguish of soul. Neither greatness nor obscurity can shield a guilty soul from the terrors of the Almighty. The aged, impenitent pauper has groaned away his dying breath in dismay on his bed of straw. Through life men often feel that they are not at peace with God, and dying they confess it. Death is commonly, though not always, an honest hour. Some hold out false signals even then, though not free from fears and terrors. At that trying moment, who would not prefer hope to fear, and peace to dismay? Yet without a change of heart and a pardon of all our sins we cannot be saved. We "are by nature the children of wrath," so that "he that believeth not is condemned already." If you, my aged friend, have not fled to Christ, you are condemned, you are lost.

But although your soul is lost, *it is not lost beyond recovery.* Blessed be God for that! "There is mercy with God, that he may be feared:" "With him is plenteous redemption :" "As I live, saith the Lord, I have no pleasure in the death of the wicked; but that the wicked turn from his way and live; turn ye, turn ye from your evil ways, for why will ye die?" I take up the words and repeat the question, Why will you die? Why will you not be saved? Will you not be saved? I trust you will. I pray you may. I know that by divine grace you can. The door of mercy is yet open, open to you. Though you have sinned long and much and grievously against God, yet he says: " To-day, if ye will hear his voice, harden not your hearts." For many years you thought it was time enough yet. Possibly this day your soul is taken in

19

some such snare. Stop and think, I pray you. Perhaps in an hour God may say: "Thy soul is required of thee." If he should, would you not be undone for ever? You know that men commonly die as they live; that a life of sin is the forerunner of endless misery; that dying regrets are a poor substitute for a life of holiness; and that a death-bed repentance is little to be trusted. No wise man will leave to his last hours the proper work of life.

But perhaps you think it is now too late to turn to God. Through hardness of heart you may not be in terrible despair. But the practical persuasion of your mind may be that God has no mercy for you, and that you have sinned too long to be forgiven. If so, let me plead with you to give up this delusion. Nowhere has God drawn up more terrible charges against sinners than in the first chapter of Isaiah, yet he concludes his address to these guilty men (and through them he speaks to you) thus: "Come, now, and let us reason together, saith the Lord; though your sins be as scarlet, they shall be as white as snow; though they be red like crimson, they shall be as wool." Could words better suit your case? and they are uttered in sincerity and truth. They are the words of God. He never mocks any of his creatures.

We have in the Bible an account of the conversion

of an old and very great sinner. Manasseh, the son of pious Hezekiah, was early instructed in the true religion. When he became king he restored idolatry, which was the highest kind of offence. He insulted God to his face by defiling the temple. He formed a league with Satan, and used enchantments and witch-craft, sins punishable with death by the fundamental law of his kingdom. He sacrificed his own children to devils. He was one of the worst of murderers. "He shed innocent blood very much, till he had filled Jerusalem from one end to another." He was obstinate and refractory under reproof. He made the nation follow his wicked practices. He seemed to be mad upon his idols and iniquities. His sin was aggravated by the example and instruction of his good father to the contrary, by his high station, by his malice and wantonness, by his stubbornness and by his long continuance in it. He ascended the throne at twelve years of age, and he lived to the age of sixty-seven. Yet when he was sixty-two years old— that is, when he had for fifty years together defiled his soul, corrupted his people, and insulted God by enormous crimes—he was brought to repentance, pardoned and saved. "Old or young sinners, great or small sinners, are not to be beaten off from Christ, but encouraged to repentance and faith; for who knows but the bowels of mercy may yearn at last upon one that hath all along rejected it?" God has vast treasures of rich mercy in store even for old and hardened sinners who will "cease to do evil, and learn to do well."

Even in our own day how many aged persons have been brought to repentance! Every old minister who has been very useful can tell of the wondrous displays of the grace of God to such. Mr. H—— was a man of good family. He was well educated, but a proud scorner. He avoided the house, the worship, and the people of God. He was profane and mingled with such. He was often intoxicated with strong drink. Yet at the age of seventy-two God's Spirit arrested him and brought him to cry for mercy. He lived for more than two years after his change, and gave the best evidence he could in that time that he was indeed a new man.

N. D—— went through nearly all the the war of American Independence with honour as a soldier, but not without injury to his morals. He was honest and truthful, but for more than fifty years of his life he seldom visited a church, and he was intemperate. God was not in all his thoughts till he was eighty-nine years old. Then he began with diligence and prayer to read the Scriptures. He went to the house of God. He sought private instruction also. After a season of great spiritual distress he was brought to settled peace of mind. I have heard his pastor say that he never saw a more lively Christian. He lived more than eighteen months after this change, and was eminently devout, humble and happy to the last. He learned to sing several hymns. Never shall I forget his appearance and voice as he sang,

"Amazing grace! how sweet the sound,
That saved a wretch like me!
I once was lost, but now am found;
Was blind, but now I see."

"That suits me, that suits me exactly!" he often said.

My aged friend, do you seek further assurances that there is mercy even for you if you will turn to God? Here they are: "Ho, every one that thirsteth, come ye to the waters, and he that hath no money; come ye, buy and eat; yea, come, buy wine and milk without money and without price." "Whosoever will, let him take the water of life freely." "Him that cometh unto me I will in no wise cast out." "The bruised reed he will not break, the smoking flax he will not quench." "A broken and a contrite heart, O God, thou wilt not despise." Say not, "It is too late." Call upon God in earnest prayer; ask others to pray for you and with you. Confess your sins to

God. If you have injured men, repair the injury as far as possible. "Seek the Lord, while he may be found." Come to Christ as you are, a poor, lost, helpless, guilty, polluted sinner, and he will save you. "He is able to save them to the uttermost that come unto God by him." But if you refuse another hour, it may be too late. This may be the last call you will ever have. Any moment you may drop into hell. Will you, will you, oh will you be saved?

Nothing but Leaves.

ANONYMOUS.

NOTHING but leaves : the Spirit grieves
    Over a wasted life—
Sins committed while conscience slept;
Promises made, but never kept;
    Hatred, battle, and strife—
      Nothing but leaves.

Nothing but leaves : no garnered sheaves
    Of life's fair ripened grain ;
Words, idle words, for earnest deeds.
We sow our seed—lo ! tares and weeds :
    We reap with toil and pain
      Nothing but leaves.

Nothing but leaves : memory weaves
    No veil to screen the past ;
As we retrace our weary way,
Counting each lost and misspent day,
    We find sadly at last,
      Nothing but leaves.

And shall we meet the Master so,
　　Bearing our withered leaves?
The Saviour looks for perfect fruit:
We stand before him, humbled, mute,
　　Waiting the word he breathes—
　　" Nothing but leaves."

God, our Help.

ISAAC WATTS, D.D.

Psalm xc.

Our God, our help in ages past,
   Our hope for years to come,
Our shelter from the stormy blast,
   And our eternal home.

Before the hills in order stood,
   Or earth received her frame,
From everlasting thou art God,
   To endless years the same.

Thy word commands our flesh to dust,
   " Return, ye sons of men ;"
All nations rose from earth at first,
   And turn to earth again.

A thousand ages in thy sight
   Are like an evening gone ;
Short as the watch that ends the night
   Before the rising dawn.

Time, like an ever-rolling stream,
  Bears all its sons away;
They fly forgotten, as a dream
  Dies at the opening day.

Our God, our help in ages past,
  Our hope for years to come,
Be thou our guard while troubles last,
  And our eternal home.

I Know that I must Die.

FROM THE GERMAN OF B. SCHMOLKE.

MY GOD! I know that I must die,
  My mortal life is passing hence;
On earth I neither hope nor try
  To find a lasting residence.
Then teach me, by thy heavenly grace,
With joy and peace my death to face.

My God! I know not when I die,
  What is the moment, or the hour,
How soon the clay may broken lie,
  How quickly pass away the flower;
Then may thy child prepared be
Through time to meet eternity.

My God! I know not how I die,
  For death has many ways to come,
In dark, mysterious agony,
  Or gently as a sleep to some.
Just as thou wilt! if but I be
For ever blessed, Lord, with thee.

155

My God! I know not where I die,
  Where is my grave, beneath what strand,
Yet from its gloom I do rely
  To be delivered by thy hand.
Content, I take what spot is mine,
Since all the earth, my Lord, is thine.

My gracious God! when I must die,
  Oh bear my happy soul above,
With Christ, my Lord, eternally
  To share thy glory and thy love!
Then comes it right and well to me,
When, where, and how my death shall be.

As Christ Chooses.

RICHARD BAXTER.

LORD, it belongs not to my care
   Whether I die or live;
To love and serve thee is my share,
   And this thy grace must give.
If life be long, I will be glad
   That I may long obey;
If short, yet why should I be sad
   To soar to endless day?

Christ leads me through no darker rooms
   Than he went through before;
He that unto God's kingdom comes
   Must enter by his door.
Come, Lord, when grace has made me meet,
   Thy blessed face to see;
For if thy work on earth be sweet,
   What will thy glory be?

Then shall I end my sad complaints,
   And weary, sinful days,

157

And join with the triumphant saints
That sing Jehovah's praise.
My knowledge of that life is small,
The eye of faith is dim;
But 'tis enough that Christ knows all,
And I shall be with him.

The Blessed Hope.

REV. AUGUSTUS M. TOPLADY.

WHEN languor and disease invade
   This trembling house of clay,
'Tis sweet to look beyond our cage,
   And long to fly away;

Sweet to look inward, and attend
   The whispers of his love;
Sweet to look upward to the place
   Where Jesus pleads above;

Sweet to look back, and see my name
   In life's fair book set down;
Sweet to look forward, and behold
   Eternal joys my own;

Sweet to reflect how grace divine
   My sins on Jesus laid;
Sweet to remember that his blood
   My debt of suffering paid;

159

Sweet in his righteousness to stand,
  Which saves from second death;
Sweet to experience, day by day,
  His Spirit's quickening breath;

Sweet on his faithfulness to rest,
  Whose love can never end;
Sweet on his covenant of grace
  For all things to depend;

Sweet in the confidence of faith
  To trust his firm decrees;
Sweet to lie passive in his hands,
  And know no will but his;

Sweet to rejoice in lively hope
  That when my change shall come,
Angels shall hover round my bed,
  And waft my spirit home.

Soon too my slumbering dust shall hear
  The trumpet's quickening sound;
And by my Saviour's power rebuilt,
  At his right hand be found.

Sweet, blessed hope! There I at last
  Shall see him and adore;
Be with his likeness satisfied,
  And grieve and sin no more;

Shall see him wear that very flesh
   On which my guilt was lain;
His love intense, his merit fresh,
   As though but newly slain.

If such the views which grace unfolds,
   Weak as it is below,
What raptures must the Church above
   In Jesus' presence know!

If such the sweetness of the *stream*,
   What must the *fountain* be,
Where saints and angels draw their bliss
   Immediately from thee!

Oh! may the unction of these truths
   For ever with me stay;
Till from her sinful cage dismissed,
   My spirit flees away.

21

Piety Exempt from the Decays of Age.

JOHN GOSMAN. D. D.

EVERY period of life—youth, manhood, and age—has its peculiar characteristics. Advanced years we naturally associate with infirmity, and consider them as those in which we have no pleasure. It is the time of retreat from the business and turmoil of life, in which, from the sinking of the bodily powers, we seem hourly to advance to the closing scene. We are deprived of many sources of delight, and are thrown, so to speak, on our own resources. As the susceptibility to pleasure is abated, and the senses lose much of their acuteness, social intercourse in a great measure ceases to charm. The gifts of mind often follow the laws of decline; the power of combining, the glow of fancy and the faculty of retention are impaired; the mind wearies and becomes perplexed. But in the case of the aged believer how changed the aspect! The spiritual principle resists decay—"it abideth for ever." The powers with which grace has endowed the soul never experience the exhaustion of debility. This happy independ-

162

ence of the mind, its capacity for enjoyment, distinct and spiritual, is seen in the vigour of perception and glow of emotion attesting its divine origin. The knowledge of advanced years is comprehensive; truths long familiar by contemplation become invested with new attractions. The glory of redemption is seen more clearly; the mind becomes assured of the certainty of the word of God; and their influence is continually advancing and diffusing its sacred power over the whole character. Like the tree, it seems to shoot deeper its roots. Like the lofty cedar of Lebanon, it stands unmoved by the tempests of earth.

The great essential truths of the word of God, of the sinfulness of our nature, the necessity of divine and gracious influence to quicken, purify and invigorate the soul are understood and felt to be true by the test most decisive—experience. Cut off from many sources of enjoyment, the aged believer finds an admirable substitute in the fellowship of the spirit with God. He can say, "Truly our fellowship is with the Father, and with his Son Jesus Christ." He has the best society, and his sympathies are more elevated than those which connect with imperfection and change. After exploring the heavens and the earth for happiness, they seem to him a mighty void, a wilderness of shadows, where all will be empty and unsubstantial without God. The language of his heart is, "Whom have I in heaven but thee? and there is none upon earth that I desire besides thee." He has inward self-enjoyment, for the good man is "satisfied from himself." There is an entrance now into the joys of the future; he enters now into peace —for what is spiritual life but the life of God in the soul of man? What are peace and joy in believing but the tranquillity of heaven brought down to earth? It is not the attribute of elevated genius alone to soar above the skies; borne on the wings of faith, the believer can adopt the language of Milton in a more exalted sense,—

> "Upled by thee,
> Into the heaven of heavens I have presumed,
> An earthly guest, and drawn empyrean air."

The enjoyments of religion are peculiar. They depend not on the senses, which may lose their quickness, or on the animal passions, which may become languid and faint, or on anything which is merely outward. They spring from the recesses of the heart. The natural eye may fade, but the eye of the spirit is vivid.

The review of the past, while it humbles the spirit, yet comes with rich and fragrant recollections of the goodness and faithfulness of God, which strengthen his confidence as to the future. An advanced believer happily expresses this trust: " I am only learning as yet the alphabet of that supernatural science which teaches us to rest in him every day, and all the day, as the ' Lord our Strength.' " His mind occupied with such grateful subjects of contemplation, his heart in repose on his covenant God, he is a stranger to the vacuity, the peevishness of caprice, and, above all, the dissatisfaction with themselves, which embitter the lives of those who, idolizing the world, find it an empty pageant. If such the joys of the believer while still imprisoned in his "house of clay," what raptures shall swell his enfranchised spirit when, dropping this decaying earthly tabernacle, he shal ascend into the immediate presence of his God!

Heaven.

ANONYMOUS.

No sickness there—
No weary wasting of the frame away—
　No fearful shrinking from the midnight air,
No dread of summer's bright and fervid ray.

No hidden grief;
No wild and cheerless vision of despair,—
　No vain petition for a swift relief—
No tearful eyes, no broken hearts are there!

Care has no home;
In the bright realms of ceaseless prayer and song
　Its billows melt away, and break in foam,
Far from the mansion of the spirit throng.

The storm's black wing
Is never spread athwart celestial skies,—
　Its wailings blend not with the voice of spring,
As some too tender flow'ret fades and dies.

No night distils
Its chilling dews upon the tender frame;
    No morn is needed there,—the light which fills
That land of glory from its Maker came.

No parted friends
O'er mournful recollections have to weep;—
    No bed of death enduring love attends,
To watch the coming of a pulseless sleep.

No blasted flower
Or withered bud celestial gardens know;
    No scorching blast or fierce descending shower
Scatters destruction like a ruthless foe.

No battle word
Startles the sacred host with fear and dread:
    The song of peace creation's morning knew
Is sung wherever angel minstrels tread.

Let us depart,
If home like this await the weary soul:
    Look up, then, stricken one,—thy wounded heart
Shall bleed no more at sorrow's stern control.

With Faith our guide,
White-robed and innocent, to lead the way,
    Why fear to plunge in sorrow's rolling tide,
And find the Ocean of Eternal Day?

Light at Eventide.

ANONYMOUS.

THE chequer'd day of life is past,
  Its varied joys, its varied cares;
The clear blue sky is overcast,
. And night a solemn aspect wears;
O thou whose smile makest all things bright,
At evening time let there be light.

Darkness has often marked our way,
  And sorrow on our souls has press'd;
But thou canst all our fears allay,
  And cheer the closing hours of rest;
Thy love is boundless as thy might:
At evening time let there be light.

Oh, shine within our hearts; reveal
  Thyself in Christ, the God of love;
Nor let one earthly cloud conceal
  The glory of the land above;
Our faith increase—our hope excite:
At evening time let there be light.

Like radiant stars that chase the gloom,
    And guide the traveller to repose,
So let thy promises illume
    The shadow which death's coming throws;
And ere our spirit takes her flight,
At evening time let there be light.

"Let there be light."   One word from thee
    Will every passing shade dispel;
Until thy face unveil'd we see,
    And in thy cloudless presence dwell.
Soon shall our faith be changed to sight :
In heaven there will be perfect light !
   22

rust.

MARTIN F. TUPPER.

"My times are in thy hand."

YET will I trust! in all my fears,
Thy mercy, gracious Lord, appears,
To guide me through this vale of tears,
          And be my strength.

Thy mercy guides my ebb and flow
Of health and joy, or pain and woe,
To wean my heart from all below,
          To thee at length

Yes! welcome pain which thou hast sent,
Yes! farewell blessing thou hast lent;
With thee alone I rest content,
          For thou art heaven.

My trust reposes safe and still
On the wise goodness of thy will,
Grateful for earthly good or ill,
          Which thou hast given.

O blessed Friend! O blissful thought!
With happiest consolation fraught—
Trust thee I may, I will, I ought—
                    To doubt were sin.

All is Well.

ANONYMOUS.

"All things work together for good to them that love God."
Rom. viii. 28.

THROUGH the love of God our Saviour,
    All will be well.
Free and changeless is his favour;
    All, all is well.
Precious is the blood that healed us,
Perfect is the grace that sealed us,
Strong the hand stretched forth to shield us,
    All must be well.

Though we pass through tribulation,
    All will be well.
Ours is such a full salvation,
    All, all is well.
Happy, still in God confiding,
Fruitful, if in Christ abiding,
Holy, through the Spirit's guiding,
    All must be well.

We expect a bright to-morrow;
  All will be well.
Faith can sing, through days of sorrow,
  "All, all is well."
On our Father's love relying,
Jesus every need supplying,
Or in living, or in dying,
  All must be well!

To the Uttermost.

REV. GARDINER SPRING PLUMLEY.

MRS. M—— was an aged woman. For eighty-four years God had spared her, though she was an impenitent, hardened sinner. Pious parents from her birth had commended her in faith to God, and with their dying breath prayed that she might meet them in heaven.

Early in life she had imbibed skeptical notions, which she loved to avow. She read her Bible to find difficulties and make objections. When personally addressed on the subject of religion, she would adroitly turn the conversation to disputed topics, and claim that she could not understand the doctrines of grace. Thus she lived with no fear of God before her eyes, and with no interest in his written and preached word, except as it furnished her with materials for argument and cavilling. Her faculties were unimpaired by age, her mind clear; and, but for her repugnance to religion, her society was agreeable.

Two successive ministers of the congregation to which her family belonged declared her to be the most hopeless individual for whom they laboured. They did not, however, neglect her. Often was her pastor found talking pointedly with her until she proposed an argument, when he would read an appropriate portion of Scripture, then pray with her, and go his way. He sometimes despaired of being at all useful to her, but was encouraged when he reflected that her parents had been faithful, that God's people were praying for her conversion, that many texts of Scripture were in her memory, and that one of her household was daily setting her a godly example.

One day, as usual, he called upon her. She seemed the same woman as ever—no penitence, no softness. She remarked, " I can't see anything wrong in what Christians call *sin*. I see evil in *ugliness* and the like; but some very good people are always talking about their *sins*. I can't tell what they mean." The Scripture statements respecting the guilt of disobeying God were held up to view, and sin was described to her as "any want of conformity unto, or transgression of, the law of God."

"Well, if there *is* such a thing as religion, I should not object to have it."

" Do you doubt, then, that there is such a thing as religion ?"

"I never saw anybody different *after*, from what they were *before*, they professed to be converted."

"Indeed! that is strange; though much younger than you, I think I have seen many. Is not your son L—— a different person from what he once was? Does he not give evidence of a great change?"

"I can't see that he does. He always was a good boy before he was pious, and he is a good son now."

"Do you not feel that you yourself need to be changed in order to meet an infinitely holy God?"

"No, I don't know as I do. I never have done any sin."

After a pause the pastor read a few verses of Scripture, and committed her to God in prayer.

Ten days afterwards he visited her again. But to his surprise he seemed to find a woman as different from Mrs. M—— as it is possible to conceive. It was Mrs. M—— as far as form was concerned, but with a subdued expression of countenance wonderful to behold. God's Holy Spirit had descended upon her, and was powerfully convincing her of sin, of righteousness, and of judgment. She was bathed in tears, and with sobbing and cries for mercy was begging God to pardon "the chief of sinners." Her pastor sought to comfort her, but she refused his consolations. " Oh, there is, there can be no mercy for me. Such a sinner, such a sinner!"

" But I thought you didn't understand what sin is—that you had never sinned? What have you been doing so bad of late?"

" Oh, do not talk so; I have committed the greatest sin that any one can commit."

" Why, what sin is that?"

" Oh, it's rejecting Christ's mercy *all these years.* Surely he will not save me now."

Jesus was preached to her as "able to save them *to the uttermost* that come unto God by him." Heb. vii. 25. It was, however, many days before she could rest upon Christ alone, and believe that he would have anything to do with *such a sinner.* Prayer was daily made for her and with her. The old elder, her neighbor, whose visits and prayers were once unwelcome, was urged by her to come as often as he could, and all other Christian friends were entreated to pray.

" The worst is," said she, " I have been sinning on and on, and opposing everything good so long; and now I am shut up in this corner, where I can do nothing but come to Christ; and *can it be possible that he will receive me when I can do nothing else?*"

" Yes, he has promised to save to the uttermost.

23

He ever liveth, he will be your Saviour eternally.
He is willing to begin to be your Jesus now. Though
aged, you are blessed with clear reason. You can
hear and understand his message: 'Believe on the
Lord Jesus Christ, and thou shalt be saved.'" Acts
xvi. 31.

At last light broke in upon her soul. She saw the
compassion of Jesus. She received him into her
heart, and found all his promises true. Then her
prayers were mingled with praises. She called upon
all about her to sing the praises of her Saviour. In
the night she would awake and request this, and on
more than one occasion succeeded in having her
friends sing "songs in the night." Old hymns long
forgotten came back to her memory, and must be
searched up and sung. The burden of those she
loved most was the power of Christ to cleanse and
save the vilest sinners. Jesus had discovered to her
her sinfulness; Jesus had made her whole. The
language of her heart was,

> "A guilty, weak, and helpless worm,
>   On thy kind arms I fall:
>   Be thou my strength and righteousness,
>   My Jesus and my all."

Here are important lessons.

1. *There is hope even for those whose case seems most*

hopeless. Never despair of such. Use all the means of grace for them. Do not argue with them. Read or repeat to them God's word, converse with them tenderly, and pray for them earnestly. Every true prayer will be answered, and every portion of truth become at last effectual.

2. *Let parents train their children for Christ, and in faith commit them to his care.* Teach them his word, set before them a godly example, and if you are taken from them, trust in God to make them his own. "I believe," said a dying Christian mother, "that all my children will be converted." And the event was in accordance with her faith.

3. *Do not delay accepting Jesus as your Saviour.* By so doing you rob God of that service which it is your privilege to render him now, and heap up sorrows for the future. Oh may you never know the pangs of remorse that follow a life of sin! If you are now convinced of your duty, and fail to do it, God may leave you to your chosen course, to sink into eternal death.

4. *The greatest sin is rejection of Christ's love.* Such is the testimony of a conscience enlightened by the Holy Spirit. Ah, sinner, beware! Are you slighting the infinite love of Jesus? Remember it was to bless *you* that he died; to make *you* for ever happy.

he bowed his head in unutterable anguish. And his power is as mighty as his love. If you believe on him, he can, he will save *you*. HE IS ABLE TO SAVE THEM TO THE UTTERMOST THAT COME UNTO GOD BY HIM.

A Little While.

HORATIUS BONAR, D. D.

BEYOND the smiling and the weeping
　　I shall be soon ;
Beyond the waking and the sleeping,
Beyond the sowing and the reaping,
　　I shall be soon.
　　　Love, rest and home !
　　　Sweet home !
　　Lord, tarry not, but come !

Beyond the blooming and the fading
　　I shall be soon ;
Beyond the shining and the shading,
Beyond the hoping and the dreading,
　　I shall be soon.
　　　Love, rest, and home !
　　　Sweet home !
　　Lord, tarry not, but come !

Beyond the rising and the setting
　　I shall be soon ;

Beyond the calming and the fretting,
Beyond remembering and forgetting,
  I shall be soon.
  Love, rest, and home!
   Sweet home!
  Lord, tarry not, but come!

Beyond the parting and the meeting
  I shall be soon;
Beyond the farewell and the greeting,
Beyond the pulse's fever beating,
  I shall be soon.
  Love, rest, and home!
   Sweet home!
  Lord, tarry not, but come!

Beyond the frost-chain and the fever
  I shall be soon;
Beyond the rock-waste and the river,
Beyond the ever and the never,
  I shall be soon.
  Love, rest, and home,
   Sweet home!
  Lord, tarry not, but come!

Peculiar Duties of the Aged.

ARCHIBALD ALEXANDER, D. D.

I HAVE no doubt that you have remarked with surprise that the impression of the reality and importance of eternal things is not increased by the nearness of your approach to the end of your course. Time glides insensibly away, and it is with us in this respect as in relation to the globe on which we reside. While other things appear to be in motion, our feeling is that we are stationary. The mere circumstance of being old seems to affect no one with a more lively concern about the salvation of the soul. None appear to be more blind and stupid in regard to religious matters than many who are tottering on the brink of the grave. This, indeed, is so commonly the fact with those who have grown old without religion that very little hope is entertained of the conversion of the aged who have from their youth enjoyed the means of grace. And it is also a fact that real Christians are not rendered more deeply

183

sensible of the awful importance of eternal things
by becoming old and infirm. The truth is, that nothing but an increase of faith by the operation of the
Holy Spirit will be effectual to prepare us for that
change which we know is rapidly approaching. Counsels and exhortations, however, are not to be neglected, as God is pleased to work by means. I
have, therefore, undertaken to address to you such
considerations as occur to me.

Having already spoken of the infirmities and sins
which are apt to cleave to us in advanced years, I
propose in this letter to inquire what are the peculiar
duties incumbent on the aged. What would the Lord
have us to do? Undoubtedly we are not privileged
to fold our hands and sit down in idleness, as if our
work was ended. Indeed, it would be no privilege
to be exempt from all occupation. Such a life to the
aged or the young must be a life of misery; for man
never was made to be idle, and his happiness is intimately connected with activity. We may be no
longer qualified for those labours which require much
bodily strength; we may indeed be so debilitated or
crippled by disease that we can scarcely move our
crazy frame, and some among us may be vexed with
excruciating pain; yet still we have a work to perform for God and for our generation.

If we cannot use our hands and feet so as to be useful in the labours which we were wont to perform, yet we may employ our tongues to speak the praises of our God and Saviour. We may drop a word of counsel to those around us; and especially the aged owe a duty to the young, to whom they may have access and who are related to them. Every aged Christian must have acquired much knowledge from experience, which he should be ready to communicate as far as it is practicable. Why is it, my dear friends, that we suffer so many opportunities of usefulness to pass without improvement? Why are we so often silent when the suggestions of our own conscience urge us to speak something for God? How is it that we consume hours in unprofitable talk, and seldom attempt to say anything which can profit the hearers? We may plead inability—we may excuse ourselves because we are unlearned and not able to speak eloquently and correctly—but let us be honest; is not the true reason because our own hearts are so little affected with these things? We cannot consent to play the hypocrite by uttering sentiments which we do not feel; and we have often been disgusted with the attempts of others, who in a cold and constrained manner have introduced religious conversation. It is easy to see where the fault lies; it is in the state

24

of our own hearts. Let us never rest, then, until we find ourselves in a better state of mind. Let us get our hearts habitually under the influence of divine things, and then conversation on this subject will be as easy as on any other. "Out of the abundance of the heart the mouth speaketh." There are companies and occasions when to obtrude remarks on religion would be unseasonable and imprudent, for we must not cast our pearls before swine; but in most cases an aged person may give utterance to seasonable and solemn truths without offence; and very often a word spoken in season has been the means of saving a soul; and the advice and exhortation of parents and pious friends are remembered and prove salutary after their heads are laid low under the clods of the valley.

I have often heard aged persons, incapable any longer of active service, express surprise that their unprofitable lives were so long protracted, while the young and laborious servants of God were cut off in the midst of their years. The dispensations of God are indeed inscrutable—"his ways are past finding out"—and we are too little acquainted with his counsels to sit in judgment on them. But I would say to those who think that they can be of no further use in the world, that they do not form a just estimate of the nature of the service which God requires, and by which he is glorified by his creatures upon earth. All true obedience originates in the heart, and consists essentially of the affections of the heart: external duties are to be performed, but are only holy as connected with holy motives. The aged man may serve God therefore as sincerely and fervently as any others, if only the heart be right in the sight of God. He can glorify God in his spirit by thinking affectionately of his glorious name, by contemplating his divine attributes, and by exercising love and gratitude towards him. His devotion might thus approach more nearly to our conceptions of the services and exercises of the saints in heaven.

It may be that the lives of some are lengthened out that they may offer up many prayers for the Church and for the world; for after all the activity and bustle and zeal apparent, there is no service which can be performed by mortals so effectual as prayer. Here there is a work to which the aged may be devoted. While Joshua and the men of war contend with the Amalekites in the battle, Moses assists by lifting up his hands in prayer; and when he is, through fatigue, no longer able to hold them up, he is assisted by Aaron on one side and Hur on the other. If you cannot preach, you can by prayer hold up the hands of those who do. You can follow the missionary who leaves all to go and labour in heathen lands with your daily and fervent prayers. It is not in vain for you to live while you have access to a throne of grace. Before the advent of Christ there were some aged persons who seem to have been preserved in life that they might pray for this event, and that they might enjoy the pleasure of seeing the answer of their prayers, and embracing him in their arms whom they had so often embraced by faith. While all around was spiritual death and desolation, and corruption and error had infected all classes, from the priesthood downward, there was a little band who had taken up their residence in the temple, or often frequented this holy place, who were waiting for the Consolation of Israel. Two of these were Simeon and Anna; but there were others of the same character; for we read that this very aged and pious widow, who departed not from the temple, but served God with fasting and prayers, night and day, " spake of Christ, after she had seen him, *to all them who looked for redemption in Israel."* The darker the the times the more closely do the truly pious adhere to each other. This little knot of praying people knew each other, and no doubt spake often one to another; and in this case the Lord hearkened and heard; for the object of their desires and prayers was given to them. Was the life of Anna an unprofitable life, although she never left the temple, and did nothing but fast and pray? Was Simeon a useless member of the Church because he was probably too old for labour? The truth was—and the same is often verified—that the true Church of God was at this time confined to a few pious souls; while the priests and the scribes and the rulers had neither part nor lot in the matter. As God preserved Simeon, according to a promise made to him, until he saw the Lord's Christ, so he may be lengthening out the lives of some of you, my aged brethren, until you may have the opportunity of seeing the salvation of Israel come out of Zion. Do you not wish to be witnesses of the rise and glory of the Church? Pray, then, incessantly for the peace and prosperity of Jerusalem. Consider it as your chief business to pray that the kingdom of God may come. What though the signs of the times be discouraging; what though you live in troublous times; what though the Church may be shaken, and the prospects of her increase be dark, yet remember that she is founded on a Rock, and the gates of hell cannot prevail against her. The vessel which carries Christ, though it be buffeted by storms, is in no danger of being wrecked. But to govern and direct does not belong to you; your duty is to pray—to pray without ceasing—to wrestle with the Angel of the Covenant, and not to let him go until he bless you. Give him no rest until he establish and make Jerusalem a praise in all the earth. You cannot offend by importunity, but by this you will be sure to prevail; for "will not God hear his own elect who cry day and night unto him?" Therefore never hold your peace, but as long as you live intercede with him to fulfil his gracious promises, and to cause the earth to be filled with the knowledge of himself as the waters cover the sea, when his people shall be all righteous, and there shall be no need any longer for any one to say to his neighbour, Know the Lord, for all shall know him from the least to the greatest.

Thanksgiving is also a duty peculiarly incumbent on the aged. In the providence of God you are spared, while most of your coevals have been cut off in the midst of their career. Some of you have enjoyed almost uninterrupted prosperity. When you consider the dispensations of God's providence towards you in the time and place and circumstances of your birth, in giving you pious and intelligent parents, who took care of your health and education, and in following you with goodness and mercy all the days of your life; giving you kind friends, faithful teachers, health and reason, together with abundant religious privileges, how thankful ought you to be! But that which above all other things enhances your obligations to gratitude is that in his own good time he effectually called you from the devious paths of iniquity, and adopted you as a child into his own household and family, and perhaps has made you the instrument of much good to others; if not on a large scale, yet in your own family, and in the church of which you are a member. If now, to all these blessings, he has given you pious children, who promise when you are gone more than to supply your place in society, or even if they have been preserved from infidelity and disgraceful immoralities, and are disposed to pay a serious attention to the preaching of the gospel, no words can express your obligations to give thanks unto the Lord, and continually to praise his name whose mercy endureth for ever and ever. " Let us therefore offer the sacrifice of praise to God continually—that is, the fruit of our lips, giving thanks to his name."

I shall Soon be Dying.

ANONYMOUS.

Ah! I shall soon be dying,
　　Time swiftly glides away;
But, on my Lord relying,
　　I hail the happy day—
The day when I shall enter
　　Upon a world unknown:
My helpless soul I venture
　　On Jesus Christ alone.

He once, a spotless victim,
　　Upon mount Calvary bled;
Jehovah did afflict him
　　And bruise him in my stead;
Hence all my hope arises,
　　Unworthy as I am;
My soul most surely prizes
　　The sin-atoning Lamb.

Soon, with the saints in glory,
　　The grateful song I'll raise,

And chant my blissful story
  In high seraphic lays.
Free grace, redeeming merit,
  And sanctifying love
Of Father, Son, and Spirit,
  I'll sing in realms above.

25

The Loss of Memory.

ANONYMOUS.

How impaired the memory becomes as we advance in years! We are constantly forgetting the little occurrences of everyday life, and our past history sometimes appears to us like an indistinct and troubled dream. The friends and associates of our youth fade from our recollection, and we are frequently unable to recall even the names which they bore. It is true that an aged person will sometimes manifest as clear and as tenacious a memory as is possessed by any one around him, but his case is a peculiar one, and does not warrant others to expect that they will be similarly favoured. For loss of memory is a common and natural infirmity of old age; and we must not be surprised, and we ought not to be impatient, at this indication, among many others, of our mortality.

The present world is not our rest, although we are too prone to live as if it were so; and our failing strength and weakened faculties are kind and neces-

194

sary remembrancers of our actual position here. And not only do they remind us that we have reached the evening of life, and should prepare for the dawn of immortality, but they tend to assist us in making that preparation, by withdrawing us from the arduous and engrossing occupations of the world, and by gradually weaning us from our natural attachment to this present state of existence. Our feeble powers, both of body and mind, unfit us for the busy engagements into which we once entered so heartily, and in our retirement from the active duties of life we have opportunity for meditation and reflection ; while the privations and trials to which we are subjected incline us to say with the afflicted patriarch, " I would not live alway ;" and thus make us willing to depart.

The failure of memory is, however, very trying and inconvenient; and it is a loss which cannot be repaired. " My memory fails day by day," writes a Christian lady in her seventieth year to her sister. " I cannot remember where I put anything, no, not for an hour ; and though the inconvenience might be prevented by having a place for everything, and being careful to put everything in its proper place— a rule good in every time of life—it is frustrated by my forgetting that I forget. No person can conceive the trial this is but they who have experienced it. It is equally distressing with regard to circumstances and dates. I must make a memorandum of everything; and then I lose the memorandum, or mislay the book in which I note down things of importance. However, I have mercies great and numerous to balance, and infinitely more than balance this; my life is hid with Christ in God; my Jesus is my surety that all will be well: *he* forgets not. All my concerns are in his hands; he will manage all, perfect all, finish all."

Oh, amidst the changes and the imperfections which are incidental to the present life, how full of comfort is the thought that Jesus forgets not! He ever remembers his people, and retains the liveliest interest in their minutest concerns. "Can a woman forget her sucking child, that she should not have compassion on the son of her womb? Yea, they may forget; yet will I not forget thee."* No lapse of time can enfeeble or destroy his perfect and perpetual cognizance of our affairs.

And although our memories are rapidly failing, although they are unable now to fulfil the trust which we once reposed in them, they can still gratefully recall the Saviour's precious name, and ardently cherish the recollection of his unspeakable love.

* Isa. xlix. 15:

The pious Bishop Beveridge, when on his death-bed, was unable to recognize any of his relatives or friends. A clergyman with whom he had been intimately acquainted visited him, and when introduced into his room, said, " Bishop Beveridge, do you know me?" "Who are you?" said the aged prelate. Being told who the minister was, he shook his head, and said that he did not know him. Another friend addressed him in a similar manner, " Do you know me, Bishop Beveridge?" " Who are you?" he again inquired. Being told that it was one of his old friends, he replied that he did not recollect him. His wife then came to his bedside, and asked him if he knew her, but the good bishop had lost all remembrance even of his wife. At last some one present said, " Well, Bishop Beveridge, do you know the Lord Jesus Christ?" " Jesus Christ!" repeated he, as if the name had produced upon him the influence of a charm; " oh, yes, I have known him these forty years; precious Saviour! He is my only hope."

> " How sweet the name of Jesus sounds
>   In a believer's ear!"

Saviour! if we forget all besides, may we remember thee! May we look to thee—rest on thee—abide in thee—and wait for that happy period when we shall be for ever with thee!

And when we have reached heaven, we shall no longer have to complain of the imperfection of memory. For then we shall remember—remember without any effort, any mistake, any omission—the way in which the Lord our God has led us so many years in the wilderness. What a retrospect will that be! The light of eternity will shine on the records of the past, and each page of our life will be clear and legible. And we shall read them without pain or regret. In this world the recollection of bygone days is often fraught with much that is sorrowful. Scenes and events come back to our thoughts on which we dare not dwell, and which we would fain forget. But it will not be so above. Perfect and vivid as that mental glance which shall survey our journey through life from the cradle to the grave will unquestionably prove, it will be accompanied by so deep and augmented an acquaintance with the loving providence of our heavenly Father, and by such sweet and entire submission to his will, as will render it impossible for the remembrances to awaken the slightest emotion of grief in our hearts. Or rather, it will furnish us with such accumulated and varied proofs of God's tenderness and care as will fill our spirits with grateful adoration. Oh, as we recall with accurate minuteness the circumstances of our earthly history, we shall see enough of God's marvellous wisdom and loving-kindness to excite our praise throughout all eternity.

Instead, then, of lamenting over our present infirmity, let us endeavour to realize that freedom from all imperfection and those superior mental faculties which we shall enjoy in a future state. We are now drawing near to the land of perpetual youth and vigour. The weakened intellect, the declining strength, the failing memory, these are tokens that it will not be very long before our weary spirits are at rest.

A poor aged widow—poor in this world's wealth, but rich in faith—in reply to the kind inquiry of her minister after her health, replied with cheerfulness, " What cause I have to be thankful! How many at my age are confined to their beds, while I am able to be about and clean my own house! I hope I may have my faculties to the last."

" You find, I dare say," he remarked, " that this earthly house of your tabernacle is being dissolved: now one pin is taken down, now another; now this part melts away, now that." " Yes, sir, I do indeed find that my poor old body is very weak; often when I only walk across the room I am extremely giddy; and my *memory* almost fails me. Sometimes I get up and go into the other room to fetch something which I want, and when I come there, I stand, and have quite forgotten for what I came."

"You remember, perhaps, what took place when you were a girl far more distinctly than what you heard or saw only last week ?"

"Oh yes, sir,; it seems to me but a few days since I was a girl; my father lived at the mill, and I remember how I used to go into the fields, and have many a game there with my little playfellows."

"Well, my dear friend, memory generally seems to be the first faculty which is taken from the aged; and God thus reminds them to forget those things which are behind, and to reach forth to those things which are before. He prevents their *looking back*, in order that they may learn to *look forward*."

Let us all "look forward ;" and as we muse on the glorious realities of heaven, can we murmur that we should forget the fading things of earth? Is it not well that the nearer we are to the joys of eternity, the less vivid and perceptible appear the vanities of time? A mist has gathered over the scenes of earth, but everlasting sunshine is about to break forth.

Prayer of an Aged Believer.

SIR ROBERT GRANT.

WITH years oppressed, with sorrows torn,
Dejected, harassed, sick, forlorn,
  To thee, O Lord, I pray;
To thee these withered hands I raise,
To thee I lift these failing eyes,
  Oh cast me not away.

Thy mercy heard my infant prayer,
Thy love, with all a mother's care,
  Sustained my childish days;
Thy goodness watched my ripening youth,
And formed my heart to love thy truth,
  And filled my lips with praise.

O Saviour, has thy grace declined?
Can years affect th' eternal mind,
  Or time its love decay?
A thousand ages pass thy sight,
And all their long and weary flight
  Is gone like yesterday.

Then e'en in age and grief thy name
Shall still my languid heart inflame,
   And bow my faltering knee;
For yet this bosom feels the fire;
This trembling hand and drooping lyre,
   Have still a strain for thee.

Yes! tuneless, broken, still, O Lord,
This voice, transported, shall record
   Thy goodness, tried so long;
Till sinking slow, with calm decay,
Its feeble numbers melt away
   Into a seraph's song.

Heavenly Realities.

FROM THE GERMAN OF J. LANGE.

WHAT no human eye hath seen,
　　What no mortal ear hath heard,
What on thought hath never been
　　In her noblest flights conferred,—
This hath God prepared in store
For his people evermore.

When the shaded pilgrim-land
　　Fades before my closing eye,
Then, revealed on either hand,
　　Heaven's own scenery shall lie;
Then the veil of flesh shall fall,
Now concealing, dark'ning all.

Heavenly landscapes, calmly bright,
　　Life's pure river, murmuring low,
Forms of loveliness and light
　　Lost to earth long time ago,—
Yes, my own, lamented long,
Shine amid the angel throng.

203

Many a joyful sight was given,
　　Many a lovely vision here,
Hill and vale, and starry even,
　　Friendship's smile, affliction's tear,—
These were shadows sent in love,
Of realities above.

When upon my wearied ear,
　　Earth's last echoes faintly die,
Then shall angel harps draw near,
　　All the chorus of the sky;
Long-hushed voices blend again
Sweetly in that welcome strain.

Here were sweet and varied tones,
　　Bird and breeze, and fountain's fall;
Yet creation's travail groans,
　　Ever sadly sighed through all;
There no discord jars the air—
Harmony is perfect there!

When this aching heart shall rest,
　　All its busy pulses o'er,
From her mortal robes undrest,
　　Shall my spirit upward soar;
Then shall pure, unmingled joy
All my thoughts and powers employ.

Here devotion's healing balm
   Often came to soothe my breast;
Hours of deep and holy calm,
   Earnests of eternal rest;
But the bliss was here unknown
Which shall there be "all" my own.

Jesus reigns, the Life, the Sun,
   Of that wondrous land above;
All the clouds and storms are gone,
   All is light, and all is love.
All the shadows melt away
In the blaze of perfect day.

Sorrows and Consolations of Old Age.*

REV. JOHN KENNEDY.

VERY mournful are some of the Bible descriptions of old age. " The days of our years are threescore years and ten ; and if by reason of strength they be fourscore years, yet is their strength labour and sorrow ; for it is soon cut off, and we fly away." This is no picture of fancy. Nor is that which Solomon gives us by way of enforcing the exhortation, " Remember now thy Creator in the days of thy youth," when he says, " While the evil days come not, nor the years draw nigh, when thou shalt say, I have no pleasure in them ; while the sun, or the light, or the moon, or the stars be not darkened, nor the clouds return after the rain ;—

> "In the day when the keepers of the house shall tremble,
> And the strong men shall bow themselves,
> And the grinders cease because they are few,
> And those that look out of the windows be darkened,
> And the doors shall be shut in the streets,

* From " Rest under the Shadow of the Great Rock. A Book of Facts and Principles." By the Rev. John Kennedy, M. A.

When the sound of the grinding is low,
And he shall rise up at the voice of the bird,
And all the daughters of music shall be brought low;
Also when they shall be afraid of that which is high,
And fears shall be in the way,
And the almond tree shall flourish,
And the grasshopper shall be a burden,
And desire shall fail: because man goeth to his long home,
And the mourners go about the streets:
Or ever the silver cord be loosed, or the golden bowl be broken,
Or the pitcher be broken at the fountain,
Or the wheel broken at the cistern.
Then shall the dust return to the earth as it was:
And the spirit shall return unto God who gave it."

Such is old age, and such its invariable ending.
And so far as its physical aspects are concerned, as
it is with the wicked, so it is with the righteous.

But the picture has another side. "The hoary
head is a crown of glory, if it be found in the way
of righteousness." Prov. xvi. 31. "The righteous
shall flourish like the palm-tree: he shall grow like
a cedar in Lebanon. Those that be planted in the
house of the Lord shall flourish in the courts of our
God. They shall still bring forth fruit in old age;
they shall be fat and flourishing; to show that the
Lord is upright: he is my rock, and there is no unrighteousness in him." Psalm xcii. 12, 15. Even
to us in Western lands, who, though we have seen
palm trees and cedars, are not familiar with them,

this description is very striking and suggestive. The ideas of majesty, and beauty, and fruitfulness, and honour, all connect themselves with the cedar and the palm tree. "The palm," we are told, "grows slowly but steadily from century to century, uninfluenced by those alternations of the seasons which affect other trees. It does not rejoice overmuch in winter's copious rain, nor does it droop under the drought and the burning sun of summer. Neither heavy weights which men place upon its head, nor the importunate urgency of the wind, can sway it aside from perfect uprightness. There it stands, looking calmly down upon the world below, and patiently yielding its large clusters of golden fruit from generation to generation. They bring forth fruit in old age." When the Psalmist says, "Those that be planted in the house of the Lord shall flourish in the courts of our God," he alludes probably to the custom of planting beautiful and long-lived trees in the courts of temples and palaces, and in all "high places" for worship—a custom still common in the East. Nearly every palace and mosque and convent in Syria has such trees in its courts, and, being well-protected, they flourish exceedingly. Solomon covered all the walls of the Holy of Holies with carvings of palm trees. They were thus represented in the very house of the Lord; and their presence there was not only ornamental, but appropriate and highly suggestive; the very best emblem, not only of patience in well-doing, but of the rewards of the righteous—a fat and flourishing old age, a peaceful end, a glorious immortality.

Old age, with all its physical infirmities and drawbacks, may then be very beautiful, very useful and very happy.

But, in order to this, the one grand essential prerequisite is that the old man should have faith in God and in his Christ. I say "in his Christ," because a mere general faith in the being and government of God is not sufficient. "How dreary would old age and illness be without the great doctrine of the Atonement!" said John Foster, when himself old and ill. He spoke as a Christian and with reference to his Christian life. The omissions and shortcomings of the best life presented themselves to his mind. "One feels," he said, "that, in the great concern of religion, much more might have been done." And it was this thought that made him revert to the great doctrine of the Atonement. Conscious that while he had "lived to God" he had lived so imperfectly, had come so far short of what he ought to be, and what he ought to have done, whither should he look for

27

peace but to that atonement through which sin is forgiven and the sinner reconciled to God? And if the Christian's condition would be dreary without free and daily access to Christ for daily cleansing and pardon, how unutterably dark must be the condition of the man who, old and feeble, has never come to Christ, and does not now come to him, but bears on his soul the load of the accumulated sins of many years! If he only thinks, let him look behind or before, and he will find nothing but darkness: behind, the darkness of a life without God; before, the darkness of an eternity without God. The darkness is such as may be felt, and the wonder is that it does not appal and overwhelm his spirit.

There is a second thing needful in order to make the old age of man, like the old age of the palm tree, fat and flourishing; it is that the old man should call into constant exercise all the principles which belong to him as a Christian, and which form his dearest heritage—that of which neither worldly adversity nor decay of nature can rob him. He is a child of God. Let him think of this. Once far from God, now made nigh; once an enemy, now a friend; once an outcast from his Father's house, now restored and pardoned: let him think of this. The relation in which he stands to God is one so full of blessing and of hope, that he has only to understand it to find in it a fountain of peace and strength. It is natural for him amidst his infirmities to look on the dark side of things, but his faith reveals to him a bright side, a very bright side, and he will do himself wrong if he does not strive habitually to look upon it. Be it that all things are transient and changing in this world, and that he now sees their emptiness more than ever, the God whom he loves, in whom he trusts, his Father as well as his God, is without change, and he is the portion of his heart, the rock of his defence, his shield, and his exceeding great reward. Be it that he has seen one generation after another passing away, rank after rank of his fellow-soldiers in the battle of life mown down by the scythe of death, and that he finds himself alone in the world, pining in solitude even though surrounded by crowds of travellers and soldiers younger than himself, his God is with him, the Father of his spirit is with him, and no fellowship can be more real or sustaining than this. Be it that he feels himself now at the very end of life, those things which were once, in the future, objects of desire and ambition, being now and for ever, in the past, stript of all their false halo—that he has come within a span of the very goal of his earthly existence, the point beyond which he can see nothing, what does it amount to but that he has reached within a span of the end of sin and sorrow, of care and toil?—that his earthly education for his heavenly state is about being finished, and that in a few more months or years he will cease to be a child, and will possess all the strength and knowledge of a man? Be it that the aged Christian shrinks, as nature will shrink, from the grave, and what men call the unknown future, let him remember that Christ hath abolished death, and brought life and incorruption to light; that the future is no longer unknown, the veil having been taken away by Christ; that, whatever may be his own helplessness in the hour of the dread transition from time into eternity, he will hear a voice, well known and loved, saying, "Fear not, for I am with thee; be not dismayed, for I am thy God."

Let the aged Christian accustom himself to meditate on these truths and hopes, and promises of the gospel, until each of them shall be as habitually present and familiar to him as the countenance of his dearest friend, and he may expect to enjoy an elevation and a cheerfulness which will triumph over the labour and sorrow of his fourscore years. Or, if there be physical causes operating involuntarily and irresistibly to depress him, he will still find that the grace of the gospel does not leave itself without a witness in this assurance: "Like as a father pitieth his children, so the Lord pitieth them that fear him. For he knoweth their frame; he remembereth that they are dust."

There is a third thing which must be kept in view to make it sure that our old age shall be character-ized by the fruitfulness and beauty of the palm tree. And it is something that concerns the young rather than the old. Whatsoever that is which we should like to be when we are old—whatsoever grace or virtue we are pleased with when we see it in others, or should like others to see in us—we must cultivate habitually all the days of our life. No sudden effort. no convulsive struggle will make us at a bound what we ought to be. Most good things are of slow growth, need much culture, and are ripened only by time. If we would have our age distinguished by patience, gentleness, lovingness, consideration towards others, and by an all-pervading faith in God, we must seek to attain these excellences in the season of health and of early life. If we are self-indulgent, self-seeking, imperious, fretful, distrustful of God throughout life, much more shall we be all this when the feebleness of age has diminished our self-control.

We are often surprised by a manifestation of unlovely tempers on the part of aged Christians. These are the results of the former want of care in spiritual culture, and obtrude themselves so painfully on those whose duty it is to nurse the aged, that observers are perplexed, and do not know how to interpret what is so unseemly in persons who are supposed to be maturing for a higher state. What a joy it is on the other hand, to see the excellences which have been conscientiously cultivated by the Christian all his life long shining brightly, and with all the freedom and spontaneousness of a second nature, in the aged! The submission to God, the grateful recognition of his hand in every gift and mercy, the holy patience, the loving self-forgetfulness, the desire to be useful to others,—these bear witness to the rich grace of God in converting the autumn of decay into a scene of spiritual beauty. Thus, but thus only, may the aged become like the palm tree, and realize the Psalmist's description.

Christian's View of Eternity.*

FROM THE GERMAN OF C. C. STURM.

I'M but a weary pilgrim here,
   Life's varied griefs sustaining;
The ills I feel, and those I fear,
   Would tempt me to complaining:
But, Lord, the hopes of joys above
The pains of pilgrimage remove,
   Or give me strength to bear them.

Oft in the silence of the night
   My soul her griefs is sighing;
And morn, with its returning light,
   No respite is supplying:
One gleam of heaven relief bestows;
That home of rest no sorrow knows,
   But joy reigns there for ever.

And when the future gives alarm
   Of evils to oppress me;

* Translated by Dr. Mills.

215

And anxious fears of coming harm
  Thick gather to distress me;
Eternity makes time so small,
Its fleeting fears and sorrows all
  No longer raise my terror.

When Death, so dreaded from afar,
  Comes nigh, my days to number,
That, free from every earthly care,
  My head may sink in slumber,
That peace and joy may banish fear,
Let then eternity appear,
  With views of future glory.

Hope, Lord, makes every burden light,
  Its strength from thee it borrows;
That glory—fit me for its sight,
  By all my pilgrim sorrows!
May it in death my doubts dismiss,
And form my endless store of bliss
  With thee, in life eternal!

Dim Eve Draws on.

ANONYMOUS.

" BEHOLD, the noonday sun of life
    Doth seek its western bound,
And fast the length'ning shadows cast
    A heavier gloom around;   .
And all the glow-worm lamps are dead
    That, kindling round our way,
Gave fickle promises of joy;
    'Abide with us, we pray!'

" Dim eve draws on, and many a friend,
    Our early path that blest,
Wrapt in the cerements of the tomb,
    Have lain them down to rest;
But *Thou*, the everlasting Friend,
    Whose Spirit's glorious ray
Can gild the dreary vale of death,
    'Abide with us, we pray!'"

The Infirmities of Age.

ANONYMOUS.

KING SOLOMON, who was a wise observer of human nature, gives us* a full description of the infirmities of age, expressed in what is called a figurative manner, the substance of which is easily understood, though, from not knowing perfectly the customs or the proverbial sayings to which he alludes, we may not be able exactly to explain every part of them.

Solomon describes old age by the darkening of the sun, the moon and the stars; and the return of the clouds after the rain. When thick and heavy clouds obscure the cheerful light of the sun by day, or of the moon and stars by night, people complain of the dulness of the weather, as it checks their pursuits both of business and pleasure; and thus it is in old age—afflictions of body and troubles of mind often produce a gloom; the days are dull, the nights are wearisome, and none of that pleasure is felt which the young, who have health, strength, and lively

* Eccles. xii. 1, 7.

spirits, generally enjoy. And then, it is added, *"the clouds return after the rain"*—that is, one pain and affliction succeeds another, as the clouds often do in a rainy season. In showery weather the clouds sometimes disperse, the clear shining of the sun succeeds for a little while; but soon the sky is overcast again, and a heavy shower descends. And thus in old age painful disorders are sometimes remitted, and the hope that health is returning is indulged; but, alas! the interval of ease is short; the pain is renewed—" the clouds return after the rain."

Another infirmity of age is thus expressed—*"The keepers of the house tremble"*—the hands and arms, like faithful watchmen, were always ready to defend the body from assaults and dangers; but these become feeble, are sometimes tremulous by palsy, and can no longer prove a sufficient guard from assaults or accidents. In like manner, *"the strong men bow themselves"*—the legs and thighs, which, in youth were like strong men, able to bear a heavy burden, are now become feeble, and too weak to bear the weight of the body, which totters from side to side, and without assistance is in danger of falling to the ground! The foresight of such a state led the Psalmist to pray, " Cast me not off in the time of old age; forsake me not when my strength faileth."

The failure of the teeth, so useful in preparing the food for its digestion in the stomach, is another infirmity of age which the wise man thus expresses: *"The grinders shall cease because they are few;"* the teeth, which in youth grind the food, like the stones in a corn mill, are decayed, or loose, or totally lost; so that some kinds of food cannot be eaten at all, and others are very imperfectly prepared for the stomach.

In old age the sight usually fails more or less, and in many mournful cases is totally lost. Solomon thus describes this affliction: *"Those that look out of the windows are darkened."* The eyes have been justly called "the windows of the soul." From these windows the mind surveys with pleasure the faces of dear relations and friends, and the delightful prospects of nature; discovers the approaches of danger, and reads the page of instruction. But all these sources of pleasure and safety are closed; the day is gone; the night, the long dark night, which will know no morning in this life, is come; and half the world, as to our enjoyment of it, is shut out for the rest of our days.

"The doors shall be shut in the streets, when the sound of the grinding is low." There seems to be an allusion here to the custom of the ancients, who, early in the

morning, as soon as the doors of the house were opened, ground their corn for the day in a hand-mill, If this refers to the grinding of food by the teeth, then it may signify the want of appetite and the refusal of food. Or it may signify their loving to stay at home, and keeping the doors of the house shut to prevent being disturbed by company. Others think it refers to "the door of the lips," and the aversion of aged people to speak much, especially in public.

"And he shall rise up at the voice of the bird." Old age is usually wakeful. Sleep, the "sweet restorer of tired nature," often departs from the eyes of the aged, or, if they sleep, they are easily disturbed. Even the crowing of the cock or the chirping of the birds will awake them; and often, unable to rest and tired of bed, they will rise at a very early hour.

"And all the daughters of music shall be brought low." Age generally loses its relish for music and singing. That which was, perhaps, a great delight becomes rather a burden; the breathing is short and the voice tremulous. Aged Barzillai, whom King David would have taken to court, declined the proposal, saying, " I am this day fourscore years old ; can I hear any more the voice of singing men and singing women ?

Wherefore, then, should thy servant be yet a burden to my lord the king?"

Another token of old age is, "*They shall be afraid of that which is high, and fears shall be in the way.*" Steep ascents are very difficult to the aged; a hill alarms their fears, for it threatens to produce much pain and weariness. Travelling now seems formidable to them. The young are often too bold, and venture into needless dangers; and the old are too timorous, and full of fear lest mischief should befall them. They prefer, therefore, staying at home, and not exposing themselves to harm abroad.

"*The almond tree shall flourish.*" The almond tree, with its white blossoms, is a beautiful emblem of the hoary head. Gray or white hairs are the common symptoms of age, and may be considered as truly ornamental, for "the glory of young men is their strength: and the beauty of old men is the gray head." Prov. xx. 29. God himself put honour upon it in the law, saying, "Thou shalt rise up before the hoary head, and honour the face of the old man, and fear thy God: I am the Lord." Lev. xix. 32. But let the aged remember that these blossoms are certain intimations of the approach of death; they have been called "churchyard flowers," which, as one says, "may serve to them that bear them, instead of passing bells, to give them certain notice whither they are shortly going."

"*And the grasshopper shall be a burden.*" This signifies the extreme feebleness of the aged, when the lightest thing may be a load—when reduced to such weakness and nervous sensibility that the least inconvenience, though it may be as trifling as the weight or the chirping of an insect, may vex and fret them.

"*And desire shall fail.*" Those animal passions and desires which in youth were so strong and violent, and too often the occasion of so much sin, now gradually decline as years increase and strength decays. And it is well it is so, for now it is high time to get the heart weaned from the world and a life of sense, and to "set the affections upon things above."

Then shall "*the silver cord be loosed—the golden bowl broken—the pitcher be broken at the fountain, and the wheel broken at the cistern.*" The whole verse seems to be a description of the functions of life, taken from a well, where there is a cord to the bowl or bucket with which the water is drawn up; a wheel by which more easily to raise it; a cistern into which it may be poured; and a pitcher or vessel to carry it away with; but now all these are broken and become useless. Thus, at death, the lungs cease to play, the heart ceases to beat, the blood to circulate; the whole surprising contrivance for forming and circulating the blood from the fountain of the heart to every extremity of the body is now entirely deranged.*

What follows this derangement? "*Then shall the dust return to the earth as it was: and the spirit shall return unto God who gave it.*" Then "*man goeth to his long home, and the mourners go about the streets.*"

How solemn are these words! They demand our most serious attention. When death takes place a separation is made between the mortal body and the immortal spirit. The body soon corrupts, must be buried out of sight, and quickly returns to its mother earth. But the spirit—the immortal spirit—what becomes of that? Does it cease to exist? No; "*it returns to God who gave it,*" to be disposed of according to his holy and sovereign pleasure. If the spirit has been renewed by grace and made meet for glory, it departs from the body to be with Christ—"absent from the body, present with the Lord;" for "blessed are the dead which die in the Lord." But if the sinner died in a graceless state, unpardoned and unrenewed, it sinks into endless perdition. The spirits

* Scott's Commentary.

of the just are made perfect, and immediately pass into glory; but the spirits of the wicked "go to their own place," as Judas did, and, with the ungodly rich man in the parable, are tormented.

"*The mourners go about the streets.*" Most men die lamented by some, either sincerely or in appearance. A funeral is a solemn sight, and ought to be conducted and viewed with deep seriousness. The mourners are conveying a dear relation, a kind friend or a valued neighbour to his "*long home*"—so the grave is here, with great propriety, styled his *long* home. The deceased had, perhaps, resided in various dwellings during the course of a long life. He removed from one habitation to another, as occasion required; but the grave is his last, his long home. Thus, as Job speaks, " Man lieth down, and riseth not: till the heavens be no more, they shall not awake, nor be raised out of their sleep." But, as St. Paul assures us, " the trumpet shall sound, and the dead shall be raised;" and then, saith Job, " Thou shalt call, and I will answer thee: thou wilt have a desire to the work of thy hands." Job xiv. 12–15.

The infirmities of age ought to teach us *the evil of sin.* If sin had not entered into the world, these infirmities would not have been known. There would have been no pains and aches, no failure of hearing

29

and sight, no wearisome days nor sleepless nights
These are all the fruits and effects of sin. If man
had not sinned, he would not have suffered by age
any more than angels do : they have lived many
thousand years, and they still enjoy all the vigour of
youth ; but man lives several years before he attains
maturity ; his manly vigour lasts but a little while,
and then he fades like a leaf or withers like a flower;
" The wind passeth over it, and it is gone, and the
place thereof knoweth it no more."   Surely, then, the
aged man should reflect on the evil of sin, which is
the sad cause of all his sufferings ; for sin is the disease, and all our afflictions are but the symptoms of
it.   In some cases the aged may perceive that particular sufferings are the effects of particular sins ;
and may cry, with one of old, " Thou writest bitter
things against me, and makest me to possess the iniquities of my youth" (Job xiii. 26) ; or, as it is in another
place, "His bones are full of the sin of his
youth, which shall lie down with him in the dust."
Job xx. 11.

The certain approach of death is another lesson
taught by the infirmities of age.   The young *may* die,
but the aged *must*.   Death may be near a man at any
age; but it must be very near the old man.   " As
the Lord liveth, there is but a step between thee and

death." It is at the door. Do not you hear it knock? Your aching limbs, your failing sight, your trembling hand, are all certain signs of the great approaching change. Are you then prepared to die? Have you believed in Christ? Have you, as a guilty sinner, fled to him for refuge? Has your heart been renewed by grace? Are you become "a new creature in Christ Jesus?" Are you "made meet," by the Spirit of God, "for the inheritance of the saints in light?"

These are some of the questions which you ought to ask yourselves. Put these questions to your hearts, and rest not without honest answers to them. If you have neglected the care of your soul till now, how deeply should you repent the shameful delay; and how earnest should you be in your prayers for the pardoning mercy of God through Jesus Christ, that now, though it be so late, even at the eleventh hour, you may obtain the salvation you have hitherto slighted and refused! Not a moment more must be lost. Oh then "seek the Lord while he may be found, call upon him while he is near. Let the wicked forsake his way, and the unrighteous man his thoughts; and let him return unto the Lord, and he will have mercy upon him; and to our God, for he will abundantly pardon."

But let the believer rejoice, for his redemption

draweth nigh. It is nearer than when he first believed. While you remain in the body, Christ will
continue to support and comfort you. God is faithful,
who will not suffer you to be tried above what you
are able to bear. As your day is, so shall your
strength be. God will give you patience to endure
all your pains and infirmities; and he has said, I will
never, never leave nor forsake you; and then, in his
own good time, he will relieve you from the burden
of the flesh, and give you an abundant entrance into
his eternal kingdom and glory.

> Yet a season, and you know
>   Happy entrance will be given—
> All your sorrows left below,
>   And earth exchanged for heaven.

Joys to Come.

FROM THE GERMAN OF H. C. VON SCHWEINITZ

WILL not that joyful be,
When we walk by faith no more,
When the Lord we loved before
 As Brother-man we see ;
When he welcomes us above,
When we share his smile of love,
 Will not that joyful be ?

Will not that joyful be,
When to meet us rise and come
All our buried treasures home,
 A gladsome company !
When our arms embrace again
Those we mourned so long in vain,
 Will not that joyful be ?

Will not that joyful be,
When the foes we dread to meet,
Every one beneath our feet
 We tread triumphantly !

When we never more can know
Slightest touch of pain or woe,
　　Will not that joyful be?

Will not that joyful be,
When we hear what none can tell
And the ringing chorus swell
　　Of angels' melody!
When we join their songs of praise,
Hallelujahs with them raise,
　　Will not that joyful be?

Yes! that will joyful be,
Let the world her gifts recall,
There is bitterness in all,
　　Her joys are vanity!
Courage, dear ones of my heart!
Though it grieves us here to part,
　　'There we will joyful be!

The Promised Strength.

ANONYMOUS.

IT is well, in every period of the Christian life, to have a right estimate of our own strength. The advanced believer is as unable by his own power to defend himself from sin and sorrow as the youthful Christian. But to each—and with peculiar force to the aged pilgrim, whose lengthened experience and deepened humility make him so distrustful of *self*—the promise comes of Almighty help and succour. "As thy days," says the God of Israel, "so shall thy strength be."* In every moment of need, "Fear thou not; for I am with thee: be not dismayed; for I am thy God."† When difficulties and dangers arise in your path, let not the thought of your own weakness and insufficiency discourage you; for "I will strengthen thee; yea, I will help thee; yea, I will uphold thee with the right hand of my righteousness."‡ "Without me ye can do nothing;"|| but

* Deut. xxxiii. 25.   † Isa. xli. 10   ‡ Isa. xli. 10.
|| John xv. 5.

231

" My grace is sufficient for thee: for my strength is made perfect in weakness."*

Take courage, aged Christian, as you listen to these cheering assurances of the most high God; and rejoice that he is able to "supply all your need according to his riches in glory by Christ Jesus."† For, remember, the strength which his promises guarantee to you is *adequate* strength. "As thy days, so shall thy strength be;" the one fully commensurate with the other. Your present necessities and your future wants might well fill you with distress and apprehension, did not God stand engaged to prepare you for every emergency and to sustain you under every burden. But since the omnipotent Creator has pledged himself to furnish his people with whatever spiritual energy they require in their perpetual conflict, you may gratefully exclaim with the Psalmist, " The Lord is my rock, and my fortress, and my deliverer; my God, my strength, in whom I will trust."‡ Yes, " trust in him at all times," " for in the Lord Jehovah is everlasting strength." Let no misgivings disturb your mind as you think of approaching and augmented trials; for with the increased demand for strength you may confidently calculate upon an increased supply. Now you are looking, perhaps, at

* 2 Cor. xii. 9.   † Phil. iv. 19.   ‡ Psa. xviii. 2.

some great trouble in the distance, and you are feeling as if, when it arrives, you must sink under it.
Ah, you are estimating your power of endurance
then by what it is now; you are supposing that, with
your present weakness, you are summoned to a more
arduous encounter than you have hitherto met with,
and you are mournfully anticipating an inevitable
failure. But do you not perceive that your conclusion is drawn from wrong premises? You will not
have to grapple with increased difficulties before you
are able to surmount them. God will never call you
to the fulfilment of any duty, nor the endurance of
any trial, without having first provided for you sufficient strength for the occasion.

But the promised strength is *daily* strength. "As
thy *days*, so shall thy strength be." You must not
expect to have a large stock on hand which will last
you for a long time; nor endeavour to make the
strength of to-day suffice for the wants of to-morrow;
but in every fresh period of conflict and suffering you
must seek for fresh strength from above. You cannot live upon past supplies, but you may safely rely
upon present and future succour. The spiritual aid
which you require will always be vouchsafed at the
right time. Each day, each season of renewed solicitude will bring with it its own appointed strength.

It may be that you are advanced, not in years only, but also in Christian experience; still you must depend as perpetually and as entirely now upon the help of God as you did at the commencement of your religious life. Day by day, hour by hour, moment by moment, you must trust in him and look to him.

And the strength which he grants to his children is *appropriate* strength. "*As* thy days, so shall *thy strength* be." The days of the spiritual life are as varied as the days of the natural life. Sometimes they are bright with hope and prosperity; sometimes they are dark with disappointment and sorrow. There are days when our path lies through green and flowery meadows; and there are days when our road is through a tangled forest or along the edge of a precipice. At one time we have to toil up the Hill Difficulty; at another, to fight our way through the Valley of the Shadow of Death. Now there is a beautiful adaptation in God's grace to the diversified circumstances of his people's history. Have you not found it to be so, dear reader? Have you not felt in your times of need that there was an exact minuteness in God's gracious dealings with you—that there was a delicate adjustment in the bestowal of his varied gifts? Expect the same considerateness in his conduct still. Believe that the strength which he prepares for you is suitable, as well as sufficient.

What day is it with you now? The day of *physical infirmity?* Is your health declining, your energy abating, your faculties one by one becoming impaired? Is yours the day so graphically described by the royal preacher, " when the keepers of the house shall tremble, and the strong men shall bow themselves, and the grinders cease because they are few, and those that look out of the windows be darkened;—when they shall be afraid of that which is high, and fears shall be in the way, and the almond tree shall flourish, and the grasshopper shall be a burden, and desire shall fail?"* Then remember God's promise, " Even to hoar hairs will I carry you."† Carry you —not leave you to bear up as you best can under the burden which old age brings with it, but uphold you with his own everlasting arm. He will help you to endure with cheerfulness and resignation the pain which is occasioned by the decay of nature.

Is it the day of *mental depression?* The infirmities and sufferings of the body often affect the mind. They cast a gloom over the spirits and throw a shadow over our prospects. " Our mind is like a stained or clouded glass, which mars the hue of what

---

* Eccles. xii. 3–5. † Isa. xlvi. 4.

is bright and deepens what is sombrous." We are discomposed and disheartened by trifles; we are frightened at shadows. All around us and before us looks dark and gloomy. Well, there is One who knoweth our frame, and remembereth that we are dust; and he can support and strengthen our disturbed and fearful spirits. We need not be ashamed to disclose to him our mental weakness; he feels for us all, nay, more than a father's tenderness; for as one whom his *mother* comforteth, so will he comfort us. "He giveth power to the faint; and to them that have no might he increaseth strength."*

Is it the day of *spiritual conflict?* Are you sore let and hindered in your endeavours to press toward the mark for the prize of the high calling of God in Christ Jesus? Do your unseen enemies seem to increase? are their assaults more malignant? and is your own heart inclined to yield to temptation? The great adversary of mankind is sometimes permitted to attack with unusual violence the soul of the aged Christian. Sins which the believer imagined were long since subdued rise up as it were into new life; thoughts and feelings utterly at variance with his renewed mind seem almost forced upon him; and the fiery darts of the wicked one are hurled at him

* Isa. xl. 29.

without intermission. Is this painful experience yours? Be not alarmed or discouraged by it. God is faithful, and he will not suffer you to be tempted above that which you are able to bear; but he will strengthen you for your last struggle with a disappointed and already vanquished foe. Clad in the panoply which God provides for you, and furnished with those weapons which through him are mighty to repel and overcome your spiritual enemies, you shall be enabled to stand in the evil day, and having done all to stand. It is true you are weak, but his strength is perfected in weakness; it is true your infirmities are many, but his power rests upon you. Fear not; look to the Captain of your salvation; follow his directions; rely upon his assistance, and you shall at last be "more than conqueror through him that loved you."*

Is it the day of *temporal distress?* Are you poor? in want of the necessaries or the comforts of life? incapable of supporting yourself by the labour of your hands, and obliged to depend on the charity of others? Or are those dear to you in adversity? are you obliged to witness sufferings that you cannot alleviate, and to hear of troubles which you can neither remove nor lighten? Or have you been bereaved of

* Rom. viii. 37.

some beloved relative, some cherished friend, with whom you were associated in the closest union, and to whom you looked for sympathy and affection. Are these, or similar afflictions, the crosses which you have to take up and carry, and do you tremble beneath their weight? Then cast your burden upon the Lord, and he will sustain you. He will strengthen your *faith* to believe that these mysterious dispensations are necessary for your real welfare; he will strengthen your *love* to receive with meekness and gratitude the discipline of a kind and tender Father; he will strengthen your *hope* to anticipate those glorious things which are unseen and eternal, and to reckon your present sufferings as unworthy of a moment's comparison with " the glory which shall be revealed."*

But there is one day rapidly approaching when you will pre-eminently require the succour and support of an Almighty hand—the day of *death*. Ah! that is a solemn day even to the believer. A darkness, a mystery rests upon our last conflict which excites feelings of seriousness and awe in all thoughtful minds. And when there is great sensitiveness of temperament and timidity of disposition, the Christian often shrinks painfully from the contemplation

* Rom. viii. 18.

of death, and through fear of it is perhaps all his life-time subject to bondage. But why should you fear the approach of the last enemy? If God promises that as your day your strength shall be, surely he will make that promise good in the day of your mortal agony. When you pass through the dark valley he will be with you; his rod and staff will guide and comfort you. When heart and flesh shall faint and fail, he will be the strength of your heart and your portion for ever.

A young Christian once said to a minister, "Although I trust implicitly in the Saviour, and rejoice in him as mine, yet I look upon death as very terrible." At that time she was in perfect health. The reply was, "Doubt not that, according to his sure word, 'As thy days, so shall thy strength be;' and that there shall be dying grace for a dying day." Not long after mortal sickness seized her, but her "peace flowed like a river;" and again and again, as her fond mother and loving sisters watched by her bed of suffering, did she exclaim, "Oh, how true do I find the assurance given me that there would be dying grace for a dying day!"

> " Yes, in your latest moments, when with death
> And Satan thou must struggle, and not yield;
> When with dim eye and quickly-heaving breath,
> Thou enterest on that solemn battle-field;

Thy Saviour, who has succoured thee through life,
Will nerve thy spirit for the closing strife;
Will lead thee on to glorious victory;
For as thy days thy strength shall surely be.''

And then there is the day of *final judgment*—that last day when all the dead shall be gathered around the great white throne of the Eternal, and hear from his lips the irreversible sentence which shall fix their everlasting destiny. Oh, the unutterable moment-ousness of that decision! How will you have courage to listen to it? How will you stand with any calmness before that awful judgment-seat, and hear the records of the past and the awards of the future? Ah, strength shall be given you in that trying hour—strength so unfailing and so indomitable that you shall meet without fear the scrutiny of him who is of purer eyes than to behold iniquity. The sweet assurance will then be yours that to those who are in Christ Jesus there is, there can be, no condemna-tion; that, clothed in the robe of his righteousness, and sanctified by the grace of his Spirit, you are faultless in God's sight. Who shall lay anything to your charge, when God himself will be your justifier?

Thus his blessed promise, "As thy days, so shall thy strength be," will never fail. Through life, in death, and before the judgment-seat, it will be richly fulfilled in your experience. Oh, the comfort of feeling sure that, however wearisome and difficult the path of duty or of suffering may prove, God will impart to us adequate and appropriate strength, and guide us in safety to the heavenly Canaan !

Dr. Doddridge was walking out one day in a very depressed state of mind. His trials were at that time peculiarly heavy; he saw no way of deliverance from them, and he was greatly discouraged. As he passed along, the door of a little cottage was standing open, and he heard a child's voice reading the words, "As thy days, so shall thy strength be." The effect produced upon his saddened feelings was indescribable; his despondency vanished, and his heart was filled with peace and joy.

Yes, one simple promise from God is enough to chase our fears and cheer our hearts. Our wants and weaknesses are many, but he knows them all, and is both able and willing to supply our every need. Then let us "seek the Lord, and his strength;"* let our earnest and constant petitions at the throne of grace be, "Give thy strength unto thy servant;" "strengthen thou me according unto thy word."† For it is they who *wait upon the Lord* that

* Psa. cv. 4.   † Psa. lxxxvi. 16; cxix. 28.

31

shall renew their strength. "Wait," then, "on the Lord: be of good courage, and he shall strengthen thine heart."* The faithfulness of his character is your security for the fulfilment of his promises; for "the Strength of Israel will not lie nor repent;"† " Hath he said, and shall he not do it? or hath he spoken, and shall he not make it good?"‡ And his conduct to his people in past days is a pledge of his readiness to help them now; for he is "the same yesterday, and to-day, and for ever."§ He has been a strength to the poor—a strength to the needy in his distress; and he is *our* refuge and strength, a very present help in trouble.

"Let us therefore come boldly unto the throne of grace, that we may obtain mercy, and find grace to help in time of need."‖ There should be no hesitation on our part to apply for the strength which we require, for there is no reluctance on God's part to communicate it. In his hand it is to give strength to *all.* A sense of our weakness, and a cry for his aid, are the only pre-requisites for its bestowal.

But *how* is this strength imparted? It is the gift of God, and through grace is laid hold of by *faith.* Faith is the hand which grasps and appropriates the

---

* Psa. xxv. 14.　　† 1 Sam. xv. 29.　　‡ Num. xxiii. 19.
§ Heb. xiii. 8.　　　　　　　　　　　　‖ Heb. iv. 16.

promises, and thus fills the soul with an all-sustaining, all-conquering energy. The Holy Spirit, by whom all spiritual blessings are bestowed, brings to the Christian just the strength which he needs, and teaches him to embrace it by faith. That faith may be weak; but its efficacy depends upon the reality, not the degree of our faith; and, therefore, if we sincerely trust in God, through Christ, we may assuredly expect that the aid which we look for, and for which we supplicate, will be granted us. Yet, while it is true that the smallest amount of true faith forms, so to speak, a channel through which God's grace flows into our hearts, it is equally true that a stronger degree of faith is more honouring to God, while it would lead us to anticipate, and prepare us to receive, a far greater measure of heavenly assistance than we now possess. "According to your faith," says the Saviour, "be it unto you;"* and, therefore, if we desire to run without weariness, to walk without fainting, and to mount up with wings as eagles towards our rest above, we should make the request of his disciples our own, "Lord, increase our faith."†

Your "wanderings in the wilderness," reader, may be now drawing towards a close. It will, then, not be long before you will be called to pass over the

---

* Matt. ix. 29. † Luke xvii. 5.

river Jordan, that you may enter the promised land. Yet, as we have seen, new trials may have to be encountered in the last stages of your lengthened and perhaps wearisome journey. There is no immunity from sorrow until you reach that blessed country, where God shall himself wipe away all tears, and give you that fulness of joy which is inseparable from his presence. But, remember, aged Christian, the promise, "As thy days, so shall thy strength be," and hold the beginning of your confidence steadfast unto the end. As you think of the evening of life, the night of death, and the solemnities of the last judgment, resolve with the Psalmist, "I will go in the strength of the Lord God: I will make mention of thy righteonsness, even of thine only."* So shall you go on from strength to strength, until you appear in Zion before your God.†

* Psa. lxxi. 16.　　　　　　　　† Psa. lxxxiv. 7.

Tarry with Me.

ANONYMOUS.

TARRY with me, O my Saviour,
  For the day is passing by :
See ! the shades of evening gather,
  And the night is drawing nigh !
Tarry with me ! tarry with me !
  Pass me not unheeded by !

Many friends were gathered round me
  In the bright days of the past ;
But the grave has closed above them,
  And I linger here the last !
I am lonely ; tarry with me
  Till the dreary night is past.

Dimmea for me is earthly beauty ;
  Yet the spirit's eye would fain
Rest upon thy lovely features :
  Shall I seek, dear Lord, in vain ?
Tarry with me, O my Saviour,
  Let me see thy smile again !

Dull my ear to earth-born music:
  Speak thou, Lord, in words of cheer:
Feeble, tottering my footstep,
  Sinks my heart with sudden fear;
Cast thine arms, dear Lord, around me,
  Let me feel thy presence near.

Faithful memory paints before me
  Every deed and thought of sin;
Open thou the blood-filled Fountain,
  Cleanse my guilty soul within:
Tarry thou, forgiving Saviour!
  Wash me wholly from my sin!

Deeper, deeper grow the shadows,
  Paler, now, the glowing west;
Swift the night of death advances;
  Shall it be the night of rest?
Tarry with me, O my Saviour!
  Lay my head upon thy breast!

Feeble, trembling, fainting, dying,
  Lord, I cast myself on thee:
Tarry with me, through the darkness!
  While I sleep, still watch by me
Till the morning; then awake me,
  Dearest Lord, to dwell with thee.

Outlived her Usefulness.

MRS. ADELINE T. DAVIDSON.

Nor till the dark waves of Jordan
  Shall close on the steps that have passed,
Not till the portals of heaven
  Shall welcome the ransomed at last,—

Not till I join in the chorus
  That sounds o'er the "crystal sea,"
May I cease to be striving and praying
  That others may enter with me.

WE were riding along very slowly, with the solemn, measured tread which compels reflection. She whose dust we were reverently depositing in peaceful rest was an aged Christian. For many years she had been foremost in every work of love and mercy. Generous, untiring, and self-sacrificing, she had passed a long life of usefulness in her family and in the church that she loved. Years of infirmity and helplessness followed, and for many weary months those hands which had ministered so cheerfully unto others could not supply her own slightest need. And then her change came.

247

"What a devoted Christian she was years ago!" was remarked; "but she has long *outlived her usefulness.* I have often wondered why such old people live. Such a one as old Mrs. J——, for instance—so perfectly helpless. She was prepared to die, we know, and yet she must have been weary of so burdensome a life."

"Did she ever express herself as being weary of life?" I asked.

"Oh! no, she was as patient as a lamb. If I were to be ill a long time, I should think it was intended to teach me patience. But she did not need such a discipline."

"And her family?"

"It may have benefited them. Mary has waited upon her grandmother so long that she has grown like her, and has become a most lovely character, so gentle and self-denying."

"Did she retain her eyesight sufficiently to read?"

"For several years past she has been quite blind. As her grandchildren would come in, she would ask them to read a single verse of the Bible, and which of the most thoughtless would refuse so small a request? Then she would in her quiet way make such varied, such beautiful application of this one text! It was a precious commentary. I think that they will never forget some of them. I know that she spent much of her time in prayer."

"Do you suppose she is praying now?"

"Certainly not. Her prayers are ended. We read of praises in heaven, but of no intercessions except those of Christ."

"Has her family been blessed apparently?"

"All her children are in the church. Her eldest son living is our most active elder, and just before her death she heard of the conversion of two of her grandsons at the West, who had been in situations of peculiar temptation."

"Do you think she remembered the church?"

"If you had known her you would not ask that. Her church was as dear unto her as the apple of her eye. She spent many a long hour in her sleepless nights in asking for blessings on the church, when the rest of the congregation were sleeping."

"Just now you wondered why God in his providence protracted the life of aged Christians when their days of active usefulness were over. And yet it seems evident that in this case it was the means of teaching patience, gentleness, a knowledge of the Scriptures, and that in answer to her prayers many of her family have been hopefully converted. No effectual, fervent prayer of the righteous is ever lost.

32

As this life is the only season for prayer, hers may have been protracted for this express purpose. For many generations, for aught you or I can tell, blessings temporal and spiritual may be granted in answer to the prayers of that helpless, bed-ridden Christian."

Said the angel of the covenant unto one who had wrestled with him all night, "As a prince hast thou power with God, and hast prevailed." Are there now no princes in prayer like him who strove at Peniel? None now who wrestle not one night only, but through long years of infirmity and suffering it may be, yet of cherished communion with God, whose prayers, presented "in the golden vial" by an almighty Advocate, are poured back in priceless benedictions?

Let us try to realize that not one day of weariness will be given to the maturest saint that is not necessary; not one sigh breathed that has not its errand. The servant of Christ need never be useless, under any circumstances, in any place, alone, on a bed of weakness, shut out from the world, deaf even, while the heart can beat with love to a dying world, or conscious thought rise to the mercy-seat.

We should shine till the last, and the brighter at the last. The nearer we draw to the Sun of Righteousness, the clearer should become our reflection of his loveliness and glory.

"*Outlived his usefulness!*" Never let such a sentence be uttered by a Christian.

A lady was urging a man in middle life to enter once more a Sabbath-school where he had formerly assisted, and where his services were greatly needed.

He declined. " I have taught for twenty years; I have served my time."

" Then your experience will be all the more valuable," was suggested.

He persisted in refusing, adding, conclusively, that " his work was done."

The next Sabbath they met in the vestibule of the church. As he greeted her she said, quietly,

" I did not expect to see you here."

"Ah! why not?"

"You told me the last time I saw you that your work was done. Now I always supposed that when our work was all done the Master would send for us. So I supposed you had gone to your reward."

The Hope of the Disconsolate.

SIR ROBERT GRANT.

WHEN gathering clouds around I view,
And days are dark and friends are few,
On him I lean who, not in vain,
Experienced every human pain;
He sees my wants, allays my fears,
And counts and treasures up my tears.

If aught should tempt my soul to stray
From heavenly virtue's narrow way,
To fly the good I would pursue,
Or do the sin I would not do,—
Still he who felt temptation's power,
Shall guard me in that dangerous hour.

When vexing thoughts within me rise,
And sore dismayed my spirit dies,
Yet he who once vouchsafed to bear
The sickening anguish of despair
Shall sweetly soothe, shall gently dry,
The throbbing heart, the streaming eye.

252

When sorrowing o'er some stone I bend,
Which covers all that was a friend,
And from his voice, his hand, his smile,
Divides me for a little while,
Thou, Saviour, seest the tears I shed,
For thou didst weep o'er Lazarus dead.

And oh when I have safely passed
Through every conflict but the last,
Still, still unchanging, watch beside
My painful bed, for thou hast died;
Then point to realms of cloudless day,
And wipe the latest tear away.

Nearer Home.

ALICE CARY.

ONE sweetly solemn thought,
  Comes to me o'er and o'er,—
I'm nearer my home to-day
  Than I've ever been before.

Nearer my Father's house,
  Where the many mansions be,—
Nearer the great white throne,
  Nearer the jasper sea.

Nearer the bound of life,
  Where we lay our burdens down,—
Nearer leaving the cross,
  Nearer wearing the crown.

But, lying darkly between,
  Winding down through the night,
To the dim and unknown stream,
  That leads me at last to the light,—

Close, closer my steps
  Come to the dark abysm,—
Closer death to my lips
  Presses the awful chrysm.

Saviour, perfect my trust,
  Strengthen the might of my faith ;
Let me feel as I would when I stand
  On the rock of the shore of death,—

Feel as I would when my feet
  Are slipping over the brink ;
For it may be I'm nearer home,—
  Nearer now than I think.

Beyond the Sunset.

REV. ROBERT F. SAMPLE.

"At evening time it shall be light."—Zech. xiv. 7.
" Thy sun shall no more go down."—Isa. lx. 20.

SHADOWS o'er the vale are creeping,
   And the sun sinks to his rest:
Twilight draws her curtains softly,
   Golden clouds hang in the west.
Hushed the noise of busy labour,
   Toil has sought its wonted rest;
Whispering trees and murmuring streamlets
   Sweetly soothe each troubled breast.

Time is fleeting, and I'm drawing
   Near the sunset of my life;
Soon will end my weary journey,
   Soon will cease all toil and strife.
Shadows o'er my path are falling,
   Earthly visions fade away,
Voices soft and sweet are telling
   Of an endless, orient day.

256

O'er the misty mountains hastens
 One I've waited long to see;
Soft as night-dew falls on meadows,
 His kind bidding, " Come to me."
Lo! the purple light of evening,
 Stealing gently up the sky,
Bears me on its wings to meet him.
 Is this death?   'Tis sweet to die.

Jesus calls me, and I'm going
 Where the shadows never come;
Now the desert lies behind me,
 And I hasten to my home—
To my home beyond the sunset,
 Far beyond the day's decline,
Where the glory is unfading,
 Where the golden portals shine.

33

The Unchanging Friend.

ANONYMOUS.

THE evening was calm and pleasant, enlivened by a gentle breeze and the rays of the declining sun. At the door of a low cottage sat an old man. His hair was white, his form was bent, and his dim eyes were fixed on the richly-tinted clouds. Was he admiring the simple grandeur of an evening sky? I think not. His features wore a sad and troubled expression, as if his mind were occupied by thoughts which had but little connection with the objects around him. And so indeed it was. He was thinking of the uncertain and unsatisfying nature of earthly friendship; he was musing over a painful proof which he had that day received of the ingratitude and unkindness of one whom he had loved and cherished in years gone by.

"It is trying, very trying," he said, "to be thus deceived and injured by an early friend. It is not an enemy that has done this, but it was my companion and familiar friend. He was the last person from whom I should have expected such treatment; I always reposed the most perfect confidence in him. Oh, what is friendship? It is like a slender reed, which, when leaned upon, often pierces us through with many sorrows."

The old man's feelings had been sadly wounded, and his mind was much disturbed. But, perhaps, just then the serene aspect of nature soothed him, or perhaps bright memories of loved and faithful ones reproached him for his indiscriminate censure; for he added, in a more cheerful tone, "Not that *all* friends prove false and changeable. Oh no! I have known and shared too much of the warm and un-selfish and continued affection of others to believe that friendship is nothing but a name. In prosperity and in adversity I have found that there are true friends. I have loved, and I have been loved; I have trusted, and I have been confided in. Life would indeed have been dreary without the sympathy and communion of friends—especially of Christian friends.

"And yet, at the best, earthly friendships are very imperfect. Liable to little mistakes—to partial interruptions; or, if unvarying in their character, incapable of entering into all our feelings, or of responding to all our emotions. And how slight is the tenure by which they are held! A few weeks, a days, nay, a few hours, and the most loved of our circle may be removed from us. Death severs the closest and the fondest ties. In yonder churchyard lie the remains of those who were once my dearest companions. Many gathered round me in early life, and set out with me on the pilgrimage to the celestial city; but they have finished their course, and now I am left alone: the grave has divided us—at least for a little while."

'Ah, in the last half of that sentence, there was a cheering truth involved, and the old man felt its sweet influence steal over him.

"For a little while!—yes, we shall meet again. They will not return to me, but I shall go to them. I sorrow not as others without hope, for I know that those who sleep in Jesus God will bring with him, and so shall we ever be with the Lord. In this world of partings, how delightful is the assurance of a speedy and lasting re-union with all those dear friends who have departed in the true faith of Christ!"

Like the sunshine bursting through a dark cloud, this bright anticipation almost dispelled the old man's sadness; and it was succeeded by a thought so full of consolation and joy that he speedily forgot the unpleasant circumstance which had lately agitated his feelings.

"Yet it is still more delightful to remember that I have an ever-living, an almighty Friend. The best earthly friends may change or die, but Jesus Christ is the same yesterday, to-day, and for ever. He will never leave me, he will never forsake me. Oh, why should I mourn over the loss or the inconstancy of earthly friends when my kind and sympathizing Saviour is ever with me?"

Reader, you cannot have advanced thus far in the experience of life without having learned, like this aged pilgrim, that instability and uncertainty are associated with all human affections. You have doubtless mourned over those friends whom time or circumstances, or death have parted from you; but have also rejoiced in the assurance of Christ's perpetual and never-changing friendship? Ah, there are many who have been deceived and disappointed in the trust which they have reposed in their fellow-creatures, and who have also never sought that heavenly Friend with whom there is no variableness nor shadow of turning; there are many who have hewn out to themselves broken cisterns which could hold no water, who have yet refused to turn, when weary and dissatisfied, to the Fountain of living waters.

"O thou who driest the mourner's tear,
    How dark this world would be,
If, when deceived and wounded here,
    We could not fly to thee!"

And it *is* dark to those who, in their hours of sorrow and desertion, have no confidence in the Saviour, no reliance on his love and sympathy. The heart that has none on earth or in heaven around whom to twine must indeed be a desolate and drooping heart. God grant that it may never be ours! Nor can it if we are united by a simple and living faith to Christ, for we are then linked with those whom he graciously calls his "friends;" and are assured that we possess at all times and under every circumstance his tender and unwavering regard. How cheering and all-sustaining, amidst the separations, the imperfections, and the declensions which mark the fairest of earthly friendships, is the consciousness that we have an unchanging and unfailing Friend, who is always ready to impart to us his sympathy and his succour.

We would not undervalue the preciousness of earthly love. It is one of the choicest gifts which God bestows upon a fallen world. It is a relic of Paradise and a type of heaven. Yet still we are taught by experience how precarious is the tie which binds us to the dearest and most loved friend   It is impossible to help feeling—without the least inclination towards misanthropy—that our affections are sometimes misplaced, that our dependence is often productive of disappointment. Imperfection and uncertainty are stamped on all the objects and relationships of earth; for "this is not our rest;" we are destined for a better country, the bright inhabitants of which are linked in pure and immortal friendship. And while we anticipate with gladness the period which shall unite us with that wholly and happy brotherhood, we will remember our best Friend—the Friend that sticketh closer than a brother—and fearlessly anchor our troubled and unsatisfied hearts in his deep and changeless love.   That resting-place for the affections never has failed—never can fail.   The circumstances which enfeeble, suspend, and terminate many of the friendships which are formed between man and man, possess no influence over the emotions which the Saviour feels towards his chosen friends, and are incapable of altering the position in which, if Christians, we stand with regard to Christ.

For instance, it frequently happens that the distance which intervenes between some friend and ourselves diminishes, and at length, perhaps, closes our friendship.   He does not intend, when separated, to forget us, but absence gradually lessens the strength of his attachment; his correspondence almost imperceptibly declines, or, through unavoidable circumstances, is hastily ended; and as time rolls on, he grows more and more indifferent towards us. Had he always remained near us, and continued the personal intercourse which once subsisted between us, he might not have changed; but in his removal he verifies the truth of the old adage, " Out of sight, out of mind." Our aged readers can doubtless confirm by their own experience the truth of this statement. They can recall to mind some, it may be several, of their early acquaintances thus geographically divided from them, who have for many years been as strangers to them.

But the Saviour, although personally absent from his people, never for one moment forgets them. From the time when he departed from his disciples at Bethany, where a cloud received him out of their sight, he gave them the most indisputable and uninterrupted proofs of his unchanged affection. He ascended then as a triumphant conqueror to heaven, and was enthroned at the right hand of God; but the glory which as the Mediator was bestowed upon him could not intercept from his view the few poor fishermen of Galilee; nor could the songs of angelic

adoration which he received hush the earnest sup-
plications that rose from that little band who were
assembled in an upper chamber at Jerusalem. No;
his love was the same in heaven as it had been on
earth; and the rich and abundant gifts which were
poured forth upon his faithful disciples were the im·
mediate results of his exaltation and intercession.
He consoled and guided them by his Spirit, and
strengthened them for the avowal and defence of his
truth. In his remonstrance with the persecuting
Saul he distinctly identified himself with his people,
estimating the injuries done to them as if inflicted
upon himself: "Saul, Saul, why persecutest thou
me?"* And he manifested the deep interest in their
welfare by his gracious appearance to the apostle of
the Gentiles, when he bade him "Be of good cheer,"
and prepared him to advocate the cause of his
Saviour in Rome.

But it is unnecessary to multiply proofs, either
from the early or subsequent history of the Church,
of the unvarying character of that regard which
the ascended Redeemer cherishes for all those who
through grace have accepted his gracious overtures
of friendship. We need only appeal to yourselves,
dear readers, as witnesses to the cheering fact that

* Acts ix. 4.

34

the love of Christ—that love which passeth knowledge—is unaffected by the withdrawal of his personal presence from amongst us.   His continued
intercessions on our behalf, his rich impartation to
us of all needful grace, and his preparation of a
place for us in his Father's house, are sure evidences
of his perpetual and affectionate remembrance.

Again, one of the causes which render human
friendship so variable is alteration in worldly circumstances.   When competency is exchanged for
poverty; when, in the expressive language of Scripture, we are " made low," what a change passes over
the little world in which we dwell!   That friendship
is indeed true and valuable which will stand such a
testing-time; for while many gather round us in
prosperity, few cleave to us in adversity.

> "The friends who in our sunshine live,
>   When winter comes are flown."

It is a bitter trial to find ourselves neglected and
forsaken when we are most in need of support and
comfort; but it is a *sanctified* trial if it teaches us
that it is better to trust in the Lord than to put confidence in man; if it endears to us that heavenly
Friend, who, though he was rich, yet for our sakes
became poor, that we through his poverty might be

made rich. Lowly indeed was his lot on earth; he had not where to lay his head; and his chosen friends and associates were from the humblest ranks of society. It was to "the poor" that he especially proclaimed the blessings of his gospel; and the sarcastic designation of his opponents, which styled him "a friend of publicans and sinners," was, in reality, beautifully expressive of his true character.

By his own position in the world, by his mingling chiefly with those who were poor and despised of men, and by the low and obscure situations in which the majority of his disciples have served him, poverty has been elevated and dignified. Not many noble, not many mighty, does the Saviour call; but he chooses the poor in this world, and makes them heirs of that glorious kingdom which he has promised to them that love him.

The wealthy and the fashionable may grow cold and distant when penury and distress enter our home; but Christ makes our season of affliction only the means of drawing us more closely to himself. Our loss of property or income, instead of raising a barrier between him and us, links us more firmly together. He soothes our spirit, sympathizes with our grief, and promises that he will never forsake us.

Or it is possible that the natural infirmities of age

and a long-declining state of health may gradually narrow the circle of our friends. Deafness, or blindness, or sickness makes our society less attractive than formerly. It is wearisome, perhaps, to sit beside us day after day and strive to interest us; and, therefore, some who were once warm and even sincere in their professions of attachment to us, grow tired of the society of an aged invalid, and their visits become few and far between. We feel sometimes, when contrasting the present with the past, that we are forsaken and alone in the world, that we are a burden to ourselves and to others. Old age brings with it a sensitiveness on this point which occasions much mental disquietude, and frequently produces a fretful and repining spirit.

Let us endeavour, in moments of loneliness and depression, to tranquilize and divert our thoughts by dwelling upon the steadfastness of Christ towards us. *He* does not cast us off in the time of old age nor forsake us when our strength fails; he is not weary of listening to the oft-repeated narrative of our wants and ailments, nor reluctant to cheer the solitude of life's evening; but he beautifully fulfils to us his own promise, "Even to hoar hairs will I carry you." As we walk with trembling steps through the valley of the shadow of death, as we miss from our side the friend on whose arm we might have leaned for support and protection; the Saviour bids us fear no evil, because *he* is with us; *his* rod and *his* staff will comfort us; and *his* presence shall perpetually abide with us. Our weakness and our infirmity may tend to loosen some of our earthly ties, but cannot diminish his kind sympathy with us. Friends may fail us, but he will never leave us.

And even should our friends prove faithful, should they retain in old age the affection which they manifested towards us in youth, yet how suddenly and irrevocably may they be parted from us by death! "Our days on the earth are as a shadow, and there is none abiding." The dearest ones around whom our affections are so firmly entwined may soon be summoned into the presence of their Maker, and leave us to tread alone the remainder of our lengthened journey. We may have to see the grave opened for those whose hands we imagined would tenderly close our eyes at the last. Stay! have we not already seen this? have not the separations of the tomb been painfully realized in our past history? The green hillock, the marble tablet, are they not cherished memorials of the departed, who still live in our hearts and are enshrined in our recollections? More eloquent than the preacher's words, more powerful than the written admonition, are the vacant seats in our households—yes, and at our firesides. Ah! the stern precept, "Cease ye from man, whose breath is in his nostrils; for wherein is he to be accounted of?"* has received frequent and practical illustration in the events of bygone days. The tolling bell has mournfully reminded us that change and decay are stamped upon all the things of earth; the cypress tree has darkly shadowed forth the solemn truth that "In the midst of life we are in death."† Well, be it so; we will not murmur that God gathers the ripest fruit and the choicest flowers from our gardens, since he gives us *himself* as our portion. We will not forget, as we sorrow over the dead, that "the Lord liveth!" While thinking of the friends whom the last enemy has snatched from our grasp, we will gratefully remember that Saviour from whom neither death nor the grave can part us. Around our desolated hearths, and in our solitary eventide, his voice is heard sweetly saying unto us, "Fear not; for I am with thee!"‡

Yes, Lord, thou art with us, our firm, our changeless, our undying Friend! "Thou art the same, and thy years shall have no end."§ Death cannot divide

---

* Isa. ii. 22.   † Prayer Book.
‡ Isa. xliii. 5.   § Psa. cii. 27.

thee from thy people, for that vanquished foe hath no power over its almighty Conqueror; and it cannot separate them from their Saviour, for its touch will only usher them into his immediate and visible presence.

"There is no death; what seems so, is transition."

Oh, we are "persuaded that neither death, nor life, nor angels, nor principalities, nor powers, nor things present, nor things to come, nor height, nor depth, nor any other creature, shall be able to separate us from the love of God, which is in Christ Jesus our Lord."*

Then let us comfort one another with this thought. Let the recollection of our indissoluble union with Christ, and of his eternal and unchanging affection for us, solace and refresh our spirits. "Having loved his own which were in the world, he loved them unto the end."† Yes, neither external circumstances, nor the decay of nature, nor even continual infirmity and sinfulness, can alienate the heart of the Saviour from those whom he has chosen, and called, and blessed. Heaven and earth may pass away, but his word—that word which assures us of the freeness and perpetuity of his love—abideth for ever.

Aged Christian! dwell much on the character and

* Rom. viii. 38, 39. † John xiii. 1.

conduct of this mighty and faithful Friend: "Cast ing all your care upon him; for he careth for you."* As life declines, let his preciousness increase; as the associations of earth gradually lessen, cling more closely and confidingly to him. Think of him as preparing a place for you in the heavenly mansions, and as coming to receive you unto himself, that where he is there you may be also. And if, while now you see him not, you can rejoice in him with joy that is unspeakable and full of glory, what will be the rapture of your emancipated spirit when you are admitted to full and uninterrupted communion with him! If now, while you only behold him as through a glass darkly, he is in your apprehension the fairest among ten thousand and the altogether lovely, how will your admiration be increased when you behold him face to face! If now, while you know him but in part, your acquaintance with him is the source of purest and inexpressible pleasure, who shall estimate the happiness and the delight which shall result from your knowing even as you are known?

* 1 Peter v. 7.

The Sympathy of Jesus.

PAUL GERHARDT.

I REST upon the ground
   Of Jesus and his blood,
For 'tis through him that I have found
   The true Eternal good.
   Naught have I of my own,
   Naught in the life I lead;
What Christ hath given me, that alone
   Is worth all love indeed.

   His Spirit in me dwells,
   O'er all my mind he reigns,
All care and sadness he dispels,
   And soothes away all pains.
   He prospers day by day
   His work within my heart,
Till I have strength and faith to say,
   Thou, God, my Father art!

   When weakness on me lies
   And tempts me to despair,

He speaketh words and utters sighs
　　Of more than mortal prayer;
　　But what no tongue can tell,
　　Thou, God, canst hear and see,
Who readest in the heart full well
　　If aught there pleaseth thee.

　　He whispers in my breast
　　Sweet words of holy cheer,
How he who seeks in God his rest
　　Shall ever find him near;
　　How God hath built above
　　A city fair and new,
Where eye and heart shall see and prove
　　What faith has counted true.

　　There is prepared on high
　　My heritage, my lot;
Though here on earth I fall and die,
　　My heaven shall fail me not.
　　Though here my days are dark,
　　And oft my tears must rain,
Whene'er my Saviour's light I mark,
　　All things grow bright again.

　　My heart for gladness springs,
　　It cannot more be sad,

For every joy it laughs and sings,
    Sees naught but sunshine glad.
    The sun that glads mine eyes
    Is Christ the Lord I love;
I sing for joy of that which lies
    Stored up for us above.

The Friend Unseen.

CHARLOTTE ELLIOT.

O Holy Saviour, Friend unseen,
　The faint, the weak on thee may lean;
· Help me, throughout life's varying scene,
　　By faith to cling to thee!

Blest with communion so divine,
　Take what thou wilt; shall I repine,
When, as the branches to the vine,
　　My soul may cling to thee?

Far from her home, fatigued, opprest,
　Here she has found a place of rest—
An exile still, yet not unblest
　　While she can cling to thee!

Without a murmur I dismiss
　My former dreams of earthly bliss;
My joy, my recompense be this,
　　Each hour to cling to thee!

What though the world deceitful prove,
  And earthly friends and joys remove,
With patient, uncomplaining love,
    Still would I cling to thee!

Oft when I seem to tread alone
  Some barren waste with thorns o'ergrown,
A voice of love, in gentlest tone,
    Whispers, "Still cling to me."

Though faith and hope a while be tried,
  I ask not, need not, aught beside;
How safe, how calm, how satisfied,
    The soul that clings to thee!

They fear not life's rough storms to brave,
  Since thou art near, and strong to save;
Nor shudder e'en at death's dark wave,
    Because they cling to thee!

Blest is my lot, whate'er befall;
  What can disturb me, who appal,
While as my Strength, my Rock, my All,
    Saviour, I cling to thee?

Youth Renewed in Age.

JAMES W. ALEXANDER, D. D.

CHRISTIAN confidence and hope in God give freshness, strength and joy, even in the period of old age. "They that wait on Jehovah," or, in modern English, they that wait *for* him, who evince their trust in his goodness and power by patiently awaiting the fulfilment of his promises—they, though no longer young, "shall renew their strength; they shall mount up on wings like eagles, they shall run and not be weary, and they shall walk and not faint." The same thought is in the thanksgiving of the one hundred and third Psalm, v. 5: "Bless Jehovah, O my soul, who satisfieth thy mouth with good things, so that thy youth is renewed like the eagle's." From both we may conclusively gather that divine grace has influences to bestow which can counteract and often annul the debilitating tendencies of old age. We are not authorized, it is true, to teach that any degree of religious affection can turn back the shadow on the dial-plate, restore its auburn beauty to the gray

273

head, or neutralize the physical causes of distress; though even here, such is the power of spirit over matter, that history shows marvels of an almost youthful gladness in blessed Christian old age. But we may and can assert that he whose habits have been formed in a perpetual waiting upon God, receives a hallowed unction of grace, which, so to speak, makes him young again, or, more properly, keeps him from waxing old within. In the most rapid survey we have considered some of the causes which make this season of life formidable. All ages have observed them; all philosophies have sought to destroy or lessen their force. The most accomplished of all Roman authors has left nothing more finished than his celebrated tract on Old Age. Short of the meridian beam of revelation and its reflections, nothing ever showed more nobly; yet the ray of its consolations is but a beautiful moonlight. In vain is the venerable Cato introduced to teach us secrets which Cato never knew. In this gem-like treatise Cicero refers the troubles of age to four classes. Old age, so he tells us, is feared because (1) it withdraws from the affairs of life; because (2) it brings infirmity of body; because (3) it abridges or ends our pleasures; and (4) because it leads to death. Already, in treating of these several heads, much is said truly, ably, and to a certain extent satisfactorily, on the first and third topics; but on the last there is nothing but melancholy conjecture. Even in regard to the other heads, of business, health and pleasure, the suggestions are infinitely below those known by the humblest Christian rustic. For what did this great and eloquent Roman know of the oil which grace pours into the sinking and almost expiring lamp?

It is not to be denied, when we come with candour to the investigation, that, as a general truth, old age withdraws men from the employments of life, and seals up the active business years. In the majority of instances, however, this retreat from labour is voluntarily sought long before the access of grave infirmity. Indeed, in prosperous communities many retire too early, under a chimerical hope of enjoying an elegant repose, for which they have made no provision by mental culture and discipline of moral habits. There is, it is true, another sort of recession from productive labours which we occasionally observe in old men, and which arises wholly from an unchastened selfishness. Let any one grow wealthy without the warming and expanding influences of benevolence, and he will more and more lose his interest in all that is going on in the world. Even wars and revolutions touch him only in their financial aspects, and the daily journal is to him not so much a courier of news as a barometer of loss and gain. Without religion, the circle becomes more contracted. Friends have departed by scores, if not by hundreds. What cares he for mighty movements in behalf of humanity and holiness around him? What cares he for posterity, the country or the world, so that he can exalt his own gate, or die worth some round sum which floats before him as his heaven? In the same degree he wraps himself in his mantle, which is daily shrinking to his own poor dimensions. This is misery indeed. Take away the blessed sun, and everything becomes wintry, frozen, all but dead: take away more blessed love, and the heart is dumb, cheerless, insulated, meanly poor, so that the Latins named such a one MISER. Let us leave him, shivering in his cave, overhung with icicles, and come out into the evening sunshine to consider the aged believer. He is, like Mnason, "an old disciple." He still learns. The Greek story tells us that when Solon lay dying, and overheard some conversation on philosophy in his apartment, he raised his head and said, "Let me share in your conversation, for though I am dying I would still be learning." Ten thousand times has this been more reasonably exemplified in dying Christians, who consider the whole

36

of this life as but the lowest form of the school into which they have been entered. And in regard to activity, while modes of service must vary with the bodily condition, we are bold to maintain that innumerable Christians now living are, in advanced life, impressing the whole engine of human affairs with as momentous a touch as at any previous stage of existence. If there is wisdom, the proper jewel of age and divine grace in its manifold actings, there need be no lack of influence. They still lift up the eagle pinion, and soar in such greatness as belongs to their nature. But the point to which we would ask more marked attention is this, that the aged believer, so far from being selfishly dead to what is going on in the world, is more vigilant and more in sympathy with all than even in his days of youth. Blessed be God, we have seen this again and again. The man who waits on God, the man of faith and hope, the man of melting benevolence, looks through the loopholes of retreat upon a world whose vast and often terrific revolutions interest him chiefly as included in a cycle of providential arrangements calculated to develop and exhibit the glory of grace. His heart beats responsive to these. The news of Christ's kingdom is as dear to him as when he was vehemently active in the field. He looks down the ages by the lamp of prophecy, and beholds events which will take place when he shall have been long in Paradise. This connects him with the cause of Christ on earth, and redeems him from that miserable, dungeon-like seclusion of soul which wastes away the aged worldling. So far is it from being true that these portraitures are figments of religious imagination, that we have been led to the choice of the subject by knowledge and recollection of this very paradox in actual example, to wit: extreme old age made light, strong and happy by community of interest in the progressive triumphs of philanthropy and missions.

When, according to the Talmudic fable, the eagle soars toward the sun, he renews the plumage of his former days. As the serene disciple withdraws himself from any personal agency in the entangling plans of life, he studies more profoundly what his Master is weaving into the web of history. No longer young, he has a heart which gushes in sympathy with the young, and he cheers them on. He places the weapons in their hands. He takes from the wall his sword, shield and helmet, and rejoices that God still has younger soldiers in the field. He lives his life over again in their achievements, and pictures to himself more signal victories after he shall have gone. Like the wounded hero Wolfe, he could even die more happy if the shout of victory should arouse his failing perception. Far from being shut up in morose, neglectful selfishness, he glories that God's cause still lives and must prevail.

Sojourning as at an Inn.

A. D. F. RANDOLPH.

I LOOK abroad upon the verdant fields,
   The song of birds is on the summer air;
Within, how many a treasure something yields
   To bless my life and round the edge of care;
      And yet the earth and air,
      All that seems good and fair,
   That still is mine or for a time hath been,
Now teach me I am but a pilgrim here,
   Without a home, and dwelling at an inn.

Not always has the outlook been so clear;
   There have been days when stormy gusts went
      by;
Nights when my wearied heart was full of fear,
   And God seemed farther off than stars and sky;
      Yet then, when grief was nigh,
      My soul could sometimes cry,

285

Out of the depths of sorrow and of sin,
That at the worst I was but pilgrim here,
  With home beyond, while dwelling at an inn.

Now I complain not of this life of mine,
  I less of shade have had than of the sun;
The gracious Father, with a hand divine,
  Has crowned with mercies his unworthy one;
        My cup has overrun,
  .   And I, his will undone,
Have changed his countless blessings into sin;
As I forgot I was but pilgrim here,
  Homeless at best, and dwelling at an inn.

Look on me, Lord! Have I not need to pray
  That this fair world, that gives so much to me,
Serve not to lead my steps so far astray
  That at the end I stand afar from thee?
        Dear Lord, let this not be;
        Nay, rather let me see
Beyond this life my happiest days begin;
And singing on my way, a pilgrim here,
  Rejoice that I am dwelling at an inn.

Dear Son of God! by whom the world was made,
  Yet homeless, had not where to lay thy head,

(Not e'en by kindred was thy body laid
  In Joseph's tomb, thou Lord of quick and dead!)
    By thy example led,
    Of me may it be said,
When I shall rest and perfect peace begin,
He lived as one who was a pilgrim here,
  And found his home while dwelling at an inn.

To an Old Disciple.

WILLIAM S. PLUMER, D. D.

My heart is drawn towards you. I too am going down the hill of life, and the longer I live the more sympathy do I feel with the aged. I have no longer the sprightliness of youth. In common with you I know the sorrow caused by the failure of hopes. A light heart carries the young swiftly along, but in us, who have passed the middle of life, the spirit is at least chastened, if not somewhat broken. Once past middle life, we seldom forget our griefs as in youth. Indeed, the memory of some sorrows never grows dim. Twenty years after his child is thought to be dead, Jacob cries out, "Joseph is not," as if he had been missing but a day or a week. We too have lost friend after friend, not only by death, but by alienation. Very few of the friends of our childhood live to love us. One said: "I walk the streets, I go to the assemblies of my brethren, but I find none who began life with me. I stand alone like a withered tree, where once was a forest clothed with verdure." We may have our descendants around us, and "children's children are the crown of old men." But sometimes children give as much pain as pleasure. Or God may have written us childless. If so, how sad are our homes! Or greedy heirs may be indecently hovering around to pounce upon our pelf as soon as we are gone. Nor care they how soon we are called away. How many of us, too, are cut off (sometimes by our own fault) from useful employment! We lack occupation. The mind, not being drawn out in healthy action, preys upon itself. Our latter years are often spent in melancholy uselessness. Our senses are often blunted as we grow old. Sweet sounds and sweet odours and delicious flavours cannot now regale us as in our younger days. To us the blue sky is no longer blue, and the green mountains are no longer green, and the voice of birds is no longer music. Great changes have come on. Times, manners, fashions, customs, habits, opinions, have all changed, nor have we changed with them. The world often seems to us to be moving too fast or too slowly, and we cry out, "What are we coming to?"

One who had long served God and his generations, seeing how things were going, thus wrote:

37

" Prophet of ills, why should I live,
Or by my sad forebodings grieve
Whom I can serve no more?
I only can their loss bewail,
Till life's exhausted sorrows fail,
And the last pang is o'er."

The pious aged have no deeper sorrows than those which spring from the memory of their sins. Job said, "Thou makest me to possess the iniquities of my youth." David cried: "Remember not against me the sins of my youth." The late Dr. Moses Hoge, of blessed memory, said: "I feel great need of offering the prayer of the old bishop, who said, 'O God, pardon my sins of omission.'" He who in old age feels no need of sorrow for past sins is no child of God. Nor can we fail to see that our time on earth is short. A few more days and our career will be run. We must bid farewell to all we have ever known; we must go to an untried eternity, and undergo the scrutiny of God. Each of us, too, has sorrows unknown to men, and, so far as we know, peculiar to ourselves. We have not breathed them to any mortal, and perhaps we never shall, but the heart knoweth its own bitterness.

Yet all is not sad in our state. We have memories of joys, of mercies, and of friends, which, though tinged with a brown shade, are dear to our hearts.

In general, too, we are treated with respect. Good men think with Solomon that " the hoary head is a crown of glory, if it be found in the way of righteousness." The respect paid us is well suited to smooth our way. We have also stores of experience, which wealth could not buy. We have been taught the art of walking in darkness and having no light, and yet trusting in the Lord. We know that all is not lost which is brought into danger. We know better than the young disciple what is meant by such texts as these: " When I am weak, then I am strong;" " he that loseth his life, shall find it;" " I have meat to eat, that ye know not of." A thousand good lessons of this sort has God taught us. We know, too, that in his providence, as in nature, the darkest hour is just before day. Why may it not be so with us, as our sky is more and more lowering? May not eternal day be ready to burst upon us? Indeed, a thousand mercies still surround us. If our hearts are right, we cannot fail to see them. Let us often count them up.

Will you permit one who is less than the least of all saints to give you a few words of counsel? If the advice given is good, follow it; if not good, reject it.

1. As long as you can, maintain habits of bod-

ily activity. If you cannot do much, do what you can.

2. Keep your mind employed. Many aged men review their youthful studies. President Edwards reviewed his Euclid every year. Some begin new studies late in life, as Dr. Scott and Dr. Bogue. Read something with care every day, or cause it to be read to you. The history of the aged is full of warnings against idleness of mind and laziness of body. Your physician and pastor can both give you many reasons in favour of activity. The average length of life among retired merchants, who have given up *all* business, is said not to exceed two or three years. If you live in idleness, life will soon be a burden. Beware!

3. If you have property, retain exclusive control of enough to keep you from want. A dependent old age may be unavoidable, and, when it is, should be borne submissively. But it is a great trial. If men will treat you well without property, they will also if you have your own means. The reverse of this is not *always* true.

4. But beware of covetousness, that universal sin. "The love of money is the root of all evil." It is very apt to grow rapidly on the aged. Be ashamed to deny to those who have a right to expect

it, a share in your estate, when you can divide it. As far as you can, be your own almoner and executor.

5. Be always trying to do good by word and deed, by precept and example. Encourage the timid, warn the reckless, visit the poor, support humane and missionary institutions, teach the ignorant, be eyes to the blind and feet to the lame, make the widow's heart to sing for joy, and do whatever will bless men and honour God. "No man liveth to himself." "As you have opportunity, do good to all men."

6. Cultivate cheerfulness of temper. Try to be pleased with your lot and your generation. Be not a murmurer and complainer. A sour old man or woman is neither happy, nor useful, nor amiable. Remember, the birds sang, the lambs skipped, and the children laughed when you were young, and they always will do it. Find not fault needlessly. "Say not thou, What is the cause the former days were better than these? for thou inquirest not wisely concerning this." Ever since Adam fell there have been wicked men and wicked deeds on earth. I exceedingly like a common saying of a pious old English bishop, "Serve God and be cheerful."

7. Yield not to tormenting despondency about the cause of Christ. The Church is safe. She is graven on the palms of her Redeemer's hands. The cause

of piety may decline in one place or at one time, but Christ's kingdom is gaining every year. The saints may lose a battle, but not the war. Christ loves the Church more than you do. "He shall not fail nor be discouraged till he have set judgment in the earth." "Hast thou not known? hast thou not heard, that the everlasting God, the Lord, the Creator of the ends of the earth, fainteth not, neither is weary?" "No weapon formed against Zion shall prosper." "The earth shall be full of the knowledge of the Lord, as the waters cover the sea, for the mouth of the Lord hath spoken it." Rest assured that Christ "shall see the travail of his soul and be satisfied."

8. Make yourself well acquainted with the promises of God, especially those which have a peculiar pertinency to you. If you are a widow, hear him saying, "A father of the fatherless, and a judge of the widows is God in his holy habitation." "He relieveth the fatherless and widow." See the Concordance under the word "widow." Are you childless? Thus saith the Lord unto the [childless] "that keep my Sabbaths, and choose the things that please me, and take hold of my covenant; even unto them will I give in mine house and within my walls a place and a name better than of sons and daughters: I will give them an everlasting name that shall

not be cut off." Are you poor? The promise is: "Thy bread and thy water are sure." "A little that a righteous man hath is better than the riches of many wicked." Are you wearied in the greatness of your way? "They that wait upon the Lord shall renew their strength." "The feeble among them shall be as David." And how was David? Though a stripling, he slew a bear and a lion, and the giant of Gath. Whatever be your condition or fears, here are the promises to all the aged pious: "They shall bring forth fruit in old age." "Even to your old age I am He, and even to hoar hairs I will carry you: I have made, and I will bear, even I will carry you and deliver you."

"What more could he say than to you he has said?"

Therefore set your hope and put your trust in God. Embrace the promises. They can never fail to those who rest upon them. Nothing but unbelief can annihilate them. Take firm hold of them, and your last days shall be your best days, and as the outward man waxes weaker the inward man shall be renewed day by day, and God himself shall be your God. "It is one of the best sights to see silver hairs adorned with golden virtues," yea, with graces more precious than gold. Have faith in God. Hope to the end.

9. Study to acquire and maintain clear views of the riches and freeness of Christ. He is a Prophet. "Learn of him." He is a Priest. Rely on his great sacrifice and intercession. His intercession is as precious as his blood. If you wish an assurance that you shall never fall into condemnation, here it is: "Simon, Simon, behold, Satan hath desired to have you, that he may sift you as wheat; but I have prayed for thee, that thy faith fail not." Christ is a King. His "throne is for ever and ever." He has all power in heaven and in earth. He is the vine, ye are the branches. Because he lives you shall live also. He is the good Shepherd, and none is able to pluck his sheep out of his hand, nor his lambs out of his bosom. He is God, and therefore counts it not robbery to be equal with God. He is man, and therefore he is not ashamed to call us brethren. He was dead, and so he made expiation. He is alive for evermore, and so we shall never perish. If sin calls for a curse, the death of Christ calls louder for pardon. If he is the Author of our faith, he is also its Finisher. Study his character and work. You cannot know too much of him. He is the desire of all nations, the delight of the sons of men, God over all, blessed for ever.

10. Endeavour to glorify God in all your sorrows,

and especially in your death. If your children give you grief, say as David in his old age: "Though my house be not so with God [as I could wish], yet hath he made with me an everlasting covenant, ordered in all things and sure." If your children are cut down in a way that makes you tremble for their souls, say as Eli: "It is the Lord; let him do what seemeth him good." If men revile you, say as the royal Psalmist: "Let him curse. . It may be God will look upon mine affliction and reward me good for this cursing." If you be under any affliction which is common to men, why should you think it strange? "Shall we receive good at the hand of the Lord, and shall we not receive evil" also? If you can say nothing to the praise of God in your afflictions, at least be "dumb and open not your mouth." If your afflictions be strange, so were Christ's. "He was tempted in all points as we are, yet without sin." "If we suffer with him, we shall also reign with him." By quietness and patience in affliction you will be prepared to honour God in your death. It is as much a duty to glorify God in death as in life. We may, by his grace, do more in an hour at death than we have done in years before. Samson's greatest achievement against the enemies of God and of his Church was in his death. Our last battle is com-

38

monly our greatest. Happy is he who is able to shout and sing, "O death, where is thy victory?" "Blessed are the dead who die in the Lord."

There is something very remarkable in the fact that the aged seldom fall into so great a decay of their faculties as to forget those things which have most engaged their affections. Nearly two thousand years ago, Cicero (in his treatise concerning old age) said that he had never heard of a miser's memory so far-failing him that he forgot where his treasure was hid. He loved that most, and he remembered it longest. I have seen a pious man who was said to be one hundred and six years old. All his faculties were greatly impaired. His memory was so far gone that he could no more learn any man's name. Yet he could repeat many of Watts' hymns, and give an intelligible account of the way of life. It is said that Bishop Beveridge in his old age, being near death, was visited by some of his old friends, who, by turns, took his hand and said, "Bishop Beveridge, do you know me?" His answer was, "No." His wife asked the same question, and received the same answer. At length one said, "Bishop Beveridge, do you know Jesus Christ?" "Yes, oh yes," said he; "I shall never forget him. When sinking in despair under the load of my sins, Jesus

Christ showed me mercy and saved me. An] he has been with me ever since."

Polycarp suffered martyrdom at Smyrna in the year of our Lord 166, aged ninety-five years. The historian says that when he appeared before the proconsul, the latter said to him, " Swear, curse Christ, and I will set you free!" The old man answered, " Eighty-and-six years have I received only good at his hands. Can I then curse my King and Saviour?" When the proconsul continued to press him, Polycarp said, " Well, then, if you desire to know who I am, I tell thee freely, *I am a Christian!* If you desire to know what Christianity is, appoint an hour and hear me." The proconsul, who here showed that he would gladly have saved him if he could silence the people, said to Polycarp, "Only persuade the people." He replied, "To you I felt myself bound to render an account, for our religion teaches us to treat the powers ordained by God with becoming reverence, as far as is consistent with our salvation. But as for those without, I consider them undeserving any defence from me."

And justly, too! for what would it have been but throwing pearls before swine, to attempt to speak of the gospel to a wild, tumultuous, and fanatical mob? After the governor had in vain threatened him with the wild beasts and the fire, he made the herald publicly announce in the circus that Polycarp had confessed himself a Christian. These words contained the sentence of death against him. The people instantly cried out, "This is the teacher of Asia, the father of the Christians, the enemy of the gods, who has taught so many not to pray to the gods and not to sacrifice."

As soon as the proconsul had complied with the demand of the populace, that Polycarp should perish on the funeral pile, Jews and Gentiles hastened with the utmost eagerness to collect the wood from the workshops and the baths. When they wished to fasten him with nails to the pile, the old man said, "Leave me thus, I pray, unfastened. He who has enabled me to abide the fire will give me strength also to remain firm on the stake." Before the fire was lighted he prayed thus: "O Lord, Almighty God! the Father of thy beloved Son, Jesus Christ, through whom we have received the knowledge of thee! God of the angels, and of the whole creation; of the whole human race, and of the saints who live in thy presence! I thank thee that thou hast thought me worthy of this day, and this hour, to share the cup of thy Christ among the number of thy witnesses!"

Thus praying, the flame was kindled, and he went to heaven as it were in a chariot of fire.

Thus God fulfils the promises: "Even to your old age I am he, and even to hoar hairs I will carry you." "I will never leave thee nor forsake thee."

Aged disciple, can you not trust him? Is he not worthy? May you not say, "I will not fear what man can do unto me;" "All the days of my appointed time will I wait till my change come;" "Lord, what thou wilt, when thou wilt, and how thou wilt;" "I know no will but thine;" "The Lord is my portion;" "Jesus, my Lord and my God, to thee I commit my spirit in life, in death, and for ever."

Only Waiting

ANONYMOUS.

A very aged Christian, who was so poor as to be in an almshouse, was asked what he was doing now. He replied, "Only waiting."

ONLY waiting till the shadows
　　Are a little longer grown ;
Only waiting till the glimmer
　　Of the day's last gleam is flown ;
Till the night of earth is faded
　　From the heart once full of day ;
Till the stars of heaven are breaking
　　Through the twilight soft and gray.

Only waiting till the reapers
　　Have the last sheaf gathered home ;
For the summer-time is faded,
　　And the autumn winds have come.
Quickly, reapers, gather quickly
　　The last ripe hours of my heart,
For the bloom of life is withered,
　　And I hasten to depart.

Only waiting till the angels
  Open wide the mystic gate,
At whose feet I long have lingered,
  Weary, poor, and desolate.
Even now I hear the footsteps,
  And their voices, far away;
If they call me, I am waiting,
  Only waiting to obey.

Only waiting till the shadows
  Are a little longer grown;
Only waiting till the glimmer
  Of the day's last gleam is flown;
Then from out the gathering darkness
  Holy, deathless stars shall rise,
By whose light my soul shall gladly
  Tread its pathway to the skies.

Friend after Friend Departs.

JAMES MONTGOMERY.

Friend after friend departs;
   Who hath not lost a friend?
There is no union here of hearts
   That finds not here an end:
Were this frail world our only rest,
Living or dying, none were blest.

Beyond the flight of time,
   Beyond this vale of death,
There surely is some blessed clime
   Where life is not a breath,
Nor life's affections transient fire,
Whose sparks fly upward to expire.

There is a world above,
   Where parting is unknown—
A whole eternity of love,
   Formed for the good alone;
And faith beholds the dying here
Translated to that happier sphere.

Thus star by star declines,
   Till all are passed away,—
As morning high and higher shines
   To pure and perfect day :
Nor sink those stars in empty night;
They hide themselves in heaven's own light.

39

Words in Season.

ANONYMOUS.

"*Cast me not off in the time of old age; forsake me not when my strength faileth.*" Psa. lxxi. 9.

Aged believer! you feel your dependence upon God for support and succour. If he should forsake you, if he should cast you off, you would indeed be helpless and hopeless. But you rejoice in the assurance that this can never be realized. You know that he will never leave you to bear up alone the pressure of your trials and infirmities; that he will never relax the grasp which enfolds you in his love. And therefore your prayer is rather the expression of confidence than the apprehension of fear. You ask for that which he has promised, which you are certain he will grant—the continuance of his gracious aid. In youthful days, it may be, in healthful hours, you found that without him you were weak and un-protected; and now in the time of old age, when your strength faileth, you are more deeply conscious of your need of his help. Well, ask and you shall

306

receive; cast your burden, cast yourself upon him, and he will sustain you. Fear not, for he is with you; be not dismayed, for he is your God; he will strengthen you; yea, he will help you; yea, he will uphold you with the right hand of his righteousness.* These things will he do unto you, and will never forsake you.

> "Why should I doubt his love at last,
>   With anxious thoughts perplexed?
> Who saved me in the troubles past
>   Will save me in the next.
> Will save—till at my latest hour,
>   With more than conquest blest,
> I soar beyond temptation's power,
>   And enter into rest."

"*Thou hast taught me from my youth: and hitherto have I declared thy wondrous works. Now also when I am old and gray-headed, O God, forsake me not.*" Psa. lxxi. 17, 18.

"Thou hast taught me from my youth." How encouraging it is to look back to our early life, and recognize the goodness of God in its varied events! He was our Guide, our Instructor, our Father. He restrained us from evil; counselled us in difficulty; directed us in uncertainty; preserved us through

* Isa. xli. 10.

danger. All the knowledge which we have gained
of his character, of his will, of ourselves, of futurity,
he has communicated to us. And how gradual, how
wise, how gentle are his teachings! How patiently
has he borne with our ignorance and forgetfulness!
how tenderly has he imparted his most difficult lessons! And though we have been dull and wayward
scholars, though we have not profited as we might
have done by his Divine instructions, yet we know,
if we are disciples of Christ, that we have *so* learned
of him as to find rest unto our souls. We have
learned to rely upon his strength, to depend upon his
faithfulness, to trust in his righteousness.

"And hitherto have I declared thy wondrous
works." Grateful for his favours towards us, we
have striven to live to his praise and show forth his
glory. It has been our aim to communicate to
others the knowledge which we have received. We
have spoken of his goodness to those around us. We
have not been ashamed of his gospel, nor indifferent
to his honour.

"Now also when I am old and gray-headed, O God,
forsake me not." "Those who have been taught of
God from their youth, and have made it the business
of their lives to serve and honour him, may be sure
that he will not leave them when they are old and

gray-headed: he is not a Master that is wont to cast off old servants."

> "In early years thou wast my guide,
> And of my youth the friend;
> And as my days began with thee,
> With thee my days shall end."

"*And even to your old age I am He; and even to hoar hairs will I carry you.*" Isa. xlvi. 4.

Ah, Christian, here is ground for your confidence in God. You have his promise that he will be with you in your old age, to support you under its infirmities, and therefore you are cheerful and tranquil. Listen to the testimony of an aged pilgrim: "What a comfort it is, as we get old and feeble, and friends drop off one after another, to remember that our God does not change! He says to us, 'I am he;' the same that I ever was; 'I am he;' the Lord who preserved and guided you from your infancy; 'I am he:' all that I have promised to be to you, all that you can possibly need. 'And even to hoar hairs will I carry you.' What tender and expressive language! How can we help trusting in such a mighty and loving Friend? Whether we look at the present or the future, there is no room for fear. Those who can walk have his rod and staff to help and comfort them; and those who cannot walk find that his everlasting arms are beneath them, and that they are borne safely onwards. We are like children, who, when they are weak and tired, are carried in a father's arms, and lifted over difficulty and danger."

"Fear not, I am with thee; oh, be not dismayed!
I, I am thy God, and will still give thee aid;
I'll strengthen thee, help thee, and cause thee to stand,
Upheld by my righteous, omnipotent hand.

E'en down to old age all my people shall prove
My sovereign, eternal, unchangeable love;
And when hoary hairs shall their temples adorn,
In the arms of my mercy they still shall be borne."

" The hoary head is a crown of glory, if it be found in the way of righteousness." Prov. xvi. 31.

Old age is honourable, and commands respect. "Thou shalt rise up before the hoary head, and honour the face of the old man."* But we cannot expect to receive true and lasting deference from others unless our *character* is calculated to win their esteem. Superiority in age should be combined with superiority in excellence. Multitude of years should teach wisdom. "The hoary head is a crown of glory, if"—mark that—"if it be found in the way of righteousness." If it be found in the way of wickedness, its honour is forfeited, its crown profaned and laid in

* Lev. xix. 32.

the dust. How is it with you, reader? Are you sanctified through faith in Christ? are you "walking in all the commandments and ordinances of the Lord blameless?"* Oh, how lovely and dignified is old age when marked by piety and consistency!

> "When piety adorns declining years,
> The hoary head a glorious crown appears;
> A dignity no earthly rank bestows
> Marks the believer then; and sweet repose
> Is stamped upon his features; all who gaze
> Revere his person, and his virtues praise."

"*Which hope we have as an anchor of the soul, both sure and steadfast, and which entereth into that within the veil.*" Heb. vi. 19.

A vessel was driving ashore. Her anchors were gone, and she refused to obey the helm. A few moments more and she would strike. If any should be saved, they must be tossed by the waves on the beach. In the midst of the general consternation there was one person quite calm. He had done all that a man could do to prepare for the worst when the wreck was inevitable; and now that death was apparently near he was quietly waiting the event. A friend of his asked the reason of his calmness in the midst of danger so imminent:

* Luke i. 6.

"Do you not know that the anchor is gone, and we are drifting upon the coast?"

"Certainly I do; but I have an anchor to the soul." On this was his trust. It entered into that within the veil. It was the ground of his confidence in the storm, and enabled him to ride securely in the view of instant and awful death.

Have you this anchor, reader? Is the hope of the gospel yours? Amidst the storms and trials of life, and in the prospect of danger and death, are you calm and trustful, assured that you will soon be admitted into the haven of everlasting peace?

Or are you destitute of this hope? Without it, how can you be happy? Without it, what will you do in the swellings of Jordan? It may be yours— yours even now—if you will seek it, if you will accept it. The *gift* of God is *eternal life.* Confidence in him—faith in Christ—will link your tempest-tossed, troubled, and perishing spirit with perpetual repose and security—with the unseen glories of heaven.

"How still, amidst commotion,
The bark at anchor cast!
Around her heaves the ocean,
The anchor holds her fast.

> So hope, an anchor of the soul,
>   How steadfast, to the saint is given:
> Though waves of trouble round him roll,
>   His hope is fixed in heaven."

"*They shall still bring forth fruit in old age.*" Psa. xcii. 14.

The palm tree, to which God's people are in this psalm compared, is remarkable for its lengthened and increasing fruitfulness. The best dates are said to be gathered when it has reached a hundred years. How beautiful an emblem of the aged believer, growing in grace and maturing in holiness to the close of his earthly existence! Each day, each year, added to his life, adds to the loveliness and perfection of his Christian virtues. His character has a mellowness and sweetness which it lacked in earlier seasons. He is ripening for heaven. In knowledge, in wisdom, in love, in humility, in gentleness, in forbearance, in peace, in usefulness, in happiness, he is steadily and constantly advancing. He is filled with the Spirit, and therefore brings forth the fruits of the Spirit.

Is this portraiture of an aged Christian yours, reader? Alas, it does not belong to all who profess and call themselves by the Saviour's name. Nay, it may be feared that there are some, really and manifestly his, to whom it bears but little resemblance.

40

They have long been "planted" in the house of the
Lord, but they do not appear to "flourish" in the
courts of our God; and as years augment they seem
to imagine that the infirmities of age are excuses for
their little fruitfulness. But they certainly never
gathered such an idea from God's word, nor rightly
studied and pleaded his promises to themselves.
Follow not their example. Rest not satisfied with
past attainments. Strive to glorify God more than
you have ever yet done. Let your last days be your
best days; your latest fruit, the richest. "And this I
pray, that your love may abound yet more and more
in knowledge and in all judgment; that ye may ap-
prove things that are excellent; that ye may be sincere and without offence till the day of Christ; being
filled with the fruits of righteousness, which are by
Jesus Christ, unto the glory and praise of God."*

> " How beautiful to see
> The clustered fruit upon the bending tree !
> Yet lovelier still the graces which adorn
> The soul that's heaven-born.
> And age does not diminish, but increase
> The precious fruits of love, and joy, and peace,
> And gentleness, and patience ; at life's close
> Each Christian virtue more luxuriant grows."

* Phil. i. 9–11.

" *My times are in thy hand.*" Psa. xxxi. 15.

Then I am sure that they will be wisely ordered. Thou hast all power in heaven and in earth; thou art, acquainted with the end from the beginning; everything is subject to thy control, and the future to thee is as the present; therefore there can be no mistake in thy purposes—no imperfection in thy plans.

" *My times are in thy hand.*" Then I will not be anxious nor distressed about the future. Varied may be the times which I have yet to experience—times of sorrow or joy; of poverty or plenty; of sickness or health; of life or death; but I can calmly leave them to thy disposal. I cannot foresee the events which thy providence appoints, but I can wait and trust. The period and the manner of my departure hence are unknown to me, but I am free from all solicitude on these points, because thou hast arranged them for the best.

> "My times are in thy hand; the night, the day,
> The moon's pale glimmering, and the sunny ray
> Are thine; and thine the midnight of the grave.
> Oh, be thou there to strengthen and to save—
> To light death's valley with thy beam of love,
> And smile a welcome to thy throne above."

" *Bless the Lord, O my soul: and all that is within*

me, bless his holy name: Bless the Lord, O my soul, and forget not all his benefits." Psa. ciii. 1, 2.

How animating is the sight of an aged Christian, who is rejoicing in hope of the glory of God, and furnishing, by daily conduct, a bright example to others of cheerfulness and gratitude! His life is a psalm of thanksgiving; his happy look and thankful spirit fill his home with sunshine, and cast their radiance on all around him. It is impossible to be long in his society without feeling gladdened and invigorated by it. You can scarcely tell why, but you feel less disposed to complain, and more inclined to rejoice, than you did before. Your own path seems to grow more hopeful and promising; you are reminded of mercies which you had hitherto forgotten; and the troubles which you thought so heavy insensibly grow lighter. The fact is, that for a time at least you have caught his spirit and imbibed his tone of mind.

A lovely instance of real and sustained cheerfulness was the late justly celebrated William Wilberforce. "A stranger might have noticed that he was more uniformly cheerful than most men of his time of life. Closer observation showed a vein of Christian feeling, mingling with and purifying the natural flow of a most happy temper; whilst those who lived

most continually with him could trace distinctly in
his tempered sorrows, and sustained and almost
childlike gladness of heart, the continual presence of
that peace which the world can neither give nor take
away. The pages of his later journal are full of
bursts of joy and thankfulness; and with his children
and his chosen friends his full heart swelled out
ever in the same blessed strains; he seemed too
happy not to express his happiness; his song was
ever of the loving-kindness of the Lord." Everything became with him a cause for thanksgiving.
When some of the infirmities of years began to
press upon him, "What thanks do I owe to God,"
was his reflection, " that my declining strength appears likely not to be attended with painful diseases,
but rather to lessen gradually and by moderate degrees! How good a friend God is to me! When I
have any complaint, it is always so mitigated and
softened as to give me scarcely any pain. 'Bless the
Lord, O my soul.' What thanks do I owe to my
gracious and kind heavenly Father!" And so, when
one of his friends had passed through a painful
operation, "Seldom," he says, "have I felt anything
so deeply. How thankful should I be to be spared
such trials, my strength not being equal to them! I
humbly commit myself unto Him who surely has

given me reason to say, 'Goodness and mercy have followed me all my days.'"

Aged Christian, do you sympathize with these feelings? do you share this thankfulness? do you manifest this gladness? "The fruit of the Spirit is love, *joy*, peace."* Every allowance must be made for natural temperament. Some persons are naturally sanguine and cheerful; others are naturally gloomy and desponding. But, in either case, the promises of the gospel, if simply believed and heartily appropriated, cannot fail to gladden the heart and influence the conduct. And it is no less our duty than our privilege to "rejoice in the Lord alway;" to "show forth his loving-kindness in the morning, and his faithfulness every night;" to "be thankful unto him, and bless his name."* We must *cultivate* this joyous and grateful frame of mind; we must strive by meditation, practice, and prayer to acquire or to strengthen it; for we ought no more to dishonour God by our unhappiness and unthankfulness than by our unholiness.

The weakness and the infirmities of old age sometimes tend to depress our spirits and dim our hopes. Therefore let us be upon our guard; and instead of giving way to discontent and despondency, let us

* Gal. v. 22.   † Psa. xcii. 2; c. 4.

count up our mercies, and look more steadfastly on the bright side of things; and as often as we do this sadness will be chased from our brow, and the self-exhortation to praise will burst from our lips: " Bless the Lord, O my soul: and all that is within me, bless his holy name. Bless the Lord, O my soul, and forget not all his benefits."

> "Farewell to sadness,
> Let every tear depart;
> Wake all to gladness,
> Wake, O my heart!
> Shall worldly triflers raise the song
> O'er pleasures they must lose ere long?
> And shall not those rejoice and sing
> Who love the heavenly King?
> Let saints on earth unite their voice
> With saints that round the throne rejoice;
> And here begin the song that through
> Eternal years is new."

"Though our outward man perish, yet the inward man is renewed day by day." 2 Cor. iv. 16.

" We must, of necessity," says a celebrated writer, " become better or worse as we advance in years. Unless we endeavour to *spiritualize* ourselves, and supplicate in this endeavour for that grace which is never withheld when it is sincerely and earnestly sought, age *bodylizes* us more and more, and the older

we grow the more are we imbruted and debased;—
so manifestly is the text verified which warns us that,
'Unto every one which hath shall be given; and
from him that hath not, even that he hath shall be
taken away.'* In some the soul seems gradually to
be absorbed and extinguished in its crust of clay; in
others, as if it purified and sublimed the vehicle to
which it was united. Nothing therefore is more
beautiful than a wise and religious old age; nothing
so pitiable as the latter stages of mortal existence,
when the world, and the flesh, and that false philosophy which is of the devil, have secured the victory
for the grave."

Aged Christian, thank God for the strengthening
and invigorating grace which he imparts to you.
Your earthly frame is weak and enfeebled; it has
lost its vigour and elasticity; it is harassed with pain
and infirmity; it must soon die. But while your
body decays your soul thrives. If the one is preparing for the grave, the other is ripening for glory.
Your faith grows firmer, your hope stronger, your
love deeper, your views clearer.

> The soul's poor cottage, battered and decayed,
> Lets in new light through chinks which time hath made.

"For our light affliction, which is but for a moment,

* Luke xix. 26.

worketh for us a far more exceeding and eternal weight of glory." 2 Cor. iv. 17.

"In visiting," writes a clergyman, "a poor man who has been bed-ridden these *twenty-five years*, I was preparing to pity him, but he called on me to rejoice. "Are you not wearied out with the length of your afflictions?" "Wearied, sir!" said he; "no, nature will soon faint, but God sustains me. I could lie here for another twenty-five years, if it pleased God. I have found this bed to be the very gate of heaven. Length of my affliction, sir! Oh, let me not call it long: it is short, very short, and will soon be over. These light afflictions, which are but for a *moment*, work for me a far more exceeding and eternal weight of glory. Is not God all love? He cannot then be unkind. Is he not all wise? He cannot then do wrong. Are not his promises yea and amen in Christ Jesus? He cannot then break his word. None who have trusted him have repented of it. Oh, sir, I dare not complain. My affliction is a mercy."

Troubled and afflicted Christian, remember, the troubles of earth will enhance the joys of heaven. And, compared with that weight of glory which is prepared for you above, are not your sorrows light? Measured by the eternity of the happiness you an-

41

ticipate, is not their duration that of a moment? Murmur not at the present; think of the future. How striking the contrast! how glorious the change!

> "The gloom of the night adds a charm to the morn;
>   Stern winter the spring-time endears;
> And the darker the clouds on which it is drawn,
>   The brighter the rainbow appears;
> So trials and sorrows the Christian prepare
>   For the rest that remaineth above;
> On earth tribulation awaits him, but there
>   The smile of unchangeable love."

"Him that cometh to me I will in no wise cast out." John vi. 37.

During his last hours a highly distinguished writer called for his chaplain and said, " Though I have endeavoured to avoid sin and please God to the utmost of my power, yet I am still afraid to die."

" My lord," said the chaplain, "you have forgotten that Jesus Christ is a Saviour."

" True," was the answer; " but how shall I know that he is a Saviour for *me?*"

" It is written, my lord, 'Him that cometh to me I will in no wise cast out.' "

" Yes, it is !" was the quick reply; "and I am surprised that though I have read that Scripture a thousand times over, I never felt its virtue till this moment; and now I die happy."

Reader, are you coming to the Saviour? Then this promise is yours.

"Jesus, the sinner's friend, to thee,
  Lost and undone, for aid I flee;
Ah, wherefore did I ever doubt?
  Thou wilt in no wise cast me out."

"*When a few years are come, then I shall go the way whence I shall not return.*" Job xvi. 22.

An approaching journey lies before me. I have to pass from time to eternity; from this world to the next. And the time of my departure, although to me uncertain, cannot be very far distant. A few years—perhaps a few days—will close my stay on earth.

It is an *unavoidable* journey. I must go. There is no choice. Willing or unwilling, when the summons for me arrives, I shall have to set off.

It is an *unknown* journey. I have never taken it before. I have no practical acquaintance with the road, the mode of transit, the dangers or the discomforts which await me. And there is no one who can clearly explain them to me. Those of my friends who have travelled that way have never come back to relate their experience.

It is a *solitary* journey. I must accomplish it alone. The most loved of my present companions cannot accompany me. They may think of me, feel for me, pray for me, but they cannot be with me. We must separate; they to remain behind, I to go forward.

It is a *momentous* journey. For at its termination I enter upon my everlasting destiny. It will convey me either to the mansions of happiness or to the abodes of misery. The narrow boundary between the present and the future state once crossed, there will be no possibility of change. " He that is unjust, let him be unjust still; and he that is righteous, let him be righteous still." Rev. xxii. 11.

It is a *final* journey. I shall go the way whence I shall not return. My pilgrimage will be for ever ended. No more parting, no more change, no more toil, no more fatigue. It will be my last journey.

And if I am a Christian how welcome is this fact! I shall have done for ever with sin and sorrow. Eternal felicity will be mine—perfect holiness, perfect happiness. This journey leads me to my home, to my father's house, to my everlasting rest.

Then I will not shrink from its approach, nor complain of its accompaniments. It may be linked with much that is painful and unpleasant, but it is the *only* way home; and therefore, although life has many ties and many joys, I feel an earnest desire to depart and be with Christ, which is far better than being here.

Death is a solemn journey, but it is a safe one to Christ's people; for he will not only receive and welcome them at its close, but he will be them as they are passing through it. Oh, it will not be lonely with him! And he is a guide who is well acquainted with the way, for he has trodden it himself, and the marks of his footsteps are visible there still. He went for the purpose of smoothing its difficulties, clearing its dangers, dispersing its terrors; and he fully accomplished his purpose: "That through death he might destroy him that had the power of death, that is, the devil; and deliver them who through fear of death were all their lifetime subject to bondage."* Therefore when I walk through the dark valley, I will fear no evil; for thou, O Jesus, wilt be with me, and thy rod and thy staff shall comfort me.

"*The spirit shall return unto God who gave it.*" Eccles. xii. 7.

Not to a stranger, not to an unknown, untried master; but to Him who has preserved and watched over it from year to year; to him who knows its struggles, its anxieties, its throbbings of hope and fear; to its own God, even the "God who gave it;"

* Heb. ii. 14, 15.

nay, more, who gave for it his only and well-beloved
Son.   Therefore, Christian reader, you need not fear
to depart.   Does the child dread to return home, to
go back to its loving parents?   Oh, happy moment!
when you shall be admitted into your heavenly Father's presence, and shall share in those pleasures
which are at his right hand for evermore!

> "Away, thou dying saint, away!
>   Fly to the mansions of the blest;
>   Thy God no more requires thy stay;
>   He calls thee to eternal rest.
>
> "Thy toils, at length, have reached a close;
>   No more remains for thee to do;
>   Away, away to thy repose,
>   Beyond the reach of sin and woe.
>
> "Away to yonder realms of light,
>   Where multitudes redeemed with blood
>   Enjoy the beatific sight,
>   And dwell for ever with their God."

The Christian's Hope.*

FROM THE GERMAN.

DEAR Saviour, when I here am blest
With prospect of that future rest
   Thy people shall inherit,
And there, by faith, see my abode;—
How light my cares!—and all their load—
   How easy 'tis to bear it!
Then, too, the fond pursuits of earth
Are in my view as nothing worth;—
Chased by the dawn of endless day,
Its glories pass like dreams away.
Lord Jesus Christ, sure ground of faith,
All this is owing to thy death.

When called the change of worlds to make
My soul shall from its fetters break—
   Thou, from on high, be near me!
Thy rod and staff be then my stay—
Through Death's dark valley guide my way,—
   With hopes of glory cheer me!

* Translated by Dr. Mills.

The splendours of the world of light,
Amid the all-surrounding night,
Shall through the clouds of darkness shine,
Revealing what shall soon be mine.
Lord Jesus Christ, with cheerful faith,
I then shall sweetly sleep in death.

But should my heart, reluctant, shrink,
The cup of Death still fear to drink,
   My sins begin to number;
Then come the thought—"My Lord has died,
My sins—atoning blood shall hide,
   Nor God will more remember!"
The hope, for sinners thou hast wrought,
Of life,—with nameless sorrows bought,
Which, God-forsaken, thou didst meet,—
'Tis this alone makes dying sweet.
Lord Jesus Christ, my only faith,
Do not forsake me at my death!

In hope my weeping eyes I'll close,
My flesh in earth shall find repose,
   Where my Redeemer rested:
And he that died, from death to save,—
His voice will call me from the grave,—
   I know whom I have trusted.

He lives!—and foes I feared below,—
The Grave and Death—his power shall know;
He lives!—and I, with saints above,
Shall know the wonders of his love.
Lord Jesus Christ, my spirit's faith,
For life prepare me by my death!

My confidence shalt thou remain
Till thou on earth appear again—
   The tombs be rent asunder:
Before thy throne I there shall be,
The Judge of all the nations see—
   Shall see with joy and wonder.
Then will thy grace to me divide
A portion always to abide,
And I shall share, by promise shown,
A glory lasting as thy own.
Thanks, Lord, to thee!—with shouts I'll sing,
"Where, Grave, thy victory?—Death, thy sting?"
   42

The Verge of Life.

PHILIP DODDRIDGE, D. D.

WHILE on the verge of life I stand,
And view the scenes on either hand,
My spirit struggles with its clay,
And longs to wing its flight away.

Where Jesus dwells my soul would be,
It faints my much-loved Lord to see;
Earth, twine no more about my heart,
For 'tis far better to depart.

Come, ye angelic envoys, come,
And lead the willing pilgrim home;
Ye know the way to Jesus' throne,
Source of my joys and of your own.

That blessed interview how sweet,
To fall transported at his feet;
Raised in his arms, to view his face,
Through the full beamings of his grace.

330

To see heaven's shining courtiers round,
Each with immortal glories crowned;
And, while his form in each I trace,
Beloved and loving all to embrace.

As with a seraph's voice to sing:
To fly as on a cherub's wing;
Performing, with unwearied hands,
A present Saviour's high commands!

Yet, with these prospects full in sight,
I'll wait thy signal for my flight;
For, while thy service I pursue,
I find my heaven begun below.

Yonder.

HORATIUS BONAR. D. D.

No shadows yonder !
  All light and song ;
Each day I wonder,
  And say how long
Shall time me sunder
  From that dear throng ?

No weeping yonder !
  All fled away ;
While here I wander
  Each weary day,
And sigh as I ponder,
  My long, long stay.

No partings yonder !
  Time and space never
Again shall sunder ;
  Hearts cannot sever ;
Dearer and fonder,
  Hands clasp for ever.

None wanting, yonder!
  Bought by the Lamb!
All gathered under
  The evergreen palm;
Loud as night's thunder
  Ascends the glad psalm.

Too Old to be Useful.

ANONYMOUS.

"WELL, it is a pleasant sight to see young people actively engaged in doing good!" said an old lady, as she watched from her parlour window some of her grand-children setting forth on their weekly errands of mercy to the poor and afflicted.

Yes; it *was* a pleasant sight to look upon these youthful Christians, full of health and energy, devoting their time and their talents to the service of God and the welfare of their fellow-creatures; and yet the old lady sighed as she finished her sentence, and did not seem quite comfortable. Why? Listen to what she is saying now:

"Ah, *I* was once as busy as any of them. I could take a class in the Sunday-school, and visit the poor, and collect for the missionary society; but now I am forced to be idle and useless. My strength and my senses are gradually forsaking me; and I am but a worn-out and unprofitable servant. But come, I must not complain; I have had my share in these

334

good works in bygone days, and I must be content to lie by now and let others labour; for I am too old to be of any use."

Was the old lady right? She meant what she said, and she meant well. She was trying to bear with patience and resignation her unavoidable exclusion from the charitable engagements of her young relatives; but old people as well as young sometimes have mistaken ideas; and it is possible that the old lady was not quite so clear upon the subject of Christian usefulness as we should like our readers to be.

It is true that the aged cannot work in God's vineyard as they used to do before infirmity or ill-health disabled them for active service, but still they are not too old to be useful.

Too old to be useful! Such words are a libel upon their characters—an insult to their capabilities. It cannot be that any Christian is continued upon earth who has not something to do as well as to suffer for his Master. Look at the closing days of the venerable Eliot, the first missionary to the American Indians. On the day of his death, when in his eightieth year, he was found teaching the alphabet to an Indian child at his bedside. "Why not rest from your labours, now?" said a friend. "Because," said the venerable man, "I have prayed to God to make me useful in my sphere, and he has heard my prayer; for now, that I can no longer preach, he leaves me strength enough to teach this poor child this alphabet."

Eighty years of age and bed-ridden! Who after this can plead their inability to do good? Who will not rather gather up their remaining time and talents and devote them to God's service? Like the widow's mite, your offering may seem poor and small; you are almost ashamed to cast it into the treasury; but bring it without hesitation—nay with gladness. What could give you more? it is your *all;* and your feeble efforts will meet with kind and gracious acknowledgment from a loving Saviour, who said, "She hath done what she could!"*

Oh, it is so delightful to labour for Christ that the true-hearted Christian would fain keep on as Eliot did to the last. The late Rev. John Campbell, of Kingsland, went one morning to attend an early committee meeting of a religious society. On his way up-stairs he found an old friend, remarkable for his devotedness to the cause of Christ, leaning on the balustrade which led to the room, and unable to proceed from a difficulty of breathing.

"What! are you here, Mr. T——? How could

* Mark xiv. 8.

you venture in your state of health? You have attended our meetings for a long time, and you should now leave the work for younger men."

His friend looked up with a cheerful smile, and replied, with characteristic energy, "Oh, Johnny, Johnny, man, it is hard to give up working in the service of *such* a Master."

How cheering then is the thought that the aged have still opportunities of usefulness afforded them! Suppose we remind our readers of a few ways in which they have it in their power to benefit others.

Well, some of you, perhaps, who cannot walk about and visit your neighbours, might send them a little tract and book occasionally. A person dies in your street—a child is born in the next house—a worldly family opposite are in trouble—a gentleman has met with an accident—a grocer's shop is open on the Sunday;—all these, and many others, are occasions when "a little messenger of mercy" might speak "a word in season." Listen to the following fact:

A man who was keeper of one of the locks on the Grand Junction Canal lived for many years apparently without any religious feelings. He possessed much personal kindness, and had been the means of saving at least twelve persons from a watery grave,

43

some of whom had plunged into the stream in seasons of frantic sorrow.   In the summer of 1841
poor Matthew met with a severe accident, and was
removed to the London Hospital.   After he had
been there a few days, he received a letter by post—
of which the following is a copy—enclosing a tract
entitled " To-day :"

" You have suffered greatly, my friend ; your poor
body calls for help and sympathy, and in the hospital you are mercifully attended to, as you could not
be at home.   How is it with your precious soul?
Are you fit to die?   Had your sufferings caused instant death, where would your soul have been?
Where, my friend? Where?   In heaven, or in hell?
Do think of this inquiry, and read the tract I en-
close, or get some one to read it to you.   Do not
neglect this friendly warning, but attend to it while
it is yet with you called ' To-day.'   Oh ! what a mercy
you were spared yet a little longer ! May it be for the
salvation of your precious soul.   The Lord Jesus is
able and willing to save all who feel their need of his
salvation.   Pray, then, afflicted friend, for the Holy
Spirit to show you your need of mercy, and of the
precious blood of the Lord Jesus Christ to cleanse
you from your sins, and to obtain your acceptance
with God.   This tract was written by a gentleman

seventy years old. May the Lord make it a blessing to your soul. He is able and willing to save you from going to hell, and willing to prepare you for the holiness and happiness of heaven.—Farewell."

There was no signature to the letter; it bore the "Stroudwater" postmark, but Matthew knew no one residing there. However, the perusal of the letter induced him to read the tract; the Holy Spirit blessed it to his conversion; and he became a consistent Christian. He wished very much that he could find out who had sent him the tract; and a kind friend to whom this interesting fact was mentioned thought that he knew the person from whom it came. He wrote accordingly, and received the following note, which proved that his conjecture was right:

"My dear sir: It was in hours of weakness, and during a long detention from the house of the Lord, that I was directed one Sabbath-day to write the letter to which you refer, to poor Matthew. It used to be a saying with myself, *to* myself, on doing any such thing, 'Well, I have cast one grain more of the good seed of the kingdom into the field of the world—that world which still lieth in wickedness.' I bless the Lord he permitted me to cast in that grain, and I praise him still more that he caused it to germinate and bring forth fruit. Glory be to his holy name that he has seen fit to glorify the riches of his grace in the salvation of a soul by means in themselves so weak and poor. When I received the supply from London, of which that tract formed one, I selected a number of that description for the purpose of enclosing in letters (now in these days of penny-postage blessedness, in which in almost every letter we write we can proclaim the glad tidings of mercy, by inserting an eight-paged tract)—and among others, poor Matthew received one. Surely it would have been a shorter journey from Paternoster Row to the London Hospital; but in this case it seemed needful that it should go from London to the country, and back again to town, to reach the object for which it was designed. Several other such grains have been cast into the field of the world. Oh, that it may please the Lord to cause them to be fruitful also!"

Now, reader, let the example of this pious invalid win you in some measure to follow it. It does not, you see, require much money, much talent, much influence, or much strength to be useful. A few kind words written, or a good tract enclosed to an acquaintance or even to a stranger, may be the appointed channel through which God's grace shall flow into their souls. "Cast thy bread upon the waters: for thou shalt find it after many days."*

Then there is the influence which you may exert over children and young persons. Not by fault-finding, or selfish requirements, or sarcastic observations; but by kind words, persuasive advice, and affectionate treatment. Your little grand-children, or your elder nephews and nieces, as they cluster round your cheerful fireside, may drink in many a gentle lesson which shall guide them in after years. If you have not any youthful relatives, you can cultivate the acquaintance of the children of your friends and neighbours. It is a lovely sight to see age and youth sweetly blending together—age tempering the gayety of youth, and youth brightening the gravity of age. The ivy adorns the oak, and the oak supports the ivy. "But young people," you may say, "are so self-willed and conceited; they think they are as wise as old folks." It is often too true, but bear with them; we have all been young in our time; and it is astonishing how grateful even the most independent among them are for a real and warm-hearted interest in their welfare. You may influence them strongly, if you are only *kind* in purpose and *judicious* in practice.

Sympathize with them in their joys and their sor-

* Eccles. xi. 1.

rows. Show them that increase of years does not necessarily blunt the feelings or narrow the affections; that the pilgrim who has almost reached his welcome and long-expected resting-place does not forget or despise those who have but lately set out on their toilsome journey. Speak to them of your own experience of actual life; of the mental and moral discipline which you have endured; of the difficulties in the path of duty which you have met and conquered; of the comfort which has sustained you in the hour of trial and bereavement. Simple facts are more impressive than mere advice. Quietly but deeply they sink into the memory, arousing no opposition, exciting no argument; in time of need they will be remembered and turned to good account. You may thus be the honoured instrument of guiding some wayward and careless heart to true peace and happiness; of imparting right principles which shall steer some perplexed spirit across the rough sea of temptation; of forming the character of those who are destined in coming years to exercise great moral power over their fellow-creatures. You may not—you will not—live to behold those happy results of your patient and prayerful efforts; but when those who die in the Lord rest from their labours, their works follow them. An aged man carefully planted several fruit-trees in his garden, that they might grow up for the use and benefit of posterity; so may you cast into human hearts that precious seed which will germinate and spring forth and bless the world long after you have departed to your rest. The destiny of future generations may be linked with your Christian endeavour to gather one youthful friend into the fold of the Saviour. God grant that you may fully appreciate and fulfil your peculiar mission to the young.

But perhaps the best way in which the aged Christian—aye, and any Christian—can benefit others is by the purity and loveliness of his *example*. You cannot now do much or say much for the good of your fellow-creatures; but "nothing speaks so loudly as the silent eloquence of a holy and consistent life;" nothing exercises such gentle and yet such powerful influence over the mind as the example of one whom we love and respect. It is a practical and perpetual sermon.

Look into that quiet and half-darkened room. In the large easy-chair sits an aged lady. She is confined by constant indisposition to her house—to her apartment; nay, even to her chair, for she cannot move herself without assistance. Her friends are forbidden to see her, as the least excitement proves injurious; and therefore a skilful nurse and a loving-hearted daughter are her only associates. But she does not wish for society; incessant pain renders her unable to converse much, and the exertion of speaking but a few words fatigues her sadly. Poor lady! the days have indeed come in which she has no' pleasure; the grasshopper is become a burden; desire has failed; and fears are in the way. Her life has been a life full of good works; and now, withdrawn for ever from her loved occupations, she must solace herself with the beautiful thought,

"They also serve who only stand and wait."

It *is* a beautiful thought; she knows its truth; she feels its preciousness; her daily, constant prayer is, "Thy will be done." Yet you must not imagine that her career of usefulness has ended—that it found its termination in that sick 'room. No; in that limited sphere, during that lingering illness, she has, perhaps, done more good than you or I have effected in our lifetime. How? That kind servant who waits upon her has lately grown thoughtful and pious, and she traces the happy change in her views and in her feelings to the sweet example of her dear mistress; not to her counsels, not to her persuasions, but to her example. She witnessed her patience,

her fortitude, her serenity, her faith in Christ, her
readiness to depart; and she felt how valuable that
religion must be which could give such peace in life,
such hope in death. She determined, with God's
help, to make that religion her own; and now her
mistress's last hours are cheered by the delightful
knowledge that her grateful attendant has chosen
that good part which shall not be taken away from
her.

Glance now inside that lowly almshouse. There
dwells a venerable man whose snow-white locks,
bended frame, and tottering steps are plain indica-
tions that his physical energies are rapidly declining.
Is he too old or too infirm to be useful? Almost,
so far as active service is concerned, for he is both
palsied and half blind; but the light of his example
shines brightly still, and sheds a holy radiance on
all who come within its reach. His upright conduct,
his cheerful demeanour, his kind feelings, and his
heaven-like spirit are perpetual living lessons to his
neighbours and friends. More than one thoughtless
visitor has left his humble abode with the impression,
"Well, there is such a thing as real religion; I wish
I were as good and as happy as that old man is."
And many wavering or weary Christians have been
strengthened for their earnest conflict through the

44

remembrance of the simple faith and devotedness of this aged servant of God.

Does your life, your example, thus influence others for good? Are you an epistle known and read of all men? Does your character and conduct commend the religion of Christ? Is it your daily endeavour to "adorn" as well as profess the doctrine of God your Saviour? Every Christian should look well to his example; it effects far more than his words, however well-chosen and well-expressed those words may be. But especially should the aged believer be careful to let his light shine brightly and steadily before men, because his sphere of usefulness being limited, he should make the most of those means which are still within his reach; and because soon, very soon, "the night cometh," and then his opportunities on earth will be closed for ever.

There is one other way that we must not overlook in which the aged Christian may advance Christ's kingdom in the world, and that way is *intercessory* prayer. Weak and infirm, you may be unable to converse about religion; poor, perhaps, in this world's riches, it is not in your power to relieve the wants of the needy; but amidst your feebleness and your poverty you can shut your door and pray to your Father who seeth in secret. You can implore his succour for the distressed; his sympathy for the sorrowful; his aid for the helpless; his instruction for the ignorant; his pardon for the sinful; his grace for the undeserving. You can plead with him on behalf of the heathen at home and the heathen abroad. You can supplicate his blessing both for the queen upon her throne and the peasant in his cottage. You can beseech him to guide into the way of truth those who have erred and are deceived, and to have mercy upon all men. Abraham interceded for Sodom; Job for his children; Moses for the Israelites; Jacob for his grandsons; the disciples for their persecuted brethren; the apostle for his beloved converts. Catch their spirit; follow in their steps; add to their success. "The effectual, fervent prayer of a righteous man availeth much."* It is impossible to tell how richly the healthful dew of God's grace may rest upon parched and barren hearts; or how appropriately the gifts of his providence may be vouchsafed to the abodes of penury and want through the instrumentality of those heartfelt petitions which you offer at the throne of grace. Eternity alone will fully disclose the blessings which have been linked with intercessory prayer.

Aged Christian! mourn not that your opportuni-

* James v. 16.

ties of usefulness are so few; rather rejoice that you are still permitted to have a place among the labourers in Christ's vineyard. Your department is a retired one; your employment is easy; but your path is marked out for you by the Master whom you serve. In wise considerateness he appoints to each labourer his position and his duties; and to all who honestly perform the work which he assigns—be it great or be it small—he will address those gracious words of commendation, "Well done, good and faithful servant:—enter thou into the joy of thy Lord."*

Yet you cannot but sigh sometimes when you reflect how little you are really able to do for the honour of God and the good of your fellow-men; your best services are so imperfect, your holiest efforts are so defiled. As life advances you grow better acquainted with your own motives, and more enlightened respecting God's character and will; and the inevitable result is that you are humbled under the increasing consciousness of your sinfulness and your failures. Oh if you could but serve God as you desire to do! How unwearied, how unselfish, how unlimited would be your joyful obedience!

Wait awhile, and your longings shall be satisfied. In heaven there will be no feebleness to retard your

* Matt. xxv. 23.

efforts, no imperfection to sully your actions. "His servants shall serve him."* Without one difficulty or defect they shall fulfil his varied behests and do his will. And as angels are now ministering spirits for the heirs of salvation, it is not improbable that glorified Christians will be frequently engaged on some errand of love to God's intelligent creatures. How welcome is this idea to those who feel half sorry when they consider that their work on earth is so near its close!

* Rev. xxii. 3.

Old Age.

JOHN WALTON.

THE seas are quiet when the winds give o'er;
So calm are we when passions are no more;
For then we know how vain it was to boast
Of fleeting things, too certain to be lost.

Clouds of affection from our younger eyes
Conceal that emptiness which age descries;
The soul's dark cottage, battered and decayed,
Lets in new light through chinks that time has made.

Stronger by weakness, wiser men become
As they draw near to their eternal home;
Leaving the Old, at once both worlds they view
That stand upon the threshold of the New.

350

Fully Ripe.

ANONYMOUS.

"Thou shalt come to thy grave in a full age, like as a shock of corn
cometh in his season."—Job v. 26.

LONG standing in the Master's field,
 Fed daily by his sun and dew,
Eager its best return to yield,
 To perfect symmetry it grew:
The storm swept over it in vain,
 Nor frost could blight its noonday heat,
Till, a fair shock of golden grain,
 It stood in perfectness complete,
       Fully ripe.

Men saw, and gave to God the praise,
 Who smiled well pleased, and passed it by,
Till in these later autumn days
 Its garner was prepared on high;
Then came the Reaper down at morn,
 Softly as feathery snow-flakes come,
To gather in the golden corn,
 And bear the precious harvest home,
       Fully ripe.

351

Ah! but the field is brown and bare,
    And heaven's great gain we grieve to lose,
For in our eyes 'twas wondrous fair,
    While fitting for the Master's use;
And for the place left desolate,
    We needs must weep; yet thanks be given,
The treasure that we found so great
    Was for a better place in heaven,
                Fully ripe.

The Hour of Departure.

REV. JOHN LOGAN.

THE hour of my departure's come,
I hear the voice that calls me home;
At last, O Lord! let trouble cease,
And let thy servant die in peace.

Not in mine innocence I trust;
I bow before thee in the dust;
And through my Saviour's blood alone
I look for mercy at thy throne.

I leave the world without a tear,
Save for the friends I held so dear:
To heal their sorrows, Lord, descend,
And to the friendless prove a friend.

I come, I come at thy command,
I give my spirit to thy hand;
Stretch forth thine everlasting arms,
And shield me in the last alarms.

45

The hour of my departure's come,
I hear the voice that calls me home;
Now, O my God, let trouble cease,
Now let thy servant die in peace.

How to Die Safely.

ARCHIBALD ALEXANDER, D. D.

Can we do anything to render our death—which cannot be far off—both safe and comfortable? No doubt, by God's assistance, we can do much to accomplish these desirable ends, if we will set about the work in good earnest.

I know that there is a feeling of despondency habitually existing in the minds of some aged persons of serious disposition, which leads them to conclude that if they are not now prepared to die they never will be. And from all the acquaintance which I have had with professors of religion, I am constrained to think that, as their near approach to the grave does not increase their impressions of the importance of eternal realities, so old age has no tendency to render the evidences of their union with Christ more clear and satisfactory. You may frequently inquire of a dozen such professors in sucession whether they have obtained a comfortable assurance of the goodness of their spiritual condition, and the probability is that four out of five, if not nine out of ten, will answer in the negative, and will express serious doubts whether they were ever the subjects of regenerating grace.

It was not, I believe, always so with those who cordially received the doctrines of grace and rested their souls upon them. To say nothing about the joyful confidence and assured hope of the apostles and primitive Christians, the members of the first Reformed Churches seem to have derived from the pure doctrines of the Bible a high degree of peace and joy. The same was the fact among the pious Puritans of Old and New England, and the Presbyterians of Scotland in the best and purest days of the Scottish Church. The question has often occurred, why does the belief of these doctrines afford less comfort now than in former times? It is not my purpose at present to attempt to account for this fact. I adduce it merely to show that most professors among us are not *actually* prepared for death. Even if their state should be one of safety, they cannot view their approaching end with confidence and comfort. And whilst their evidences of genuine piety are so dubious, they of course cannot know that they are in a safe condition. It is then of the utmost importance that all professors of the above description, and especially the aged, should be importunately urged "to give diligence to make their calling and election sure." I am aware that some Christians who enjoy very comfortable evidences of being the adopted children of God are not willing to profess that they have arrived at full assurance. They suppose that they who have attained to this high privilege are in a state of uninterrupted joy, and that no shadow of doubt ever passes over their minds. The truth is, they do possess a solid assurance, although their frames of mind are not always equally comfortable, and although the evidence is not so great that it cannot be increased. I recollect, when very young, to have heard a judicious minister conversing with an eminently pious old lady, who had belonged to the church under the care of the Rev. Samuel Davies, in the county of Hanover. In answer to some inquiry respecting the comfort which she enjoyed in the service of her divine Master, she said, after expressing lively feelings of faith, penitence and gratitude, "But, my dear friend, I have never yet attained to the faith of assurance; all I can say is, that I have the faith of reliance." "Well," said the minister "if you know that you have the faith of reliance, that is assurance." The degrees of evidence possessed by different Christians are various, from the feeblest hope up to strong confidence, and the clearness of the evidence to the same person varies exceedingly; but in general there seems to be in our Church a sad falling below *par* in respect to this matter. It has, however,. often been correctly observed that we are not to expect *dying grace* before the dying hour arrives. God gives strength as we need it; and when the believer is called to severe trials or to difficult duties, he commonly receives aid proportioned to the urgency of his wants, and is surprised to find himself held up by a power not his own. Thus we have often seen the sincere, humble Christian, who, during life, was subject to bondage through fear of death, triumphing in the dying hour. This expectation of special aid ought to be encouraged. It is, indeed, a part of that preparation which we should make; and if we confidently rely on the great Shepherd to meet us and comfort us while walking through the valley and shadow of death, he will not disappoint us.

But, in dealing with professors troubled with doubts, we are too apt to proceed on the assumed principle that, notwithstanding their sad misgivings and fears, they are at bottom sincere Christians, and have the root of the matter in them; while in regard to many this may be an entire mistake, and we are in danger of cherishing in them a fatal delusion. Here the skill and fidelity of the spiritual watchmen are put to the test; and while they should not deviate a hair's-breadth from the rule of the divine word, it is better that the pious Christian should suffer some unnecessary pain than that the false professor should be bolstered up with delusive hopes. I must say, therefore, that the true reason why many professors have no comfortable evidence of their religion is because they have none. They have never experienced the new birth; and being still dead in trespasses and sins, it is no wonder that they cannot find in themselves what does not exist. I abhor a censorious spirit, which, upon slight grounds, judges this and that professor to be graceless; but all my experience and observation lead me to believe that in our day, as well as in former times, the "foolish virgins" constitute a full moiety of the visible Church.

What I would urge, therefore, on you my aged friends, and on myself, is a more serious, impartial, and thorough examination into the foundation of our hope of heaven than perhaps we have ever yet made. Let us go back to the commencement of our religious course, and see whether in our present more mature judgment we can conclude that we were then the subjects of a saving change. I do not ask you whether you had an increase of serious feelings, or whether your sympathies were strongly excited and experienced some change from a state of terror or distress to comfort; for all these things may be experienced, and have been experienced, by unregenerate persons. Let us carefully inquire whether the habitual tenour of our lives has been such as to satisfy us that a new nature was received. If we have fallen into sin, have we deeply and sincerely repented of it? Have we wept bitterly for our sin, like Peter? or have we mourned in deep sorrow, like David? Not such repentance as some experience, who, after all their convictions and confessions, return again to the same course of iniquity. But, after all examinations of past .experience, the main point is, What is the present habitual state of our hearts? Do we now love God as his character is exhibited in his word? Do we hunger and thirst after holiness or a complete conformity to the law of God? Would we be willing that that law should be relaxed in its demands to afford us some indulgence? Do we seek our chief happiness in the favour of God, and in communion with him in his word and ordinances? Is his glory

uppermost in our desires, and do we sincerely wish
and determine to do all that we can to promote the
kingdom of the Redeemer? Do we sincerely love
the people of God, of every sect and name, because
they bear his image and are the redeemed children
of God? Again: what is the ground on which we
expect the pardon of sin and the favour of God? Is
it because we are better than many others? Is it
because we have had what we esteem great experiences? Is it on account of our moral demeanour or
charitable benefactions? Dare we trust in any measure to our own goodness and righteousness? If we
build on any of these, or on any similar grounds,
then are we on a sandy foundation, and all our tow-
ering hopes must fall.

But methinks I hear the humble penitent saying,
"All these things I count loss for Christ—I feel that
I deserve to die—I never was more convinced of
anything than that it would have been perfectly just
for God to send me to hell. And now all my trust
and all my hope, if I know my own heart, is in the
LORD JESUS CHRIST, and in his perfect righteousness
and intercession; and all my confidence of being able
to serve God hereafter, or to persevere for a single
day, is in the grace of the Holy Spirit." The whole
evidence of Christian character may be reduced to

46

two particulars—entire trust in Christ for justifica-
tion, and a sincere and universal love of holiness,
with a dependence on the Holy Spirit for its existence, continuance and increase. If, my friend, you
have these evidences *now*, you need not perplex yourself by a multitude of scruples. You may dismiss
your doubts. God's word will never deceive any who
rely upon its guidance. You may not know the day
nor even the year when spiritual life commenced in
your soul; and yet, if you now feel its warm pulsa-
tions—if you breathe its genuine aspirations—if your
heart's treasures are in heaven, and if the cause of
God is dearer to you than any other interest—if his
people are dearer to you than any other people—if
your most constant and supreme desire is to glorify
God your Redeemer, whether by living or dying—
then may you welcome death. He is no king of terrors to you. You may say, "Come, Lord Jesus,
come quickly!"

Perhaps some of you are afraid of the pangs of
death. You have heard of the convulsive struggle—
the dying groans—the difficult breathing—and the
ghastly countenance. Well, it must be confessed,
the scene is appalling; but it is soon over, for ever.
I am of opinion, however, that often there is the appearance of dreadful suffering where the patient is

unconscious of any very acute pain; and very frequently the departure of the immortal spirit is, at the
last, like falling into a gentle sleep. And not un-
frequently, while the body is racked with pain, or
with what would produce pain in other circumstances,
the soul is so supported and comforted by the sweet
peace of God poured into it, that the disorders and
convulsions of the body are scarcely thought of. And
in many instances God takes his people away by a
sudden stroke;—they know nothing about it until
they awake in heaven. Oh what a transition! Or,
if it be necessary to let in the light of glory gradually, God, who knows our constitution, will order all
things well.

I would advise you to meditate much on death.
Collect and have in memory a number of precious
promises for the occasion. Put up many prayers for
grace and strength for a dying hour. Beg an interest
in the intercessions of your Christian friends. Keep
your minds calm, and yield not to perturbing cares.
Be found at your post when the summons comes,
with your loins girded and lights burning.

Our Beloved have Departed.

FROM THE GERMAN OF J. LANGE.

OUR beloved have departed,
While we tarry broken-hearted
　　In the dreary, empty house;
They have ended life's brief story,
They have reached the home of glory,
　　Over death victorious!

Hush that sobbing, weep more lightly;
On we travel, daily, nightly,
　　To the rest that they have found:
Are we not upon the river,
Sailing fast, to meet for ever
　　On more holy, happy ground?

On we haste, to home invited,
There with friends to be united
　　In a surer bond than here;
Meeting soon, and met for ever!—
Glorious hope, forsake us never,
　　For thy glimmering light is dear.

Ah! the way is shining clearer,
As we journey ever nearer
  To the everlasting home.
Comrades, who await our landing,
Friends, who round the throne are standing,
  We salute you, and we come.

Confidence in God.

PAUL GERHARDT.

BITTER anguish have I borne,
Keen regret my heart hath torn,
Sorrow dimmed my weeping eyes,
Satan blinded me with lies;
    Yet at last am I set free;
    Help, protection, love to me
    Once more true companions be.

Ne'er was left a helpless prey,
Ne'er with shame was turned away,
He who gave himself to God,
And on him had cast his load.
    Who in God his hope hath placed
    Shall not life in pain outwaste;
    Fullest joy he yet shall taste.

Though to-day may not fulfil
All thy hopes, have patience still;
For perchance to-morrow's sun
Sees thy happier days begun.

366

As God willeth march the hours,
Bringing joy at last in showers,
And whate'er we asked is ours.

When my heart was vexed with care,
Filled with fears, wellnigh despair;
When, with watching many a night,
On me fell pale sickness' blight;
    When my courage failed me fast,
    Camest thou, my God, at last,
    And my woes were quickly past.

Now as long as here I roam,
On this earth have house and home,
Shall this wondrous gleam from thee
Shine through all my memory.
    To my God I yet will cling,
    All my life the praises sing
    That from thankful hearts outspring.

Every sorrow, every smart,
That the eternal Father's heart
Hath appointed me of yore,
Or hath yet for me in store,
    As my life flows on, I'll take
    Calmly, gladly for his sake—
    No more faithless murmurs make.

I will meet distress and pain,
I will greet e'en death's dark reign,
I will lay me in the grave
With a heart still glad and brave.
      Whom the Strongest doth defend.
      Whom the Highest counts his friend,
      Cannot perish in the end.

The Banks of the River.

ANONYMOUS.

" Now I further saw that betwixt the pilgrims and
the gate of the city was a river; but there was no
bridge to go over, and the river was very deep. At
the sight of this river the pilgrims were much
stunned; but the men that went with them said,
'You must go through, or you cannot come at the
gate.' The pilgrims then began to inquire if there
was no other way to the gate? to which they answered,
'Yes; but there hath not any, save two, Enoch and
Elijah, been permitted to tread that path since the
foundation of the world, nor shall until the last trumpet shall sound.' The pilgrims then began to de-
spond in their minds, and looked this way and that,
but no way could be found by them, by which they
might escape the river."*

Ah, how true and how touching is this description
of the emotions which are often excited in the Christian pilgrim's breast as he stands on the banks of

* Pilgrim's Progress.

the river! He fears to cross its deep, dark waters; he shrinks from the strange, and, it may be, the stormy passage to eternity. Oh, if he could but reach the celestial city without having to cross the stream of death!

It cannot be. When the summons for his departure arrives, he must enter that cold flood and meet its terrors. None can disregard the call, nor choose any other mode of transit. "It is appointed unto men once to die."*

Yet why should the Christian be afraid? Solemn and mysterious as the last change undoubtedly is, even to the child of God, he may rest assured that a wise and loving Saviour will shield him from every danger, and guide him in safety through it. And if Christ himself is with him then, if his rod and staff support and comfort him, what evil can he fear?

Aged reader, as you gaze upon the river which rolls between you and the promised land, is your mind filled with gloom and apprehension? Is it not because you look *only* at death? You do not at the same time fix the eye of faith upon your Saviour. You seem to think that, unaided and alone, you will have to struggle through its waves, instead of joyfully remembering his promise, " When thou passest

* Heb. ix. 27.

through the waters, I will be with thee; and through the rivers, they shall not overflow thee."* Oh! he who lays hold upon this sweet assurance may safely shut his eyes, and leave himself to the entire disposal of infinite love, and faithfulness, and wisdom.

Does nature recoil from the physical suffering of the last mortal conflict? It is true that the pains of death are sometimes so severe as to occasion the deepest distress and anguish; but in the greater number of instances how easy and tranquil are the closing moments of life! How many pass from time to eternity as calmly as an infant falling asleep on its mother's bosom! But should it be otherwise—should your dying hour be one of extreme suffering—is not the *manner* as well as the time of your departure hence appointed by your heavenly Father? and will he suffer you to be tried above that which you are able to bear? He knows your frame; he remembers that you are dust, and feels the tenderest parental compassion for those who fear him; and therefore you may be assured that the trials which his love ordains, whether in life or in death, are *necessary* trials, and that he will give you support under them. And if your strength is proportioned to your burden, is it not the same in effect as if that burden were re-

* Isa. xliii. 2.

moved? Listen to the testimony of an eminent minister of Christ, whose sufferings were intense, but whose spirit was filled with rejoicing in the midst of them: "I have suffered twenty times, yes—to speak within bounds—twenty times as much as I could in being burnt at the stake; but my joy in God so abounded as to render my sufferings not only tolerable, but welcome. The sufferings of the present time are not worthy to be compared with the glory that shall be revealed. God is my all. While he is present with me no event can in the least diminish my happiness; and were the whole world at my feet trying to minister to my comfort, they could not add one drop to the cup. Death comes every night, and stands at my bedside in the form of terrible convulsions, until every bone is almost dislocated with pain; yet while the body is thus tortured, the soul is perfectly happy and peaceful—more happy than I can possibly express to you."

How easily might we multiply proofs like these—proofs of God so sustaining and elevating the soul of the believer above the pressure of physical suffering as that it was comparatively unheeded and unfelt! And can he not do the same, reader, for you? Is not his grace sufficient for you as well as for others? Oh, trust yourself to him; repose with confidence upon his promises; and believe that in a dying hour, your succour shall be equal to your need. Do not test your preparedness for that hour by the strength and comfort which you now possess, but by the solemn engagement which Christ has made never to leave nor forsake you. He is with you now, to help you to glorify him by your life; when death comes he will be with you then, and help you to glorify him by your death. Dying grace will not be vouchsafed until a dying hour; you do not want it now, but it will be abundantly vouchsafed then. Wait for it in faith. "Death is somewhat dreary," said Bishop Cowper to his weeping friends, "and the streams of that Jordan which is between us and our Canaan run furiously; but they stand still when the ark comes."

But perhaps your anxiety respecting death is occasioned by the thought of the separation which must take place between the soul and the body. You dread the entrance upon an unknown and untried state of existence. It is not what you know, but what you do not know of the future, which causes your distress. If any one could return from the unseen world, and tell you exactly what he experienced in the moment of his departure from earth, and clearly describe to you the sensations which he felt when he found himself absent from the body, your mind, you think, would be relieved of much of its disquietude. But it is the uncertainty, the blank, the mystery lying before, in the awful distance, at which you tremble. Like a child in the dark, because you cannot see, you are afraid. The imaginary objects which fill you with awe and trepidation would disappear if there were light enough to reveal to you the true state of things. Why, then, you ask, is that light withheld? Could not God have unfolded to us in his word the nature of our future existence, and the mode of our introduction to it? He must have foreseen the suspense and the agitation which would arise through our ignorance, and yet he has not sought to allay our fears by a clearer and fuller revelation of things to come. Why is it? The fact of God's silence upon this point is a sufficient reply. We may be sure, since he is Love, that the knowledge which he has reserved is neither requisite nor desirable for us. It is probable that, in our present state of existence we could not comprehend more than he has already told us about another world, or the full blaze of light which we desire, had it been granted, might have proved injurious to us. We are as yet only in the infancy of our being, and do not know what is best for us; but our Maker knows,

and he has acted accordingly. "He has said enough
to awaken curiosity, to enkindle desire, to inspire
hope, to encourage confidence and expectation; and
we must wait for the rest. God calls us to honour
him by our faith, by our belief, at all times and under
all circumstances, in his wisdom and goodness. It
is as though we were allowed to give to the universe
a proof of the firmness of our dependence upon him,
such as no heavenly spirits can give, to show that we
are not afraid to trust him even when he bids us
die." Oh, shall we not willingly prove how unshaken
is our reliance on his love, by resigning ourselves in
the hour of death, without one fear, to his care? The
way before us is dark and mysterious, but we will
cheerfully follow where he leads us. And how
gently, how tenderly will he lead us! The act of
dying which we so greatly fear may be a gentle and
painless slumber—a quiet falling asleep in Christ;
and the light of eternity will dawn upon us like the
tranquil beams of the morning which now gladden
our waking eyes.

"Hast thou ne'er looked on a little child
    When he first awakes from rest,
And smiles to think how his dream beguiled
    While he slept on a parent's breast?
So calm and so sweet shall the waking be
In the radiant dawn of eternity."

There is, it is true, something strange and inexplicable in the idea of our existence without a body; we are apt to fancy that a disembodied spirit must at first feel as it were unclothed and unprotected. But it is a mistake to suppose that the soul owes its defence from external harms and hardships to the body in the same manner as the body does to the clothes it wears. The very contrary is true. It is here exposed to many more harms and hardships by means of its union with the mortal body; and, consequently, its disunion from that will be its freedom from them. The operations and conceptions of the liberated soul will be inconceivably more perfect, free, and unbiassed than they now are, while subject to so many impediments and interruptions from its connection with animal nature. This is evident from the fact that even *now* we find our soul in the best frame for thinking when it is least affected by the body. How rapid, how strong, how clear, then, will be the flow of its thoughts when they meet with nothing from without to obstruct them!

The dread of death, however, may arise from other causes. It may result from apprehensions as to our eternal happiness. We fear, sometimes, whether our names are written in the Lamb's book of life—whether we have any warrant to look forward to a participation in everlasting joys; and therefore we cannot bear the thought of meeting our Judge face to face, and would fain retard the moment when our everlasting destiny must be fixed. Were we *sure* that there was a mansion prepared for us, and a crown of glory laid up for us in heaven, oh we should not mind passing through the river of death, even though its waters were deep and tempest-tossed. But how can we be sure?

What saith the Scripture?—"There is now no condemnation to them which are in Christ Jesus." "He that believeth on the Son hath everlasting life." "I am the living bread which came down from heaven; if any man eat of this bread he shall live for ever." "My sheep hear my voice, and I know them, and they follow me: and I give unto them eternal life; and they shall never perish." "I will come again, and receive you unto myself; that where I am, there ye may be also."*

But precious as these assertions are, they do not exactly relieve our distress. Our fear is not whether true believers are everlastingly saved, but whether we are among their number. We hope we are, but it is so easy to deceive ourselves; we may be mistaken; and how terrible to wake in eternity and find

* Rom. viii. 7; John iii. 36; vi. 51; x. 27; xiv. 3.

48

ourselves excluded from the bliss of the redeemed, beyond the possibility of change; for, what we are then, we must be for ever

Our dread, then, of death—or rather of the consequences of death—may be traced to the weakness of our faith or to imperfect views of the gospel of Jesus Christ. It cannot, therefore, be removed until our faith becomes stronger and our views clearer. We must study the word which God has given us, and ask for the teaching of his Spirit, that we may be enabled to understand and to apply to ourselves the heart-cheering truth, "Christ is all, and in all;" "Ye are complete in him." We must strive to lay aside the reasonings, the prejudices, and the unbelief of our own hearts, and receive with simplicity and thankfulness the full and free promises of our Saviour. As we become better acquainted with that loving Saviour, and understand more perfectly the design of his all-sufficient atonement, our anxious forebodings about the future will gradually pass away as the gloom of midnight fades before the rising sun, and the God of hope will fill us with all joy and peace in believing.

It will tend to mitigate the alarm with which we regard the solemn change of death, if we look at it in its true character, as a continuance of the present, rather than as the commencement of a new state of existence. Heaven and hell are not so much the reward (using the word in its scriptural sense) of our past life as the necessary sequence of it. It will be *what* we are, not *where* we are, which will constitute our felicity or our woe; and therefore if we are conscious now that we love the Saviour and trust in him, and follow after holiness, or even that we heartily desire and strive to do this, is it not plain that we have within us the germ of true happiness— a heart that is touched with the love of Christ, and longs for conformity to his likeness? With this principle implanted in our hearts, how could we be for ever miserable? It is impossible! not only because God will never falsify his own word, nor condemn those who put their trust in his Son, but because the elements of lasting peace and joy are already ours. "He that believeth on the Son *hath*— not *shall have*—everlasting life." Meditate on this declaration, dear reader, and take the consolation which it is calculated to impart to all who are placing their reliance upon the atonement of Christ.

But in the contemplation of a dying hour a tender and affectionate spirit is sometimes deeply affected at the prospect of parting with beloved relatives and friends. There are some, perhaps, to whom we are a solace and a support, who have always been accustomed to lean upon us in their weary march of life, and to look to us for counsel and sympathy; how will they do without us? how can we leave them to struggle on alone and sorrowful? Or there are others for whose salvation we are deeply concerned, and over whose wanderings we often shed bitter tears; how shall we bear to take our farewell—it may be our last farewell—of them? How keen will be the anguish of our dying hour as we reflect that they are still unchanged, unsaved, and that we dare not cherish the hope of meeting them again!

Oh how painful are the separations of the grave! How hard it is to sever, if only for a few years, the ties which bind us so closely to the *dear* ones around us! Many Christians, *aged* Christians too—for old age does not quench the ardency of the affections—can respond to the touching desire of a youthful disciple of the Saviour: "Oh, mamma! I wish we could all die and go to heaven together."

Yet why should you dwell only on the dark side of the picture? It may never be presented to you. Your heavenly Father, in his compassion for your weakness, may spare you the sorrow which you anticipate. You may pass away from this life as in a quiet slumber.

"Nor bear a single pang at parting;
  Nor see the tear of sorrow starting;
  Nor hear the quivering lips that bless you;
  Nor feel the hands of love that press you."

Or, if not—if fully conscious in your last moments that you are parting from those whom you love—God will so strengthen and animate your dying spirit as that you shall be enabled with calmness, nay, with cheerfulness, to resign the objects of your affection to his merciful guidance and protection. You will feel that he who has watched over you so many years in the wilderness, and brought you safely through every danger, can surely do as much for those whom you are leaving behind; that he who has taught you to pray so earnestly and so perseveringly for their spiritual welfare will not suffer your prayers to remain unanswered, although he calls you home before you have witnessed their fulfilment. And you will also realize your happy and speedy re-union with your dear friends in another world. Death will not long divide you; the remainder of their appointed time on earth will pass rapidly away as a tale that is told, and then you will meet them again—meet to part no more!

"With the prospect of meeting for ever,
  With the bright gates of heaven in view,

From the dearest on earth we may sever,
And smile a delightful adieu."

Aged believer, you are standing now on the banks
of the river; fear not, only believe. Remember that
one of the reasons why Jesus Christ manifested himself in human nature was for the express purpose of
dispelling that gloom which naturally overspreads
the mind as we look upon the dark waters of death.
"Forasmuch as the children are partakers of flesh
and blood, he also himself likewise took part of the
same; that through death he might destroy him that
had the power of death, that is, the devil; and deliver them who through fear of death were all their
lifetime subject to bondage."* Then seek deliverance from that fear, and expect deliverance. Christ
suffered not in vain; all the purposes of his death
have been fully accomplished; and he would have
his people even now to participate in his triumph;
and without waiting for the actual encounter to join
in the ascription of the apostle, "Thanks be to God
which giveth us the victory through our Lord Jesus
Christ!" Then

"Shudder not to pass the stream,
Venture all thy care on him—
Him whose dying love and power
Still'd its tossing, hushed its roar.

* Heb. ii. 14, 15.

Not one object of his care
Ever suffered shipwreck there;
See the haven full in view;
Love divine shall bear thee through."

Is it granted to you to possess that strong faith, that calm assurance which elevates the mind above the fear of death? Can you say with gladness, " The time of my departure is at hand: I have fought a good fight, I have finished my course, I have kept the faith: henceforth there is laid up for me a crown of righteousness which the Lord the righteous Judge shall give me at that day?"* Thank your Saviour for this glorious hope—this hope which is as an anchor of the soul, sure and steadfast—for he is its author and its bestower. It is because he has abolished death and brought life and immortality to light through the gospel, that you are now enabled to look forward with composure to your conflict with the last foe, and triumphantly to ask, " O death, where is thy sting? O grave, where is thy victory?"† Well may you rejoice, for your life is hid with Christ in God, and you are safe for ever—safe amidst the infirmities and perils of old age; safe in the swelling waters of Jordan; safe when you stand before the solemn judgment-seat; yes, safe throughout eternity. No-

* 2 Tim. iv. 6–8. † 1 Cor. xv. 55.

thing in earth or hell can separate you from the love
of God which is in Christ Jesus, or pluck you from
the grasp of your ever-living Saviour. He upholds
and comforts you now in the evening of life; and
"by-and-by, leaning upon his arm, you shall come
down to the river. Not a ripple shall be on its
bosom; its clear waters shining in heaven's own light
shall allure to the crossing. *His* feet shall but touch
the stream, and, lo, a way for the ransomed to pass
over." "Blessed are the dead which die in the
Lord;" "Precious in the sight of the Lord is the
death of his saints."*

But our remarks about the river of death have
been addressed to true Christians; are you, reader,
one of their number? If not, you have no right to
appropriate to yourself the consolations which are
designed only for them. There is no sight more
painful than that of an aged individual on the borders of the grave, on the threshold of eternity, unrenewed, unsanctified, and yet undismayed by the
terrors of the future, and confident of the joys of
heaven. May God preserve us from so fearful a delusion! "Be not deceived; God is not mocked: for
whatsoever a man soweth, that shall he also reap."†
A life of carelessness — of worldliness — of self-

* Rev. xiv. 13; Psa. cxvi. 15.   † Gal. vi. 7.

righteousness, cannot prepare us for a life of glory. "Except a man be born again, he cannot see the kingdom of God." "He that believeth not the Son shall not see life; but the wrath of God abideth on him.* "Without holiness no man shall see the Lord "† A change of heart, faith in Christ, the fruits of holiness, are the precursors of the believer's assurance of eternal felicity; what do you know of them in your own experience? Examine yourself, whether you are in the faith, or whether you have only a name to live while you are dead. The absence of alarm, or even the possession of joy, as you draw near to death and eternity, is not of itself an indication of safety. It may be but the deadly calm before an awful tempest; a fatal slumber on the edge of a frightful precipice. IGNORANCE trembled not when he came to the river-side and prepared to cross it; he got over it with less difficulty than Christian, for one VAIN HOPE helped him with his boat; but when he reached the other side, the King commanded his servants to bind him hand and foot, and to cast him into outer darkness.

Yet while this should warn the presumptuous and the self-confident, it should not discourage the awakened sinner who feels that life is receding be-

* John iii. 3, 36.   † Heb. xii. 14.

neath his tread, and that his feet have as yet found no sure resting-place. The language of the gospel is language of peace to all who really desire salvation from the peril and the dominion of sin. "Come unto me," says the Saviour whom it proclaims, "all ye that labour and are heavy-laden, and I will give you rest."* It is never too late to turn to him, to seek forgiveness at his cross. God's promises of salvation are made without exception of time; for whenever a sinner repents of his sins, he has promised to put away his wickedness out of remembrance. They are made without exception of sins; for, "The blood of Jesus Christ cleanseth us from all sin;"† and, "All manner of sin and blasphemy shall be forgiven unto men."‡ They are made without exception of persons; for, "Whosoever shall call on the name of the Lord shall be saved;"§ "Whosoever will, let him take the water of life freely;"‖ "Him that cometh to me I will in no wise cast out."¶

Aged reader! "Behold the Lamb of God which taketh away the sin of the word." Look unto him and be saved. How else will you pass through the swellings of Jordan? how else will you stand at the judgment-seat of Christ?

---

* Matt. xi. 28.   † 1 John i. 7.   ‡ Matt. xii. 31.
§ Acts ii. 21.   ‖ Rev. xxii. 17.   ¶ John vi. 37.

Heavenward.

FROM THE GERMAN OF B. SCHMOLKE.

HEAVENWARD doth our journey tend,
   We are strangers here on earth;
Through the wilderness we wend
   Towards the Canaan of our birth.
Here we roam a pilgrim band,
Yonder is our native land.

Heavenward stretch, my soul, thy wings,
   Heavenly nature can'st thou claim;
There is naught of earthly things
   Worthy to be all thine aim;
Every soul whom God inspires
Back to him, its Source, aspires.

Heavenward! doth his Spirit cry,
   When I hear him in his word,
Showing thus the rest on high,
   When I shall be with my Lord:
When his word fills all my thought,
Oft to heaven my soul is caught.

Heavenward ever would I haste,
  When thy table, Lord, is spread;
Heavenly strength on earth I taste,
  Feeding on the Living Bread.
Such is e'en on earth our fare
Who thy marriage feast shall share.

Heavenward! Faith discerns the prize
  That is waiting us afar,
And my heart would swiftly rise,
  High o'er sun and moon and star,
To that Light behind the veil
Where all earthly splendours pale.

Heavenward Death shall lead at last,
  To the home where I would be;
All my sorrows overpast,
  I shall triumph there with thee,
Jesus, who hast gone before,
That we too might heavenward soar.

Heavenward! Heavenward! Only this
  Is my watchword on the earth;
For the love of heavenly bliss
  Counting all things little worth.
Heavenward all my being tends,
Till in heaven my journey ends.

When wilt thou Die?

ANONYMOUS.

NOT in the solemn night,
When dim and shadowy all things appear;
When thoughts are tinged with mournfulness and
fear,
And nature's fairest scenes are veiled from sight;
For darkness only throws a deeper gloom
Around the opening tomb.

But let the gladsome day
Smile upon my departure; let the bright
And glorious sunshine image forth that light
Which soon shall beam with pure and fadeless ray
Upon my ransomed spirit; let no cloud
Life's closing scene enshroud.

Not in the hour of health,
Without one kind adieu or parting token,
When suddenly the chain of life is broken,
And our last messenger comes as by stealth;—
From quick transition to eternity,
Good Lord, deliver me.

Calm be my last farewell
To all the joys and cares and griefs of earth;
On themes of precious and immortal worth
    In peaceful contemplation let me dwell;
As gradually fades the light of day,
        So let me pass away.

Not in a distant land,
Or on the bosom of the lonely sea,
Where stranger forms would coldly bend o'er me;
    Far, far from the loved and home-linked band;
Without one friend my dying hours to bless,
        And soothe my weariness.

But gather round my bed
The loved ones who have gladdened life's past hours:
Let cherished objects, fondly-tended flowers,
    And well-known faces, comfort round me spread;
And gentle words of counsel and of love
        Point me to hopes above.

Saviour! thou wilt not chide
These simple wishes twined around the grave;
And yet 'tis better that on death's cold wave
    My trembling vessel thou shouldst launch and guide,
How, when, and where thou wilt: what should I fear
        With thee, my pilot, near?

Through all life's troublous way
Thou hast sustained me.   Thou wilt keep me still.
Veiled is the future, yet I fear no ill;
  But ready stand thy summons to obey.
It matters little what the path may be,
      So that it leads to thee.

The Aged Believer's Triumph.[*]

REV. WILLIAM ROMAINE.

It is appointed unto men once to die. The time is fixed by an immutable decree. The days of our years are threescore years and ten, and if by reason of strength they be fourscore years, yet is their strength labour and sorrow: for it is soon cut off, and we flee away. If some be permitted to live longer, yet the infirmities of old age must arrive, bringing with them labour and sorrow, the forerunners of death. Circulation will become languid. The senses of the body will grow dull and heavy. The faculties of the mind will be impaired, and they will discover it by not remembering proper names.

In this decline of life believers are subject to the same infirmities with other men; they have no exemption from pain, or sickness, or death; but they have that which keeps up their spirits and makes them patient and joyful. The consolations of God are then most needed, and he has promised them, and

* From "Triumph of Faith."

he is faithful: he never failed them who trusted in
him. He has suited his promises to all the infirmities of age. He knows our frame perfectly, and has
described it with an unerring pen (Eccles. xii.), that
when we feel the signs of old age we may apply to
to him for grace to profit by them. The symptoms
there given are infallibly true and just, and are as so
many monitors, warning the man that the vigour of
life is declining, and that the body is returning to the
earth from whence it came. Happy is he who takes
this warning, and remembers his Creator in the days
of his youth, before the wearisome days come of
weakness and pain. He has fled to Jesus for refuge,
and finds and experiences what he has engaged to
do for his people when heart and flesh begin to fail
them. Blessed be his grace for the abundant provision which he has made for their faith and patience: he says to them, "I will be with you, I will
never leave you nor forsake you: so that you may
boldly say, The Lord is our helper, and we need not
fear what the infirmities of age can do unto us." One
of them, the Christian hero, thus encouraged himself
in the Lord his God: "Thou art my hope, O Lord
God: thou art my trust even from my youth. By thee
have I been holden up from the womb; thou art he
that took me out of my mother's bowels; my praise

50

shall be continually of thee. I am a wonder unto many, but thou art my strong refuge." This was his trust; and God did not forsake him. He remembered his word unto his servant, whereon he had caused him to depend. There failed not aught of any good thing which the Lord had spoken unto him. Oh what great encouragement have believers to follow the steps of his faith! For his God is their God, the same yesterday, to-day, and for ever, to young and old, who put their trust in him. His promise to the Israel of God cannot be broken. Thus he pledges his word of truth to them, giving them a warrant to pray unto him: " Let my mouth be filled with thy praise, and with thy honour all the day; cast me not off in the time of old age; forsake me not when my strength faileth." To this prayer the Lord inclined his ear, and vouchsafed this gracious answer: " Hearken unto me, O house of Jacob, and all the remnant of the house of Israel, which are borne by me from the belly, which are carried from the womb: and even to your old age I am he; and even to hoar hairs will I carry you: I have made, and I will bear; even I will carry, and will deliver you." These are some of his rich cordials for the aged, which he provided for them in his love, and he is sensibly touched with the feeling of their in-

firmities in administering them; for he himself
took our infirmities and bare our sicknesses. His
compassions bind him to comfort and relieve his old
disciples; and when they apply to him in time of
need, he is ever present to grant them his promised
help; yea, so suited to their case as to make them
grow in grace as they grow in years. They bring
forth fruit in their old age, the rich fruit of humility
and the ripe fruit of thankfulness—fruit that endureth unto everlasting life.

We have a happy instance of this in God's goodness to an ancient believer who lived to be an hundred and seventy-five years old. He was the friend
of God, who had blessed Abraham through life, and
that in all things, and who even to hoary hairs
loaded him with blessings. For God had promised
him, "Thou shalt go to thy fathers in peace, thou
shalt be buried in a good old age;" and the sacred
historian, relating the fulfilling of the promise, says,
"He gave up the ghost, and died in a good old age,
an old man, and full of years, and was gathered to
his people." His old age was good in body and soul.
Whatever infirmities he had, they were intended for
good, and actually did him good. He was a very
cheerful, pleasant old man. The peace of his mind
had a sweet influence upon his temper and beha-

viour. It kept him from being fretful and peevish in his family. He was loving to his children and kind to his servants, God himself being witness. He was also happy in his last years; for he spent them in faith, and when they came to an end he died in peace; with his last breath he committed his spirit into the hands of him who had redeemed it, *full of years;* it is in the original one word—*he was satisfied;* so it is rendered, Psa. xvii. 15, "As for me I shall behold thy face in righteousness; I shall be satisfied when I awake with thy likeness." He was satisfied with what he had enjoyed of the favour and friendship of his God; who had been his shield to defend him from all sins and enemies, and also had promised to be his exceeding great reward. This he obtained when he was gathered to his people, to the general assembly and Church of the first-born, and to the most blissful communion of the Three-One Jehovah. All the children of faithful Abraham, treading in the steps of his faith, have the same God to deal with, who keepeth promise for ever. It is recorded of Isaac, the heir of the same promise with his father, that he died in the same faith an old man. He was tried with many infirmities, but we read of no complaints, though he was an hundred and eighty years of age. He expired in praise and thankfulness, satisfied with life, and happy in the prospect beyond death. And his son Jacob, an hundred and forty-seven years old, when he was dying declared that he had waited for the salvation of God. Waiting faith is strong faith. And after he had blessed his children, and had given commandment concerning his bones, he quietly, as if he had been going to sleep, gathered up his feet into the bed and died in peace, an old man and satisfied. All these lived in the world, strangers and pilgrims, looking for a city that hath foundations, whose builder and maker is God. And they were not disappointed of their hope; they all died in faith—in an act of faith—and were gathered to their people, to the general assembly and Church of the first-born. When they came to the end of their faith they came to heaven. The moment they expired they entered the city which God had prepared for them; and their bodies sleeping in the dust are in the covenant of life, and shall be raised and glorified in the morning of the resurrection. For our Lord proves that the dead shall rise from this very circumstance; he says to the Jews: "Have ye not read in the books of Moses, how in the bush God spake unto him, saying, I am the God of Abraham, and the God of Isaac, and the God of Jacob? He is not the God of the dead, but the God of the living."

In this faith the patriarchs died; being children of the resurrection, they left their bodies in the hand and care of a covenant God, well assured that he would raise them up to glory and life everlasting, according to that good word wherein he had caused them to put their trust.

These examples of the loving-kindness of God to ais aged servants were recorded for our learning, that believers, if God by his providence should bring them to old age, might be encouraged to trust in the God of Abraham, Isaac, and Jacob, with such a confidence of their hearts as not to doubt of the divine truth or of the divine power. Whatever he was to them, he is the same to us—our God as well as theirs —our covenant God engaged to glorify both body and soul; on whom we are commanded to cast all our cares and concerns in extreme old age. If what is of nature be failing, what is of grace cannot. If the life of sense be dying, the life of faith should flourish the more; it is a life that cannot die; for the branches thrive and bring forth fruit in their old age, not of themselves, but because they are engrafted into the heavenly vine, in which they live for ever. " I am the vine," says Jesus, " ye are the branches; he that abideth in me, and I in him, the same bringeth forth much fruit; for without me ye can do nothing." But through his Spirit strengthening you, he will make you bud and flourish, and fill the face of the world with fruit. He will so fill you with the fruits of righteousness which are through Christ Jesus, to the glory and praise of God, that your last days shall be your best days.

In this view of old age, it may become a favourable time for exercising and improving faith, because the activity of the life of sense is abating, and thereby many things are removed which before obstructed the growth of the spiritual life. Now is the time to learn to walk by faith, and not by sense. A believer, young in years and young in experience, is often tempted to judge of himself by his feelings more than by the word of God. In a good frame he is a good believer. Then all is well with him. But when he is walking in darkness he is very apt to question his state—" If all be right with me, why am I thus? My present frame is very dull and uncomfortable ; I am not so lively as I used to be in prayer or in ordinances ; my delight in God, and the things of God, is far short of what it was formerly—perhaps I have been deceiving myself, and crying, Peace, peace, when there was no peace for me."

From this temptation age itself is a sort of deliverance ; self-activity is weakened, and thereby,

through grace, self-dependence. The believer, if he
be a good scholar, will now learn to walk more by
faith and less by sight. The vigour of his senses is
decaying. The high spirits of youth are abating.
His present lesson is very plain and simple, and
while he attends to what is passing in him and about
him, he has a thousand monitors calling upon him
now to learn and practise a perfect dependence on
those things which are always one and the same, without any variableness or the least shadow of turning
—one record of God—one Saviour—one Spirit—one
faith, of which the Saviour is the author and the finisher. This faith is made to grow and flourish, as
there is less dependence on other things; and as age
itself tends to weaken this dependence, it becomes, in
the hand of the Holy Spirit, a favourable time to
live less upon the things which are seen, and more
upon the things which are not seen. Less of sense,
more of faith. One scale rises as the other falls
The outward man dying, the inward man grows more
lively—yea, grows up into Christ Jesus, and that in
all things. O blessed old man! thou hast lived to
a good time when this is thy experience; when in the
prayer of faith thou canst cast all thy burdens on
thy Saviour: "Lord, keep me, a poor helpless creature; now I feel that of myself I can do nothing as

I ought or as I wish to do. Glorify thy grace in me, and strengthen me mightily by thy Spirit in the inner man, that I may bless thee for thy salvation, and for the things which accompany salvation. Into thy faithful hands, for life and death, I commit myself and all my concerns; for thou hast redeemed me, O Lord, thou God of truth."

But it must be remembered that old age does not produce these happy effects of itself. It is not of nature, but entirely of grace, that any one is able to gain such spiritual profit from bodily infirmities. The mere natural man, fortify him with all his boasted aids of reason and philosophy, yet cannot help murmuring when age brings weakness, and sickness brings pains. He becomes peevish and fretful. Having no friendship with God, he cannot look up for divine supports when all human begin to fail him. Under a severe fit of the stone, or a long fit of the gout, he is often out of all patience. Uneasy in himself, he is out of humour with everybody and everything. How different is the believer in the same circumstances! His body feels pain as others' do; but his mind is comfortable and at ease. Happy in God, he has patience given him to bear his sufferings, and grace to profit from them; yea, the peace of God rules in his heart always and by all means.

. An old man with this peace, which surpasseth all understanding, ruling in his heart, will be so far from complaining, that he has everything to be thankful for which can render him blessed of the Lord. He is provided with an infallible antidote against all that old age can try him with. It is true, I have an infirm body, but, thank God, I have a sound mind. Age has brought upon me great weakness, but this makes more room for the power of God, that it may be perfected in my weakness. I have many pains, but not so many as he has comforts to give me; in the worst of them he keeps me patient. " Father, thy will be done." I have an afflicted body, but I have a happy heart; although the outward man be perishing, yet I faint not, because the inward man is renewed day by day. My supports are great, the consolations of God not a few. I feel the symptoms of old age warning me daily of my approaching dissolution. Through grace I take the warning. They find me living, and I hope they will find me dying, in the faith of the Son of God. The earthly tabernacle is taken down, but he does it with much tenderness and love, and assures me that he has prepared for me a house not made with hands, eternal in the heavens. May he who keeps it for me, and me for it, never leave me nor forsake me, till I be

with him, where he is, and be like him, and enjoy
him for ever and ever! Yet a very, very little while
—hold on, faith and patience—and I shall see Jesus
in his glory, which is the heaven of heavens.

O thou merciful and faithful High Priest, Jesus
Christ, I bless thee for thy kind promises to the
aged. Thou hast suited them in great mercy to all
their infirmities, and thou art always with them to
help in time of need. I begin to feel the sad effects
of sin in my body, weakening it and tending to
bring it down to its appointed end. To thee I look,
almighty Jesus, for thy promised grace. O grant
me constant supplies of thy Spirit, that I may profit
by my infirmities, may exercise and improve my
faith in thee, that they may keep me humble, and I
may pray more in faith; and keep me thankful,
that I may be more in praise. Thine arm is not
shortened, nor can thy compassions fail. Stand by
me then, and hold me up according to thy word.
Make me strong in thy strength, that I may daily
put more honour upon thy love and thy power. In
the decline of life let me not doubt of thy faithfulness to support, and, when thou seest it best, to comfort me. Vouchsafe me the consolations of God;
when my heart and my flesh fail me, then be thou

the strength of my heart and my portion for ever. When I am weakest in myself, then make me strongest in the Lord; and if it be thy holy will that I should become quite helpless, an infant again, make me to lie quiet in thy hand without murmuring or repining, but believing that thou art all my salvation, and enjoying in thee all my desire. Grant me this, Lord Jesus; for thy mercy's sake, let me die in faith. Amen and Amen.

A Little Way.

MISS JOSEPHINE POLLARD.

A LITTLE way—I know it is not far
To that dear home where my beloved are;
And yet my faith grows weaker, as I stand
A poor, lone pilgrim in a dreary land,
Where present pain the future bliss obscures;
And still my heart sits like a bird upon
The empty nest, and mourns its treasures gone;
  Plumed for their flight,
  And vanished quite.
Ah! me, where is the comfort?—though I say
They have but journeyed on a little way!

A little way—at times they seem so near,
Their voices ever murmur at my ear;
To all my duties loving presence lend,
And with sweet ministry my steps attend,
And bring my soul the luxury of tears.
'Twas here we met, and parted company;
Why should their gain be such a grief to me?
  This sense of loss!
  This heavy cross!

405

Dear Saviour, take the burden off, I pray,
And show me heaven is but—a little way.

These sombre robes, these saddened faces, all
The bitterness and pain of death recall;
Ah! let me turn my face where'er I may,
I see the traces of a sure decay;
And parting takes the marrow out of life.
Secure in bliss, we hold the golden chain,
Which death, with scarce a warning, snaps in twain,
    And never more
    Shall time restore
The broken links;—'twas only yesterday
They vanished from our sight—a little way!

A little way!—this sentence I repeat,
Hoping and longing to extract some sweet
To mingle with the bitter. From thy hand
I take the cup I cannot understand,
And in my weakness give myself to thee!
Although it seems so very, very far
To that dear home where my beloved are,
    I know, I know,
    It is not so;
Oh! give me faith to feel it when I say·
That they are gone—gone but a little way!

Support in Death.*

FROM THE GERMAN OF N. HERMANN.

WHEN now the solemn hour is nigh
   That from this world shall call me,
On what, O Lord, can I rely,
   While terrors would appal me ?
My soul and body, to the last,
I'll on thine arm of mercy cast,—
   'Tis safe to trust thy mercy !

My sins may seem in number more,
   While conscience shall recount them,
Than sands upon the ocean shore,—
   Thy grace can still surmount them.
I'll think, dear Saviour, of the death
Sustained by thee ;—and thus my faith
   From sinking shall uphold me.

I am a branch of thee, the Vine ;
   My strength from thee I borrow ;
Round thee my tendril hopes shall twine
   In death's drear night of sorrow :

* Translated by Dr. Mills.

And when 'tis over, thou wilt give
An endless life with thee to live
   In bliss thy sorrows purchased.

My Lord o'er death triumphant rose,
   From earth to God ascended;
His victory yields my heart repose,
   The fear of death is ended;
For where he is, I too shall come,
And find with him a joyful home:
   Why should I fear to follow?

With outstretched arms I'll welcome Christ.
   That he from earth may take me:
I'll leave my flesh in hope to rest,
   Till from the grave he wake me;
But Christ himself will go before,—
Of heaven for me throw wide the door,
   And bless my soul in glory.

The Heavenly Rest.

ANONYMOUS.

How welcome to the aged Christian is the thought of heaven! As the toil-worn labourer hails with gladness the hour of rest; as the wave-tossed mariner discerns with thankfulness the haven of safety; as the weary exile approaches with feelings of rapture his native country; so does the believer rejoice in the immediate prospect of eternal glory. He loves to think of that moment when he shall be absent from the body and present with the Lord; when the cares, the conflicts, and the corruptions which surround him here will be exchanged for the peace and purity which pervade the everlasting abode of the redeemed. Varied are the attractions which draw his thoughts and affections thither. Deliverance from trouble, freedom from sin, increase of knowledge, separation from the ungodly, intercourse with the holy, communion with his Saviour,—these and other delineations of the heavenly state make him ready, willing, eager to depart from the present life, and to enter upon that new and noble existence.

"My chief conception of heaven," said Robert Hall, who was an almost constant sufferer from acute bodily pain, "*is rest.*" And many sons and daughters of affliction can respond to his remark. They have so much to do and to suffer, they see so much misery and discord around them, their spiritual foes are so powerful and persevering, that the sigh of the Psalmist is often heard from their lips: "Oh that I had wings like a dove! for then would I fly away, and be at rest."* Rest! Where? In heaven: there the weary are at rest.

They rest from *toil.* From physical exertion and from mental labour. The hand no longer has to procure bread for the sustenance of life, and to provide things honest in the sight of all men; the head no longer has to plan for avoiding difficulties and distress, and to strive after a temporary relief from some of the cares of daily life. "They shall hunger no more, neither thirst any more."† "They rest from their labours; and their works do follow them."‡ All fatigue and anxiety are for ever ended.

They rest from *pain.* The inhabitant of that heavenly city shall not say, I am sick; "neither shall there be any more pain: for the former things are passed away."§ "I shall soon be at home now,"

* Psalm lv. 6.   † Rev. vii. 16.   ‡ Rev. xiv. 13.   § Rev. xxi. 4.

said an aged Christian woman, who had been for many years afflicted with a painful disease, "and then all suffering will be over. I hope I am not impatient; I am willing to bear whatever God sends, and as long as he sends it; I know he is love. But it is very sweet sometimes, when my poor body is racked with pain and I cannot get a minute's relief, to think that I am every day nearer heaven, and to feel that the sufferings of this present time are not worthy to be compared with the glory that shall be revealed. What a change it will be!"

They rest from *sorrow.* "God shall wipe away all tears from their eyes; and there shall be no more death, neither sorrow, nor crying."* Yes; God himself shall wipe away their tears. The days of their mourning will be for ever ended, and sorrow and sighing shall flee away. Want, disappointment, care, unkindness, injustice, bereavement, and every other source of earthly distress, are unknown in heaven. The waves of grief cannot pass the confines of eternity. The clouds of sadness cannot float in the clear atmosphere of heaven. The voice of lamentation and weeping can never mingle with the songs of the redeemed.

They rest from *spiritual conflict.* Life is a period

* Rev. xxi. 4.

of warfare and trial. The foes of the Christian are
many and they are mighty. His own unsubdued
passions, the world, with its temptations on the one
hand and its reproaches on the other, and the great
adversary of mankind going about as a roaring
lion, seeking whom he may devour, are continually
arrayed against him; and he must be always upon
his guard, always ready for the encounter. Nor does
he, except in occasional moments of discomfiture and
depression, shrink from the battle-field. It is his
earnest desire to fight the good fight of faith, and to
endure hardness as a good soldier of Jesus Christ.
To ask for victory and rest from a mere love of selfish
ease is inconsistent with his principles and feelings.
God has called him to the contest, and when he sees
fit will call him to his reward; till then he is willing
to wait and toil and struggle on. His prayer is that
when his Lord comes he may find him watching.
This is a right spirit. We ought not to grow weary
in well-doing. We ought not to wish for our crown
before our conflict is ended. But at the same time
we may look forward to our rest with hope and gladness. In the midst of our conflict with evil we may
soothe and refresh our spirits with the thought of
final victory. As we press forward in our heavenward journey, encompassed by difficulties and beset

with dangers, we may rejoice in the consideration
that

> "We nightly fix our moving tent
> A day's march nearer home!"

Yes: our warfare will soon be over—our rest attained.

And how cheering is the reflection that *holiness* as
well as rest is linked with our anticipations of
heaven! Nothing that defileth can enter there. The
Church above is " a glorious Church, not having spot,
or wrinkle, or any such thing; but holy and without
blemish."* The Christian, it is true, is already sanctified by the indwelling of the Holy Ghost. Sin has
no longer dominion over him; for the grace of God,
which bringeth salvation, teaches him to deny un-
godliness and worldly lusts, and to live soberly, right-
eously and godly in this present world. His heart
is purified by faith. He has put on the new man,
which, after God, is created in righteousness and true
holiness. He has been adopted into God's family,
renewed in his image, and made a partaker of his
holiness. But as yet how imperfect is the resem
blance which he bears! how feeble are the attainments which he has made! While he delights in
the law of God after the inward man, he sees another

* Eph. v. 27.

law in his members warring against the law of his mind, and bringing him into captivity to the law of sin, so that in the anguish of his spirit he exclaims with the apostle, "O wretched man that I am! who shall deliver me from the body of this death?"[*] Day by day he presses toward the mark for the prize of the high calling of God in Christ Jesus, but he is often sore let and hindered in running the race that is set before him; sometimes he stumbles and falls; and sometimes he wanders into some by-path which leads him into distress and danger; and although he never gives up, although each revival of the sin which so easily besets him—each temptation to which through unwatchfulness and self-dependence he yields—only prompts him to more prayerful and vigorous efforts for the future, can we wonder if he anticipates with eagerness and delight the moment when he shall be freed from the defilement and imperfection of his present condition, and be perfectly conformed to the image of his Saviour? Oh, to have his will entirely absorbed in God's will; to have every thought in unison with his mind; to have self for ever lost sight of in the radiance of his glory; to be holy and unblamable, and unreprovable in his presence! How delightful is this prospect!

* Rom. vii. 24

how all-sustaining is this hope! And as years increase, as life declines, his desire after perfected holiness grows stronger and stronger, until it overcomes his fear of death and weakens the fondest ties which link him to earth. He is ready to leave all around him, and to press through all before him, in order that he may be separated from sin and be completely assimilated to the likeness of Christ. "We shall be like him!" is the thought—the glorious thought—which makes heaven so precious in his estimation. He longs more for purity than he does for rest. He wants to be holy, sinless, perfected.

His desire will soon be granted, his hope realized. "Blessed are they which do hunger and thirst after righteousness; for they shall be filled." Filled? Satisfied? Yes. When? In part now, in completeness hereafter. In heaven they hunger no more, neither thirst any more: they are restored to the image of their God, and are faultless before his throne.

And then how delightful to the thoughtful and inquiring Christian—and every Christian ought to sustain this character—is the assurance that in a future state our *knowledge* will be greatly increased! In this world how limited are our highest acquirements! We are like children playing on the sea-shore. and diverting ourselves, now and then finding a smoother pebble or a prettier shell than ordinary, whilst the great ocean of truth lies all undiscovered before us. But what we know not now, we shall know hereafter. Now we see through a glass darkly; now we know but in part; but then we shall see face to face, and know even as we are known. Many deeply interesting and important questions which are unanswered now will be solved then. Many difficulties which perplex us now will be explained then. How numerous are the mysteries in Providence, both in connection with our own history and with the history of others, which will then be unravelled! How varied are the mysteries in religion which will then be clear to us as the light of noonday! And our knowledge will be ever increasing. The first glance into eternity will not reveal to us all that it has to unfold. We shall be always learning something new—continually making fresh discoveries of the wisdom and power and goodness of God. And this without weariness, without effort, without disappointment.

Associated with the perfected development and probable augmentation of our intellectual powers, is the noble and uninterrupted service in which we shall oe engaged above. Alas! how feeble and how poor are our best attempts now for the fulfilment of God's will and the promotion of his glory! How little, comparatively have we done; how little can we do to make him known and loved among our fellow-men! Frequently do we mourn over our weakness and apparent uselessness, and feel that we are indeed unprofitable servants. But in heaven our service will be vigorous, perpetual, untiring. There the weary will be at rest, not because they cease to labour, but because labour brings no fatigue; and they that "have entered into rest" will find this to be their rest, that "they rest not day and night."[*]

Each glorified servant will doubtless be occupied in the manner which is most accordant with his individual bias and qualification. As the cherubim and seraphim are supposed to have their separate and appropriate offices, though all stand round the throne, so may we expect that holy engagements will be distributed in amazing diversity among the white-robed saints. But this will be the delight, that each one occupies his own, his proper, his favourite employment—that for which his being is made; no nerve strained; no part burdened; no power taxed; but all easy, enjoyable, delicious, the very part he would have chosen; the part he loves; the part he can do

* Rev. iv. 8.

best, assigned to him for ever and ever. And in this, his own proper province, each one will exercise his whole perfected being. Whatever he loves he will understand, and whatever he understands he will love; and both his mind and his will will take effect through the instrumentality of a body which is in complete unison with his spirit; never cumbering it, never darkening it, but instant and capable to do everything which the thought desires or the heart suggests; so that it will be a perfectly intelligent affection, performing without diminution and without delay all it thinks and all it feels. Then shall we understand, in that entire concurrence of all the properties which make the creature, what is the meaning of that service of which Christ spoke, when he said, " God is a Spirit; and they that worship him must worship him in spirit and in truth."*

And as we think of all the high functions and happy services of those in glory, shall we not remember those loved ones among their number who were once co-workers with us here, and rejoice in the thought that we shall ere long share in their holy occupations and participate in their fadeless joys? The communion of saints on earth is sweet, but what will it be in heaven? Here there is much to mar

* John iv. 24.

and interrupt it; there it will be perfect and perpetual. We shall be associated with "the glorious company of the apostles, the goodly fellowship of the prophets, and the noble army of martyrs;" we shall sit down with Abraham, Isaac, and Jacob in the kingdom of God. We shall share in the high and holy converse of those esteemed by us on earth for the beautiful graces and gifts which adorned their character, and become intimately acquainted with others long endeared to us by their labours and their worth, but who, through time or varied circumstances, were personally unknown to us. And there will be no discord, no prejudices, no rivalry to disturb the harmony of our intercourse. We shall dwell together as the children of one Father, as the brethren of one family, as the loved and loving inhabitants of one eternal home.

But dearer, far dearer, than the thought of this complete and tender sympathy with all the redeemed in glory, is the prospect of that perfect and constant communion with our Saviour which his promises now unfold to our view. "I will come again and receive you unto myself; that where I am, there ye may be also;" "Father, I will that they also whom thou hast given me be with me where I am; that they may behold my glory which thou hast given me."* Well might one of Christ's tried and honoured servants, in the simple meditations which she penned as she waited for her summons to pass over the river, write: " To be where thou art, to see thee as thou art, and to be made like unto thee ; the last sinful motion for ever past; no more opposition; no more weariness, listlessness, dryness, or deadness; but conformed to my blessed Saviour, every way capacitated to serve him, to enjoy him,—this is heaven." And well might her glowing words animate the faith and hope of that devoted missionary of the cross who was called, when at the foot of Mount Lebanon, to encounter the last enemy. His friends having proposed to pray with him, he replied, " Yes ; but first I wish you to read some passages from 'Mrs. Graham's Provision for Passing over Jordan ;' " and on hearing the words, " To be where thou art, to see thee as thou art, to be made like unto thee," he anticipated the conclusion, and said, with an expressive emphasis, " That is heaven !"

Yes, to be with Christ, to see him as he is, that indeed is heaven. In our converse with him now by faith we rejoice with joy that is unspeakable and full of glory; what, then, will be our emotions when that glory is realized and his presence is attained?

* John xiv. 3; xvii. 24.

"Not all things else are half so dear
  As converse with the Saviour here;
    What must it be in heaven?
'Tis heaven on earth to hear him say,
As now I journey day by day,
Poor sinner, cast thy fears away:
    Thy sins are all forgiven.

"But how will his celestial voice
  Make my enraptured heart rejoice;
    When I in glory hear him!
While I before the heavenly gate
For everlasting entrance wait,
And Jesus on his throne of state
    Invites me to come near him."

Reader, is this happy, this heart-cheering anticipation yours? What proof can you give of your
title to mansions in the skies? Is "Christ in you,
the hope of glory?"* Have you "the earnest of the
Spirit?"† Are you *made meet* to be partaker of
the inheritance of the saints in light?"‡

Then, "rejoice in hope of the glory of God."§
Your warfare will soon be accomplished, your labours
ended, your rest begun. Now is your salvation
nearer than when you believed. A little while and
you shall tread the golden streets of the holy city;
you shall eat of the tree of life which is in the midst
of the paradise of God, and drink of the pure crystal

* Col. i. 27.   † 2 Cor. v. 5.   ‡ Col. i. 12.   § Rom. v. 2.

river which proceeds out of the throne of God and
of the Lamb. A crown of glory shall be yours, and
the waving palm of victory; you shall hear the
voice of harpers harping with their harps, and you
shall join in their ever-new and triumphant song:
" Worthy is the Lamb that was slain to receive
power, and riches, and wisdom, and strength, and
honour, and glory, and blessing."* "In thy presence
is fulness of joy; at thy right hand there are pleasures for evermore."†

Wherefore, beloved, seeing that ye look for such
things, be diligent that ye may be found of him in
peace.‡ "Walk worthy of God, who hath called
you unto his kingdom and glory."§ Remember,
that "without holiness no man shall see the Lord."||
And the well-grounded hope of future blessedness
necessarily leads to present sanctification. " Every
man that hath this hope in him purifieth himself,
even as He is pure."¶ The "exceeding great and
precious promises" are given to us, not only that we
may be gladdened and comforted by them, but also
that we may be made partakers of the divine nature,
and escape "the corruption that is in the world
through lust."** "When Christ, who is our life,

* Rev. v. 12. † Psa. xvi. 11. ‡ 2 Pet. iii. 14. § 1 Thess. ii. 12.
|| Heb. xii. 14. ¶ 1 John iii. 3. ** 2 Pet. i. 4.

shall appear, then shall ye also appear with him in glory. Mortify, *therefore*, your members which are upon the earth."*

Weary and sorrowful pilgrim, the sufferings of the present time are not worthy to be compared with the glory that shall be revealed. Let the radiance of coming joys illumine the clouds of present grief; let the melody of heaven-breathed songs soothe the agitation of your troubled spirit. Oh, your " light affliction is but for a moment," and it " worketh for you a far more exceeding and eternal weight of glory; while you look not at the things which are seen, but at the things which are not seen: for the things which are seen are temporal; but the things which are not seen are eternal."†

Aged Christian, the time of your departure is at hand. The sunset of life and the night of death usher in the dawn of immortality. The earthly house of your tabernacle is about to be dissolved, but you have a building of God, a house not made with hands, eternal in the heavens. " Blessed be the God and Father of our Lord Jesus Christ, which according to his abundant mercy hath begotten us again unto a lively hope by the resurrection of Jesus Christ from the dead, to an inheritance incorruptible

* Col. iii. 4, 5.　　　　† 2 Cor. iv. 17, 18.

and undefiled, and that fadeth not away, reserved in heaven for you, who are kept by the power of God through faith unto salvation ready to be revealed in the last time: wherein ye greatly rejoice!"*

Listen to the words of your ascended and glorified Saviour: "Surely I come quickly!" What is your earnest and heartfelt response? "Amen. Even so, come, Lord Jesus!"†

* 1 Pet. i 3–6.   † Rev. xxii. 20, 21.

The Aged Believer at the Gate of Heaven.

THOMAS GUTHRIE. D. D.

I'm kneeling at the threshold, weary, faint and sore;
Waiting for the dawning, for the opening of the
door;
Waiting till the Master shall bid me rise and come
To the glory of his presence, to the gladness of his
home.

A weary path I've travelled, 'mid darkness, storm
and strife;
Bearing many a burden, struggling for my life;
But now the morn is breaking, my toil will soon be
o'er;
I'm kneeling at the threshold, my hand is on the
door.

Methinks I hear the voices of the blessed as they
stand,
Singing in the sunshine in the far-off sinless land;
Oh, would that I were with them, amid their shining
throng,
Mingling in their worship, joining in their song!

The friends that started with me have entered long
    ago ;
One by one they left me struggling with the foe ;
Their pilgrimage was shorter, their triumph sooner
    won ;
How lovingly they'll hail me when all my toil is
    done !

With them the blessed angels that know nor grief
    nor sin ;
I see them by the portals, prepared to let me in.
O Lord, I wait thy pleasure ; thy time and way are
    best ;
But I am wasted, worn, and weary ; O Father, bid me
    rest.

A Better Country.

REV. JOHN NEWTON.

THE promised land of peace
　　Faith keeps in constant view:
How different from the wilderness
　　We now are passing through!

Here often from our eyes
　　Clouds hide the light divine;
There we shall have unclouded skies,
　　Our Sun will always shine!

Here griefs, and cares, and pains,
　　And fears distress us sore;
But there eternal pleasure reigns,
　　And we shall weep no more.

Lord, pardon our complaints;
　　We follow at thy call;
The joy prepared for suffering saints
　　Will make amends for all.

427

Grandma is Dead.

A. D. F. RANDOLPH.

OUR grandmamma is dead, Aggie: hear, Aggie, what
   I say :—
My dear grandma is dead, and now her soul is gone
   away.
It seems so strange without her, how strange I can-
   not tell ;
She was often sick and tired, she is rested now and
   well.

Sometimes I stop and wonder that her face I do not
   see,
And sometimes I forget myself and ask where can
   she be?
She never made a bit of noise, she talked so sweet
   and low ;
And yet our house seems stiller now, no matter where
   we go.

She loved us children, Aggie; there are three of us
    in all;
The oldest is my sister Jane; and Will is strong and
    tall;
And I am twelve; and all of us she used to rock to
    sleep,
When we were little, tiny things, and couldn't even
    creep.

I miss her more and more, Aggie,—don't wonder
    that I cry;
She went without my kissing her—I did not say
    good-bye;—
For on the morning that she died, so did my father
    say,
She shut her eyes and went to sleep, and slept her
    life away!

I'd like to tell her, if but once, and so would brother
    Will,
We are sorry for our naughty ways,—how much we
    love her still.
That's where she used to sit, when he would creep
    behind the place,
And take the glasses from her eyes and feel her
    wrinkled face.

She was very old and very lame, Aggie; sometimes
 was full of pain;
She never once was cross to us, or really did com-
 plain:
Once, long ago, when she was sick, she said, I heard
 it so,
"Come, Lord, and take me home to heaven, for now
 I long to go."

The day she died was stormy, and when my father
 prayed,
He thanked the Lord for helping her that she was
 not afraid:
I knew she was not; many a time she did us children
 tell
That those who love him when they die shall go with
 Christ to dwell.

Now when I read the Bible, and about that happy
 place,
I think that she is there, and not a wrinkle on her
 face;
I know she is not lame or old, that there she has no
 pain;
Yet somehow I keep wishing she was back with us
 again!

Oh, how my mother misses her! I often see her
    cry ;—
My father tries to comfort her, and so do Jane and I;
I do not wonder, it's so strange with grandma gone
    away,
But God is good, my father says, and so she used to
    say !

I keep trying to remember that he is our Father too,
And like my father here, I'm sure he nothing wrong
    will do ;
So, Aggie, though I can't but cry, it is all right, you
    know ;—
The Lord he wanted her to come, and she was glad
    to go

Longing after Heaven.

DE FLEURY.

YE angels, who stand round the throne,
   And view my Immanuel's face,
In rapturous songs make him known;
   Tune, tune your soft harps to his praise.
He formed you the spirits you are,
   So happy, so noble, so good;
While others sunk down in despair,
   Confirmed by his power ye stood.

Ye saints, who stand nearer than they,
   And cast your bright crowns at his feet,
His grace and his glory display,
   And all his rich mercy repeat;
He snatched you from hell and the grave,
   He ransomed from death and despair;
For you he was mighty to save,
   Almighty to bring you safe there.

Oh, when will the period appear
   When I shall unite in your song?
432

I'm weary of lingering here,
　And I to your Saviour belong.
I'm fettered and chained up in clay;
　I struggle and pant to be free;
I long to be soaring away,
　My God and my Saviour to see.

I want to put on my attire,
　Washed white in the blood of the Lamb;
I want to be one of your choir,
　And tune my sweet harp to his name:
I want—oh I want to be there,
　Where sorrow and sin bid adieu,
Your joy and your friendship to share,
　To wonder and worship with you.

55

Crossing the River.

REV. ROBERT F. SAMPLE.

"When thou passest through the waters," &c.—Isa. xliii. 2.

SOLEMN and still are the watchers pale,
　And quietly steal the hours away;
Heavily droopeth the empty sail,
　Silent the green where the children play.

The curtains are drawn in the chamber of death,
　Through the sheltering vine faint sunbeams fall;
The watchers bowing, with long-drawn breath,
　Wierd shadows cast on the dusky wall.

On poised wings, lo! the angels wait,
　And the Ancient of Days is there,
Who pointeth afar to a golden gate,
　As faltering lips move in fervent prayer:

　　"Jesus, my All-in-all!
　　　To thee I cry;
　　The deep'ning shadows fall
　　　From yonder sky.

434

Lead me, O Saviour dear,
    Through death's dark rolling tide,
Let faith not yield to fear,
    But strong abide.

"Thy footsteps, Lord, I see
    Along the shore,
And here I wait for thee
    To guide me o'er.
Lead me, O Saviour dear,
    To yonder sunlit land;
Let faith not yield to fear;
    Take thou my hand.

"Higher the waters rise,
    The billows roll;
Oh calm the stormy skies,
    Save thou my soul!
Ah! now I see thy face,
    Thy loving words I hear,
I praise thee for thy grace,
    I shall not fear."

"It shall be well," said the dying saint,
    And Jesus took his outstretched hand,
Who uttered words of tenderest cheer,
    And sweetly spake of the glory-land.

Enraptured we watched till the curt'ning clouds
　　Concealed them all from our wondering sight;
Then the ringing of bells, and anthems loud,
　　Of the welcome told from saints in light.

  *   *   *   *   *   *

Solemn and still are the mourners pale,
　　And quietly steal the hours away;
Heavily droopeth the empty sail,
　　Silent the green where the children play.

There's a new-made grave in the churchyard old,
　　At the family hearth a vacant chair;
There's gloom in the home, on field and wold,
　　But radiant glory in the voiceless air.

Liveth the sire in love's inner shrine,
　　Cherished shall be the mem'ries of yore,
Linked with the light that was wont to shine
　　On the old arm-chair by the cottage door.

Heaven.

HORATIUS BONAR, D. D.

THAT clime is not like this dull clime of ours:
    All, all is brightness there;
A sweeter influence breathes around its bowers,
    And a far milder air.
No calm below is like that calm above;
No region here is like that realm of love;
Earth's softest spring ne'er shed so soft a light;
Earth's brightest summer never shone so bright.

That sky is not, like this sad sky of ours,
    Tinged with earth's change and care;
No shadow dims it, and no rain-cloud lowers;
    No broken sunshine there!
One everlasting stretch of azure pours
Its stainless splendour o'er those sinless shores;
For there Jehovah reigns with heavenly ray;
There Jesus reigns, dispensing endless day.

The dwellers there are not like those of earth—
    No mortal stain they bear;

437

And yet they seem of kindred blood and birth,—
    Whence and how came they there?
Earth was their native soil; from sin and shame
Through tribulation they to glory came;
Bond slaves, delivered from sin's crushing load;
Brands, plucked from burning by the hand of God.

Those robes of theirs are not like those below;
    No angel's half so bright!
Whence came that beauty, whence that living glow?
    Whence came that radiant white?
Washed in the blood of the atoning Lamb,
Fair as the light those robes of theirs became;
And now, all tears wiped off from every eye,
They wander where the freshest pastures lie,
Through all the nightless day of that unfading sky.

Here and There.

ANONYMOUS.

Here, 'mid death and danger, mournfully we stay,
Everything around us yielding to decay;
But in the better country, sin's dark triumph o'er,
All things are enduring—life for evermore.

Here, with weary footsteps, in a desert waste,
Strangers in a strange land, we pass through in
      haste;
There our rest awaits us, our hearts are gone before,
In that land of brightness—rest for evermore!

Here our courage faileth in the storms of life,
Our hearts are sad and anxious, ruffled in the strife;
There the tempest endeth, the billows cease to roar,—
All is calm and tranquil—peace for evermore!

Here amid our sadness silence often reigns,
Or our voices mingle in low and plaintive strains;
There no chord of sadness shall wake an echo more,—
Heaven itself resoundeth—song for evermore!

Here amid our sorrow sighs are often heard,
Fondest hearts are parted, sick with hope deferred;
There no tear-drop falleth, hearts are never sore,
All is joy and gladness—joy for evermore!

Here 'mid deepening shadows, wearily we roam,
Looking for the day-star, the bright light of home;
There the clouds shall vanish, the night of weeping
   o'er,
When the sun ariseth—light for evermore!

Only a little longer have we to trust and wait
E'er we reach the portals, pass the pearly gate,
Hear the shout of welcome from loved ones gone be-
   fore,
In our Father's mansion—home for evermore!

That Land.

FROM THE GERMAN OF UHLAND.

THERE is a land where beauty will not fade,
  Nor sorrow dim the eye;
Where true hearts will not sink nor be dismayed,
  And love will never die.
Tell me—I fain would go,—
For I am burdened with a heavy woe;
The beautiful have left me all alone;
The true, the tender, from my path have gone,
And I am weak and fainting with despair;
Where is it? tell me, where?

Friend, thou must trust in Him who trod before
  The desolate path of life;
Must bear in meekness, as he meekly bore,
  Sorrow, and toil, and strife.
Think how the Son of God
These thorny paths has trod;
Yet tarried out for thee the appointed woe;
Think of his loneliness in places dim,
When no man comforted or cared for him;

Think how he prayed, unaided and alone,
In that dread agony, " Thy will be done !"
Friend, do thou not despair,
Christ, in his heaven of heavens, will hear thy prayer.

Prayer for One Nearing Another World.

ARCHIBALD ALEXANDER, D. D.

O MOST merciful God! I rejoice that thou dost reign over the universe with a sovereign sway, so that thou dost according to thy will in the armies of heaven and among the inhabitants of the earth. Thou art the Maker of my body and Father of my spirit, and thou hast a perfect right to dispose of me in that manner which will most effectually promote thy glory; and I know that whatsoever thou dost is right and wise, and just and good. And whatever may be my eternal destiny, I rejoice in the assurance that thy great name will be glorified in me. But as thou hast been pleased to reveal thy mercy and thy grace to our fallen, miserable world, and as the word of this salvation has been preached unto me, inviting me to accept of eternal life upon the gracious terms of the gospel, I do cordially receive the Lord Jesus Christ as my Saviour and only Redeemer, believing

443

sincerely the whole testimony which thou hast given respecting his divine character, his real incarnation, his unspotted and holy life, his numerous and beneficent miracles, his expiatory and meritorious death, and his glorious resurrection and ascension. I believe, also, in his supreme exaltation, in his prevalent intercession for his chosen people, in his affectionate care and aid afforded to his suffering members here below, and in his second coming to receive his humble followers to dwell with himself in heaven, and to take vengeance on his obstinate enemies. My only hope and confidence of being saved rests simply on the mediatorial work and prevailing intercession of the Lord Jesus Christ; in consequence of which the Holy Spirit is graciously sent to make application of Christ's redemption by working faith in us and repentance unto life, and rendering us meet for the heavenly inheritance by sanctifying us in the whole man, soul, body, and spirit. Grant, gracious God! that the rich blesssings of the new covenant may be freely bestowed on thy unworthy servant. I acknowledge that I have no claim to thy favour on account of any goodness in me by nature, for, alas! there dwelleth in me, that is in my flesh, no good thing; nor on account of any works of righteousness done by me, for all our righteousnesses are

as filthy rags. Neither am I able to make atonement for any one of my innumerable transgressions;
which, I confess before thee, are not only many in
number, but heinous in their nature, justly deserving
thy displeasure and wrath, so that if I were immediately sent to hell thou wouldst be altogether just
in my condemnation. Although I trust that I have
endeavoured to serve thee with some degree of sincerity, yet whatever good thing I have ever done, or
even thought, I ascribe entirely to thy grace, without
which I can do nothing acceptable in thy sight.
And I am deeply convinced that my best duties have
fallen far short of the perfection of thy law, and
have been so mingled with sin in the performance
that I might justly be condemned for the most fervent prayer I ever made. And I would confess with
shame and contrition that I am not only chargeable
with sin in the act, but that there is a law in my
members, warring against the law of my mind, aim-
ing to bring me into captivity to the law of sin and
death. This corrupt nature is the source of innumerable evil thoughts and desires, and damps the
exercise of faith and love, and stands in the way of
well-doing, so that when I would do good, evil is
present with me. And so deep and powerful is this
remaining depravity that all efforts to eradicate or

subdue it are vain without the aid of divine grace. And when at any time I obtain a glimpse of the depth and turpitude of the sin of my nature I am overwhelmed, and constrained to exclaim with Job, "I abhor myself and repent in dust and ashes." And now, RIGHTEOUS LORD GOD ALMIGHTY, I would not attempt to conceal any of my actual transgressions, however vile and shameful they are, but would penitently confess them before thee; and would plead in my defence nothing but the perfect righteousness of the Lord Jesus Christ, who died, the just for the unjust, to bring us near to God. For his sake alone do I ask or expect the rich blessings necessary to my salvation. For although I am unworthy, he is most worthy; though I have no righteousness, he has provided by his expiatory death, and by his holy life, a complete justifying righteousness, in which spotless robe I pray that I may be clothed; so that thou, my righteous Judge, wilt see no sin in me, but wilt acquit me from every accusation, and justify me freely by thy grace, through the righteousness of my Lord and Saviour, with whom thou art ever well pleased. And my earnest prayer is, that JESUS may save me from my sins, as well as from their punishment; that I may be redeemed from all iniquity, as well as from the condemnation of the law; that the work of sanctification may be carried on in my soul by thy word and Spirit, until it be perfected at thine appointed time. And grant, O Lord! that as long as I am in the body I may make it my constant study and chief aim to glorify thy name, both with soul and body, which are no longer mine, but thine; for I am "bought with a price"— not with silver and gold, but with the precious blood of Christ, as of a lamb without blemish and without spot. Enable me to let my light so shine that others, seeing my good works, may be led to glorify thy name. Oh make use of me as an humble instrument of advancing thy kingdom on earth and promoting the salvation of immortal souls. If thou hast appointed suffering for me here below, I beseech thee to consider my weakness, and let thy chastisements be those of a loving father, that I may be made partaker of thy holiness. And let me not be tempted above what I am able to bear, but with the temptation make a way for escape.

O most merciful God! cast me not off in the time of old age; forsake me not when my strength declineth. Now, when I am old and gray-headed, forsake me not; but let thy grace be sufficient for me, and enable me to bring forth fruit even in old age. May my hoary head be found in the ways of rightcousness! Preserve my mind from dotage and imbecility, and my body from protracted disease and excruciating pain. Deliver me from despondency and discouragement in my declining years, and enable me to bear affliction with patience, fortitude, and perfect submission to thy holy will. Lift upon me perpetually the light of thy reconciled countenance, and cause me to rejoice in thy salvation and in the hope of thy glory. May the peace that passeth all understanding be constantly diffused through my soul, so that my mind may remain calm through all the storms and vicissitudes of life.

As, in the course of nature, I must be drawing near to my end, and as I know I must soon put off this tabernacle, I do humbly and earnestly beseech thee, O Father of mercies, to prepare me for this inevitable and solemn event. Fortify my mind against the terrors of death. Give me, if it please thee, an easy passage through the gate of death. Dissipate the dark clouds and mists which naturally hang over the grave, and lead me gently down into the gloomy valley. O my kind Shepherd, who hast tasted the bitterness of death for me, and who knowest how to sympathize with and succour the sheep of thy pasture, be thou present to guide, to support, and to comfort me. Illumine with beams of heavenly light the valley and shadow of death, so that I may fear no evil. When heart and flesh fail, be thou the strength of my heart and my portion for ever. Let not my courage fail in the trying hour. Permit not the great adversary to harass my soul in the last struggle, but make me a conqueror and more than a conqueror in this fearful conflict. I humbly ask that my reason may be continued to the last, and, if it be thy will, that I may be so comforted and supported that I may leave a testimony in favour of the reality of religion, and thy faithfulness in fulfilling thy gracious promises; and that others of thy servants who may follow after may be encouraged by my example to commit themselves boldly to the guidance and keeping of the Shepherd of Israel.

And when my spirit leaves this clay tenement, Lord Jesus, receive it. Send some of the blessed angels to convoy my inexperienced soul to the mansion which thy love has prepared. And oh! let me be so situated, though in the lowest rank, that I may behold thy glory. May I have an abundant entrance administered unto me into the kingdom of our Lord and Saviour Jesus Christ; for whose sake and in whose name I ask all these things. Amen.

God of my Youth.

ISAAC WATTS, D. D.

God of my childhood and my youth,
    The guide of all my days,
. I have declared thy heavenly truth,
    And told thy wondrous ways.

Wilt thou forsake my hoary hairs,
    And leave my fainting heart?
Who shall sustain my sinking years
    If God, my strength, depart?

Let me thy power and truth proclaim
    Before the rising age,
And leave a savour of thy name
    When I shall quit the stage.

The land of silence and of death
    Attends my next remove;
Oh may these poor remains of breath
    Teach the wide world thy love!

By long experience have I known
  Thy sovereign power to save;
At thy command I venture down
  Securely to the grave.

When I lie buried deep in dust,
  My flesh shall be thy care;
These withered limbs with thee I trust,
  To raise them strong and fair.

I would not Live Alway.

WILLIAM A. MUHLENBERG, D. D.

I WOULD not live alway,—I ask not to stay
Where storm after storm rises dark o'er the way;
The few lurid mornings that dawn on us here
Are enough for life's woes, full enough for its cheer.

I would not live alway, thus fettered by sin,
Temptation without, and corruption within;
The rapture of pardon is mingled with fears,
The cup of thanksgiving with penitent tears.

I would not live alway—no, welcome the tomb!
Since Jesus hath lain there, I dread not its gloom;
There sweet be my rest, till he bid me arise,
To hail him in triumph descending the skies.

Who, who would live alway, away from his God,
Away from yon heaven, that blissful abode,
Where rivers of pleasure flow o'er the bright plains,
And the noontide of glory eternally reigns,—

452

Where saints of all ages in harmony meet,
Their Saviour and brethren transported to greet;
Where anthems of rapture unceasingly roll,
And the smile of the Lord is the feast of the soul?

The Lord's my Shepherd.

ROUSE.

Psalm xxiii.

THE Lord's my Shepherd, I'll not want,
　　He makes me down to lie
In pastures green: he leadeth me
　　The quiet waters by.

My soul he doth restore again,
　　And me to walk doth make
Within the paths of righteousness,
　　E'en for his own name's sake.

Yea, though I walk in death's dark vale,
　　Yet will I fear no ill;
For thou art with me, and thy rod
　　And staff me comfort still.

Goodness and mercy all my life
　　Shall surely follow me,
And in God's house for evermore
　　My dwelling-place shall be.

The Pilgrim's Song.

ANONYMOUS.

I'M but a stranger here;
  Heaven is my home.
Earth is a desert drear;
  Heaven is my home.
Danger and sorrow stand
Round me on every hand;
Heaven is my Father-land;
  Heaven is my home.

What though the tempest rage!
  Heaven is my home.
Short is my pilgrimage;
  Heaven is my home.
And time's wild wintry blast
Will soon be overpast;
I shall reach home at last;
  Heaven is my home.

There, at my Saviour's side—
  Heaven is my home,

I shall be glorified ;
      Heaven is my home.
Then with the good and blest,
Those I loved most and best,
I shall for ever rest ;
      Heaven is my home.

Therefore I'll murmur not—
      Heaven is my home.
Whate'er my earthly lot,
      Heaven is my home.
For I shall surely stand
There, at my Lord's right hand ;
Heaven is my Father-land ;
      Heaven is my home.

𝔚orn and 𝔚eary.

S. ROBERTS.

My feet are worn and weary with the march
 Over the road and up the steep hill-side;
Oh! city of our God, I fain would see
 Thy pastures green, where peaceful waters glide.

My hands are weary toiling, toiling on
 Day after day for perishable meat;
Oh! city of our God, I fain would rest—
 I sigh to gain thy glorious mercy-seat.

My garments, travel-worn and stained with dust,
 Oft rent by briars and thorns that crowd my way,
Would fain be made, O Lord, my righteousness,
 Spotless and white in heaven's unclouded day.

My heart is weary of its own deep sin,—
 Sinning, repenting, sinning still again;
When shall my soul thy glorious presence feel,
 And find, dear Saviour, it is free from stain?

Patience, poor soul! the Saviour's feet were worn;
 The Saviour's heart and hands were weary too,
His garments stained, and travel-worn, and old,
 His vision blinded with a pitying dew.

Love thou the path of sorrow that he trod;
 Toil on, and wait in patience for thy rest!
Oh! city of our God, we soon shall see
 Thy glorious walls,—home often loved and blest!

As thy Days.

LYDIA H. SIGOURNEY.

WHEN adverse winds and waves arise,
And in my heart despondence sighs;
When life her throng of cares reveals,
And weakness o'er my spirit steals,
Grateful I hear the kind decree,
That " as my day, my strength shall be."

When, with sad footsteps, memory roves
'Mid smitten joys and buried loves,
When sleep my tearful pillow flies,
And dewy morning drinks my sighs,
Still to thy promise, Lord, I flee,
That " as my day, my strength shall be."

One trial more must yet be past,
One pang—the keenest and the last;
And when, with brow convulsed and pale,
My feeble, quivering heart-strings fail,
Redeemer! grant my soul to see
That " as my day, my strength shall be."

459

The Heavenly Rest.

WILLIAM B. TAPPAN.

THERE is an hour of peaceful rest
  To mourning wanderers given;
There is a joy for souls distressed—
A balm for every wounded breast;
  'Tis found above—in heaven!

There is a home for weary souls,
  By sin and sorrow driven—
When tossed on life's tempestuous shoals,
Where storms arise and ocean rolls,
  And all is drear but heaven!

There faith lifts up the tearful eye,
  The heart with anguish riven;
And views the tempest passing by,
The evening shadows quickly fly,
  And all serene in heaven!

There fragrant flowers immortal bloom,
  And joys supreme are given;
There rays divine disperse the gloom:
Beyond the confines of the tomb
  Appears the dawn of heaven!

Thy Will be Done.

CHARLOTTE ELLIOT.

My God, my Father, while I stray
Far from my home in life's rough way,
Oh teach me from my heart to say,
    "Thy will be done!"

Though dark my path, and sad my lot,
Let me be still and murmur not,
But breathe the prayer divinely taught,
    "Thy will be done!"

What though in lonely grief I sigh,
For friends beloved, no longer nigh,
Submissive still would I reply,
    "Thy will be done!"

If thou should'st call me to resign
What I most prize—it ne'er was mine;
I only yield thee what was thine—
    "Thy will be done!"

Should pining sickness waste away
My life in premature decay,
My Father, still I strive to say,
　"Thy will be done!"

If but my fainting heart be blest
With thy sweet Spirit for its guest,
My God, to thee I leave the rest—
　"Thy will be done!"

Renew my will from day to day,
Blend it with thine, and take away
All that now makes it hard to say,
　"Thy will be done!"

Then when on earth I breathe no more
The prayer oft mixed with tears before,
I'll sing upon a happier shore,
　"Thy will be done!"

Our Home.

ANONYMOUS.

LIFE's sun a longer shadow throws,
And all things whisper of repose;
Our toilsome journey soon will close,
　　And we shall reach *our home!*

Here we no resting-place have found;
Unnumbered dangers lurk around,
Temptations, snares, and griefs abound;
　　Earth cannot be *our home.*

On let us press with cheerful haste,
Nor precious moments idly waste;
For, oh! we long those joys to taste
　　Which are reserved *at home.*

Only a narrow stream doth flow
Between this dreary waste of woe
And that fair land where richly grow
　　The lovely flowers *of home.*

Its peaceful waters softly glide,
And Christ through them our steps will guide,
And land us on the other side,
　　Where we shall be *at home.*

Some cherished friends have gone before;
Their conflicts and their toils are o'er,
And we shall meet to part no more,
　　When we have gained *our home.*

Their songs of welcome, sweet and clear,
Will soon be falling on our ear;
For we are drawing very near
　　Unto *our happy home.*

No clouds of sorrow gather there;
Hushed is the latest thought of care;
Perpetual joys those loved ones share
　　Within *our Father's home.*

Life's sun a longer shadow throws,
And all things whisper of repose;
Our toilsome journey soon will close,
　　And we shall reach OUR HOME.

THE END.